THE BEAR PAW HORSES NO

THE BEAR PAW HORSES

Will Henry

Chivers Press • G.K. Hall & Co.
Bath, Avon, England • Thorndike, Maine, USA

This Large Print edition is published by Chivers Press, England, and by
G.K. Hall & Co., USA.

Published in 1995 in the U.K. by arrangement with the author's estate.

Published in 1995 in the U.S. by arrangement with the Golden West
Literary Agency.

U.K. Hardcover ISBN 0-7451-2698-7 (Chivers Large Print)
U.S. Softcover   ISBN 0-7838-1121-7 (Nightingale Collection Edition)

The text of this Large Print edition is unabridged.
Other aspects of the book may vary from the original edition.

Set in 16 pt. New Times Roman.

Printed in Great Britain on acid-free paper.

British Library Cataloguing in Publication Data available

Library of Congress Cataloging-in-Publication Data

Henry, Will, 1912– / ?7/
    The Bear Paw horses / Will Henry.
        p. cm.
    ISBN 0-7838-1121-7 (alk. paper : lg. print)
    1. Dakota Indians — Fiction.   2. Large type books.   I. Title.
[PS3551.L393B43   1995]
813′.54 — dc20   94-34002

For Melville W. Beardsley
trusted friend of
boyhood and all the years between

HISTORICAL FORENOTE:
Where the Red Man Rode

Today is the day of the Horseback Indian remembered. The seekers along the fading pony tracks of a hundred winters gone are hungry to know about the places where these warbonneted ghost riders actually did the things the history books say they did.

People want to have a pinch of earth from precisely where the Sioux killed George Armstrong Custer. They inquire after the exact battlefield of Tongue River, where General Patrick Connor wished he had not surprised Black Bear and the Arapaho. They spend hours tromping down the desolate sage on Red Fork of Powder River where Ranald Mackenzie burned the Cheyenne lodges of tragic Dull Knife. They demand to be shown the specific hole made by Red Cloud when he thrust his lance into the ground at Laramie and cried out to Indian Commissioner E. B. Taylor, 'The Great Father sends us presents and wants a new road (the Bozeman Trail) across our lands, but the Eagle Chief goes with his soldiers to steal that road before the Indians say yes or no.' And sightseers have virtually worn away Massacre Hill, up south of Sheridan, Wyoming, where dashing W. J. Fetterman, 'with fifty men I could ride through the whole Sioux Nation,' tried it and got himself and seventy-eight men wiped out by two thousand Cheyenne, Arapaho, Miniconjou, and Oglala Sioux, under the implacable Crazy Horse.

One of the most singular of such Indian place-names, however, is not celebrated in the white man's history books. It is not even marked in the tourist guides that, for one dollar plus tax, tell the entire truth about Little Big Horn, Powder River, Massacre Hill, or wherever.

High Meadow is the name of this forgotten milepost along the lost trail of the Indian past.

Should one seek today to find it, he will require Indian assistance. If the red man that he asks is old enough in years and still, as his people say, 'calm in his mind' (not senile), here will be the misty answer called up from the smokes of lodge fires long since banked, their ashes blown away:

Let the searcher begin his quest a certain number of miles in a given direction from historic old Hat Creek station on the vanished Cheyenne Deadwood stage road of a hundred winters gone. There, when he has climbed enough blind ridges, he will come to the rock-walled pasture of the Bear Paw horses. Let him stand there quietly, thinking back to yesterday. Doing this, he will come to see in his mind's eye how it was that long-ago night of the great snowstorm when the old man Crowfoot and the young squaw Twilight, with the ancient bell mare Speckledbird and no other aid, rounded up and drove out over Bad Face Pass the 397 restolen Oglala ponies that were the substance of Crazy Horse's dream of escape for his people from Fort Robinson, Nebraska.

The searcher may see, too, with that same eye of the mind, the fateful message the Indians say the warchief sent from Red Cloud agency to Spotted Tail agency the night of his wounding, and directed there to his most trusted counselor, the Oglalan medicine priest Kangi-siha, known as Crowfoot:

'Go and take back our horses from where they are hidden by that white man and those others who stole them from us as we came into the reservation,' the dying warchief charged Crowfoot. 'Tell no one of your plan, not even my wife who is ill in your care, but take the horses to meet our red brother Joseph and his Nez Perces at Cow Island as we promised them, to aid them in their hard fighting toward the Land of the Grandmother.

'Do not make the ground bloody over there at your agency as the soldiers have done with my blood here. Only go and get back our horses. When the Oglala see the brave thing you have done, they will take new heart and break away from Fort Robinson and go to be free with Sitting Bull and the Hunkpapa in Canada, even as Joseph and the Slit Noses are trying to do.

'Touch-the-Clouds is with me and will carry these words to you. My old father and mother sit by my blanket. They pray for me, but they are looking at me under their hands. For I am bad hurt and I have told Touch-the-Clouds to tell the people it is no use to depend on me anymore. The soldiers have put their bayonets into both my kidneys. I am cold, I cannot see now, and I am much afraid...'

Thus, the final testament of Ta Sunke Witko, Crazy Horse, strange man of the Oglala Bad Face Sioux. Its legacy began September 13, 1877, in High Meadow, Wyoming. It ended on the fifth of October, 1877, at the Bear Paws in Montana's lonely Milk River buffalo country. What appears of it here is the Indian story of the twenty-three days and 575 miles between.

W.H.
High Meadow, Wyoming

CHAPTER ONE

It was the sixth of May, 1877. Custer had been a year less fifty days in his grave beside the Greasy Grass, the Little Big Horn. Of all the Sioux leaders who had put him there, only Crazy Horse remained defiant. The others were either dead or had surrendered or fled to Canada.

American Horse was gone, killed by the raiding Captain Anson Mills. The great warrior's forty-eight-lodge village was destroyed to the last buffalo hide, burned to the last blanket. General 'Red Beard' Crook was back in the country, called up from far Arizona to lead the hunt for the Sioux survivors of the Little Big Horn. Colonel Nelson A. Miles, known as Bear Coat to the Sioux, was down in the Yellowstone drainage with a big force, stopping retreat to the south. The wily Sitting Bull had twice slipped in to council with Miles, a man respected by the Sioux. But the second meeting had ended in a shooting fight, and peace was put beyond reach.

The white chiefs in Washington, meanwhile, made a law that said that until the Sioux gave up all claims to the Powder River country and the Black Hills—all of the best buffalo pastures of the northern homeland—no rations would

1

be issued to them, and no shelter given on the reservations. Starving, after the hard winter of war and hot pursuit following the massacre of Longhair Custer and his Seventh Cavalry, the Sioux of all hostile bands, Oglala, Hunkpapa, Brûlé, Miniconjou, all the fighting families, were coming in and signing.

Red Cloud, that pompous pawn, had been deposed at the Fort Robinson agency bearing his name. A second Sioux agency had been established separate from it under famed Brûlé statesman, Spotted Tail. Troops had been put on battle alert at Fort Robinson, located in the extreme northwestern corner of Nebraska, where it guarded both Red Cloud and Spotted Tail agencies. Revolt and countering violence were in the air. But the Indians were starving. Their women and children were ill. The ponies were dying. The best horses were being butchered so that the people might eat one more day. Even the buffalo failed. It was the poorest spring for fat cow in red memory. The winter before it had been cruel with killing winds.

In the depths of its terrible cold, Colonel Ranald Mackenzie had attacked and burned the sleeping village of Dull Knife, Crazy Horse's 'Cheyenne brother,' in last resistance to white surrender. Women, children, old people, had been shot down pleading for life. The fabled Last Bull, chief of the Cheyenne Dog Soldiers, had been killed. His death

2

disorganized the Cheyenne. The survivors, under Little Wolf, fled through the arctic weather seeking asylum with the Oglala Bad Face Sioux, who were winter camped not far away.

The Cheyenne, freezing, bleeding, starving, stumbled at last into the haven of the Sioux lodges. They were made welcome, given food, warm shelter, sympathy. But Crazy Horse, Ta Sunke Witko, whose village it was, had an unpleasant surprise for the desperate Cheyenne. They would not be turned away by the Sioux but neither would the Sioux join them in their vengeance on the white soldiers. Little Wolf would have to make that fight by himself. Crazy Horse was thinking of going in and giving up.

Little Wolf departed with his wounded tribesmen swearing revenge on Crazy Horse and the Oglala that would know no ending. The famed Cheyenne would go to Fort Robinson and offer his services to the Army as a scout in the field against his old friend and blood brother, Ta Sunke Witko.

As good as his word, Little Wolf enlisted on the side of the white man, and the fate of Crazy Horse and all the hostile Indians yet free upon the North Plains was thus sealed. When brother turned on brother, it was the finish.

The cold diminished. The new grass sprang up. Crazy Horse moved his camp to Reno Creek, 160 miles northwest of Fort Robinson.

Sitting Bull with two hundred lodges left the country with the late spring thaws. He retreated into Canada, safe from all American army pursuit. The word wafted back down south that he was living happily with the Red River Mixed Bloods up there in the Land of the Grandmother, the Sioux name for Queen Victoria's country of the redcoats. Unlike the Americans, the British soldiers never fired first. Their justice was the same for an Indian as for a white man. No wonder the mastermind of the Little Big Horn slaughter was happy! Maybe all the Sioux should go up there and live with the Mixed Bloods.

But the Oglala loved their American homeland; they would not go to Canada with their Hunkpapa cousins.

Crazy Horse had made his decision.

Old Spotted Tail had come out from Fort Robinson under auspices of Red Beard Crook, whom the Sioux listened to and called an honest man. Spotted Tail had talked hard with his nephew Ta Sunke Witko, Crazy Horse. He had made the fiery warchief understand that the old days were gone forever and that the Indian must change or die—starved or murdered in his old free-roving camps—and that the buffalo pastures were white man's grass now and would so be for all time to come.

Crazy Horse called his people to him.

'My uncle, Spotted Tail, has said to me that there is no use fighting anymore,' he began.

4

'You all heard him say it, and he is right. I have fought a long time now and I still love this Land of the Spotted Eagle which is our land. But I am tired and the white man is too many. I am done now, I am going in. I have asked Sitting Bull if he will surrender, too. He said, "I do not wish to die yet."

'That is all he said. Then he struck his lodges to go and live with the Mixed Bloods up on Red River. His trail is wide and plain to see. Those who will may follow it. I say, let them go now. But that trail is not my trail. The Land of the Grandmother is not my land. My home is where I stand. I will not run away. These are my lands and they have been taken from me. But I am going in as Spotted Tail said. I will go first to Red Cloud agency and talk to Red Beard Crook. Some fool has told him that I mean to sneak in close to him over there and kill him. I must tell Red Beard what a lie this is. He will understand.'

Crazy Horse paused, looking out over the people.

'I have promised my uncle Spotted Tail all of this,' he said. 'Go with me if you will. Who knows what trail is best?'

The following morning the lodges were struck. Half of them disappeared to the north, going to join Sitting Bull in Canada. The others, about one hundred lodges, moved slowly eastward with Crazy Horse, bound for Fort Robinson and the white man's road.

'Maybe,' said Crazy Horse, 'we will be happy there.'

Kangi-siha, Crowfoot, his old adviser, riding knee and knee with him, said, 'maybe,' and no more. Yet one hundred words, or one thousand, could not have revealed more poignantly the despair that remained unspoken in the hearts of both dark-skinned horsemen.

The sunrise of the final day that would bring them down upon Red Cloud agency and Fort Robinson would be the last thing of wild free beauty or of nomad happiness that any of them would know. The only other matter they would remember about that fateful day would be its date: May 6, 1877.

Oh, yes, and the time of that day: The sun, Old Anpetuwi, was straight overhead, filling the loveliness of the springtime buffalo pastures with fragrances and excitements.

High noon for the last of the fighting Sioux.

CHAPTER TWO

At Red Cloud, Tasina Sapewin, Black Blanket, the wife of Crazy Horse, fell ill with the Pale Eye's lung sickness, tuberculosis. Having little resistance to the germ, the woman weakened steadily. Crowfoot, who, as medicine priest of the band, tended her, knew that unless a white doctor's skills might be brought in Tasina was doomed. Such a doctor was known to

Crowfoot and Crazy Horse. This was V. T. McGillycuddy, whom the histories of both red and white man were to remember kindly.

But the excellent physician was then stationed at the Spotted Tail agency, a long day's pony ride to the east, and could not be called upon.

Crowfoot took council with his Indian conscience.

Tasina Sapewin was not merely one more victim of the Custer vengeance.

She was a Mixed Blood woman, granddaughter of the old man who nursed her. Moreover, she had with her a younger sister made homeless by the Little Big Horn bloodshed. This one, H'tayetu, Twilight, for all her ripe body and thrusting teats, was a girl only, homesick and much afraid. For this child of her same blood, the young wife of Crazy Horse feared more than she did for her own life. It was this concern that hampered Crowfoot in his decision. That made him hesitate to go to the warchief and tell him what he knew—that Tasina Sapewin was going to Wanagi Yata, the Land of the Shadows, unless she might be gotten to Dr McGillycuddy in time. Even then, the gamble was of high order. Tasina was far gone. The white man's medicine might prove no more effective than that of Crowfoot. Nor was that the only risk, nor even the gravest, involved in telling Crazy Horse the truth: If the warchief understood that his young wife's only chance lay in her reaching Dr McGillycuddy down at Spotted Tail, then no power on the white man's earth could stop him from taking his woman there.

This was the danger, for Crowfoot knew that it was precisely just such a request that the army would blindly refuse. Though the officers never spoke of it to him, Crazy Horse was a prisoner at Red Cloud. He could not leave the camp, nor the sight of the camp, without express permission. He was watched night and day. Should he make one move, the commander at Fort Robinson would certainly order his arrest by force, a thing inconceivable to Crazy Horse. The warchief would as surely react and the ground would be again made bloody with the Sioux supplying the blood.

So it was not only the life of poor Tasina that Crowfoot weighed in his heart.

Four moons had passed since the Oglala had come in to Fort Robinson. It was now September. In the weeks of those moons the wife of Crazy Horse was not the only one who sickened. The warchief himself was ill within his wild breast. But it was not with any white man's disease. He suffered the red man's wasting affliction, the fever for personal liberty. Like a caged animal he paced the confines of the agency raging to be free. And like a caged animal the angers of his flesh began to invade and poison his mind.

Crazy Horse had always hated the white man. Now he thought of nothing else but escape and revenge. He furtively worked to arouse support among his followers. By that autumn he believed that, with strong inclusions of Sans Arc and Brûlè brothers among his loyal Oglala, there were, between Red Cloud and Spotted Tail agencies, more than two thousand persons prepared to die with him. Crowfoot had attempted in every way he knew to dissuade him of this delusion. The old adviser knew that the number of those desperate enough in their own hearts to go with Crazy Horse in a breakout and blood vengeance would be nearer to two hundred than two thousand. Yet the tortured warchief schemed on.

As was inevitable, the army learned of his conspiring through Indian informers. Even General Crook, that old friend of the fighting Indians, believed the reports of Crazy Horse's planned uprising in the inflated terms falsely given by the warchief's enemies, of two thousand Indians ready to rise up and strike for Canada.

It was the old story, brother against brother. The Sioux informers who told Crook of the thousands yearning to join Crazy Horse and his Oglala troublemakers knew, as well as old Crowfoot knew, that they lied. But Crazy Horse was still the hero of the people. The other chiefs were jealous. Less wild and more wily than the warchief, they turned on him actually hoping to have him sent south, out of the way of their own maneuvering for power among the agency Sioux.

All this was known to Crowfoot. Yet even knowing it and adding to it the burden of watching the warchief's wife waste and die of the white man's lung sickness, he could not bring himself to warn Crazy Horse and so risk the lives of many more Indians than Tasina.

Not so wise as the old man, Tasina's younger sister Twilight reached a different decision. No longer could she bear the sight of Tasina's suffering, knowing that the white man's medicine might save her sister's life.

Before Crowfoot could stop her, she was at the door-flaps of the lodge. 'I am going to tell the warchief,' she whispered. 'Do not awaken my sister, but be ready.'

It went then as the old man knew it must.

Crazy Horse stormed into the office of the commandant at Robinson demanding permission to take his wife to see Dr McGillycuddy over at Spotted Tail agency. The permission was summarily refused. Without a word the warchief turned away. Within the hour, he had Tasina in a travois behind an aging mule and, with Twilight and old Crowfoot for companions, was dragging his dying woman toward the agency of his uncle, Spotted Tail. If Tasina must die, she would not do so because the white man refused her the decency of a doctor's attentions. If the warchief must die helping his woman, then so be it. And the young sister and the old Sioux grandfather would die with him. It was the Oglala way, freedom or death.

Twenty Indian government scouts, many of them enemies of Crazy Horse, were sent at the gallop to arrest the warchief and return him to Red Cloud. Secret orders had been given Crook to send the war leader out of the country, 'down to the hell of the Dry Tortugas for life imprisonment.' Word of this treachery had somehow reached Crazy Horse. Perhaps it was even the prime reason for his desperate move toward the Spotted Tail agency. What life had a man to lose whose life had already been taken from him by such a terrible future? In this mood, when the Indian police rode up to arrest him, the warchief whirled upon them like a cornered panther.

'I am Ta Sunke Witko!' he cried, 'Crazy Horse.' The words exploded with the force of pistol shots in the suddenly stilled air. 'Do not dare to touch me! I am not running from you.'

His fury was too strong in its medicine for the shamed scouts. There were not war honors enough among the full score of them to match a tenth of those belonging to Crazy Horse. Not one of them was entitled to lay the smallest of his red fingers on this brave and undefeated man. They all knew it.

They fell into the dust of the travois of

Tasina Sapewin and rode as an honor escort for the warchief and his doomed wife the remaining miles to the eastern agency.

There, Crazy Horse's wise old blood uncle came riding out to meet the caravan. Spotted Tail wanted to give some advice to his nephew out there on the trail, where the people of his agency would not be present to embarrass the great fighter. The elder statesman of the surrendered Sioux understood that the 'crazy' in Crazy Horse's name was no mere accident of Indian descriptive powers. He knew his dangerous nephew well.

'Listen to me,' he said to the warchief, holding up his hand to halt the travois. 'We never have trouble over here in my camp. The sky is clear. The air is still and free from dust. You have come here and you must hear me and what I say for my people. I am the chief here. We keep the peace. We, the Brûlés, your own red brothers, do this willingly. My people obey me. And every other Indian who comes here must obey me also and must listen.'

Spotted Tail again motioned with his hand continuing.

'You say you want to come to this agency and live at peace,' he said, and all could read the doubt in his words. 'All right, come on, then. But if you stay here you will listen to me. That is all. Bring your sick woman and be welcome.'

During this speech, seeming to appear from

nowhere, no less than one hundred armed Brûlè warriors had drifted up to sit their restless ponies behind Spotted Tail. In the silence following the old chief's warning and welcome to Crazy Horse, the flat steel sounds of cocking rifle hammers carried clearly to the dark-faced war leader.

It was a sound he understood, which needed no translation.

Yet he was still the warchief.

Saying not a single word in answer to the greeting of Spotted Tail, he whirled his pony and kicked it in the ribs, heading the little animal toward the packed ranks of the Brûlè riflemen. He rode straight into them and they parted swiftly before him, making a clear path, and wide, so that none might need to touch him.

But at the agency another power waited, and it knew no fear of any Indian.

Major Jesse M. Lee, of the Ninth Infantry, was a just man but firm. He was the agent at Spotted Tail, and he ran it as a tiny white island in a sea of red men with but a hundred troopers. The secret of his power was his word. It was as strong as an Indian's word, and Lee convinced Crazy Horse that he must return at once and in all peace to Fort Robinson and Red Cloud agency.

'Your woman will be cared for,' he promised the warchief. 'But you cannot stay here; you must go back.'

Crazy Horse believed him, asking only that Lee ride with him. This the officer readily agreed to do. More than that, he said that he and the warchief would ride alone. No one else with them. Just the two of them, white man and red. Armed only by their honors and their words.

'*Hau, kola?*' said the white man. 'Have we an agreement between friends?'

'*Ha-ho,*' answered Crazy Horse, 'thank you. Yes.'

The officer looked at him a moment, then nodded.

The two men left, Lee riding in an army ambulance, Crazy Horse permitted to use his war pony.

All along the route of the return journey to Red Cloud groups of agency Indians appeared out of the hills, falling silently into place about and behind Crazy Horse. By the time they neared Red Cloud, no less than two hundred Brûlè 'friendlies' were riding along with the warchief. Crazy Horse did not know them, and learned only too late, the answer to their true allegiance. He believed until the very end that they had 'thought all things over' and had decided to support him. It never entered his savage mind to suspect that his brothers had in fact surrounded him. He sat very tall upon his Sioux pony as the cavalcade drew down upon Fort Robinson.

But he was wrong again. It was not a

14

cavalcade that he headed. It was a cortege.

CHAPTER THREE

Coming under the guns of the post, Crazy Horse grew uneasy. 'Why do all these Indians follow us?' he asked Lee.

The major, who was in fact as disturbed as his Oglala charge by the unwonted gathering, did his best to dissemble. The scores of silent escorts came in tribute to their warchief, he told him. But even as he said it, he saw the ramrod pride go out of Crazy Horse riding beside the army wagon, and he knew that the warchief knew.

'I am sorry, my chief,' he said quietly, making certain that none of the watchers might hear his words. 'You must trust in me. I shall do my best. Keep your word and I will keep mine.'

Crazy Horse did not reply.

He was looking far away over the heads of his mounted brothers who came to see him in his shame. He was looking over the lodges of the agency encampment. Beyond the pine-plank and small-log structures of barracks building and officers' quarters there at Fort Robinson, Nebraska, was freedom. Did it still wait for him in the restless wind? He did not know. He could only ride on and be ready.

Unseen by Major Lee, his hand slid beneath

the snow-white buckskin shirt that was his tribal trademark. There, the sinewed fingers gripped the knife secretly passed to him, in parting, by his wife's young sister, Twilight. If it were the warchief's time to die, others would take the long trail with him.

By this time it was fully dark. The pace had been slow all day and night had come upon the caravan from the Spotted Tail agency. On every hand the false-tongue stories flew. Famed Lieutenant W. P. 'White Hat' Clark, that most overcredited of Indian fighters, a man who hated Crazy Horse as much as the warchief despised him, had done his work well in spreading the lie that Crazy Horse still planned to 'get in close' and murder General Crook. With this vicious story, of course, went no explanation of how Crazy Horse intended to win past the soldiers who guarded the general. Red Beard Crook was, in actual fact, the good friend of the Oglala chief and of every Indian. All the rumor hinted was that Crazy Horse would, with his attack on Crook, thus give the signal for the start of the Sioux uprising at Red Cloud.

Lethal companion to the Clark canard was the true report of the Dry Tortugas order for Crazy Horse's capture and life imprisonment in Florida. The warchief's friends were now appearing on the line of his approach to Fort Robinson. They called to him, warning him of these treacheries, but their appeals echoed

16

hollowly.

If Crazy Horse heard them, he gave no sign, no reply. He was like a man in a medicine trance. He kept looking over the heads of all out toward the place where freedom waited, where the winds of liberty blew for those who would risk everything to ride out to follow them.

His friends saw this and their own mood grew ugly.

Crazy Horse had been promised a direct meeting with General L. P. Bradley, Ninth Infantry, commanding the district of the Black Hills, embracing all of the Indian lands of forts Laramie, Fetterman, Sheridan, and Robinson. But they had been told that General Bradley was not even in his office that night to receive the warchief; only his adjutant was there, a man of little rank absolutely unfit to accept the return of Crazy Horse. A guttural sound of vast unease swept the growing ranks of the true friends. Something stank upon the rising wind of this bad night.

All could feel the presence of Yunke Lo, the God of Death. Some began to sing low prayers, others to cock hidden guns, grasp arcane blades beneath leather shirts.

But these friends were outnumbered and their time in history was past. Many more were those who watched them scowlingly. Crazy Horse had made nothing but trouble for all of them. He stirred up the dust wherever he went.

17

The agency Sioux were weary with his hatred, his plottings.

'*Wagh!*' they growled to one another. 'If that damned Ta Sunke tries anything here, he will get big trouble!'

In the lampshine fronting General Bradley's headquarters, Major Lee halted his wagon. Crazy Horse slowed his pony.

'Get down,' said the white officer. 'Walk with me to the general's office. I will be with you. It is all right.'

They started up the planked walk to the door of the office. The door opened and the adjutant stepped out briskly halting them with upraised arm.

'Major Lee,' he snapped, 'General Bradley directs you to turn Crazy Horse over to the officer of the day. You are to do this without delay. Now, major. It's an order.'

Lee paled. He took the young adjutant roughly by the arm, literally dragging him out of earshot of the warchief.

'My God, man!' he rasped. 'I can't obey that order.'

'You will have to obey it, sir.'

'I will not obey it!' said Lee. 'I have promised this man that he could talk to General Bradley. I had the general's word on that. This is the only reason Crazy Horse came along in peace. He wants to tell his side of the story, and by God, sir! I have pledged him my word that he will be permitted to do so.'

'I'm sorry, major. The general was definite. He put it as an order. Crazy Horse is under arrest.'

Lee drew back, his face white. 'Then that Dry Tortugas story is true?'

'I've seen it myself, major. The arrest order, I mean.'

Lee peered about desperately. A familiar shadow moved in pacing silhouette against the drawn shades of the office.

'Why, that is General Bradley,' accused the agent from Spotted Tail. 'We were given to understand he was absent.'

'He is,' nodded the adjutant. 'That's an order, too.'

Lee's heavy face writhed.

'The hell,' he said, his voice low. 'Get out of my way.'

He went back to Crazy Horse. 'Will you go into the other little room there,' he said, indicating the adjutant's outer office cubicle, 'and wait for me? I am going in to talk to the general myself. Everything will be all right.'

Crazy Horse nodded soberly, shook hands with Major Lee, went quietly into the smaller office. With him went his true friends High Bear, Touch-the-Clouds, Swift Bear, Black Crow, and Good Voice. Missing was the trusted adviser Crowfoot, still at Spotted Tail with Tasina and Twilight. An odd thing happened, too, the moment that the warchief went into the adjutant's office. Indian police

19

moved in swiftly and stood outside the door, rifles ready.

A growl of anger went up from the watching Oglala.

What was this?

A trap?

No. A moment later Major Lee came out of General Bradley's quarters. Even though his face was as blank as a buffalo's sheathed in blizzard sleet, his words did their best.

'General Bradley says the night has grown too late for counciling,' he told Crazy Horse. 'He asks that you go with the officer of the day, as the adjutant has requested. We will talk tomorrow. General Bradley says to tell Crazy Horse that not one hair of his scalp will be harmed.'

This was a bald lie. Bradley had in fact refused point-blank to hear a word from Crazy Horse. He showed the 'arrest and imprison' order to Lee, and that was that. In fairness to the Spotted Tail agent, however, the lie was the best that he could do in the moment's danger, which was entirely real, and he doubtless spared far more blood than now came to darken the ground at Fort Robinson.

Crazy Horse's few friends were happy with the falsehood. They crowded around their fierce-eyed leader.

'You see, Ta Sunke? No reason for worry after all. Do you not feel foolish now? You thought they were making a trap for you, didn't you? The soldier chief's heart was good all along. Tomorrow he shall hold that council with Ta Sunke and things shall be cleared up. *Woyuonihan!*"

It was the Sioux word of deepest respect, and Crazy Horse acknowledged it with one of his rare dark flashes of a smile. He put out his hand to shake hands with Captain Kennington. But the officer of the day was not smiling and did not take the proffered hand. He and two armed troopers led the warchief away, marching stiffly. Crazy Horse went with them, trusting them. Had not the general given his word?

But the anger sound among the Oglala now ran more ugly than before. Kennington and the troopers were not taking their guest to some warm barracks or to the safety of a friend's lodge in the camp of Red Cloud nearby. They were marching the warchief toward the post guardhouse.

And he did not even realize it was a prison!

The bare earthen yard in front of the dingy building was well lighted. It was filled, as well, with armed soldiers. The Indians saw clearly enough the tragedy that would come now. From among the stilled ranks a guttural Oglala voice arose. '*H'g-un! H'g-un!*' it cried aloud— the Bad Face word for 'have courage.' The echo of that pathetic plea was the last salute to a warrior whose kind would ride the northern plains no more. Crazy Horse acknowledged the tribute with a wave, still not understanding

21

where he was going. He stepped toward the door; it swung open before him and he was halfway through when he saw the iron bars within and knew that the white man had at last and indeed put him into a *wickmunke*, a trap.

Too late the proud Oglala read the treachery of the prison bars. His dark fingers slid within the white buckskin shirt, reaching for the hidden blade. The warchief would die fighting for that freedom, and for the last, least chance of yet winning past the white man into the blackness of the night.

One way or another, Ta Sunke Witko would go free.

CHAPTER FOUR

It was just within the guardhouse door that Crazy Horse whirled, knife in hand. At the door Captain Kennington barred his escape with drawn saber. Outside, the two bayonet-armed troopers of the guard detail held fire for fear of hitting the officer. For a tragic instant the tableau was etched against the glare of the yard lanterns, back-lighted by the feeble lamp within the prison structure. Then Crazy Horse struck.

Straightaway the warchief leaped at Kennington. The young officer demonstrated more sense than he had so far shown by getting completely out of the field. He dove to the side making no effort to employ his sword nor to obstruct in any manner the flight of his prisoner. Thus he lived to add his own lies to the pack of tall stories that white man's history would call 'the truth' of what transpired that night at the Fort Robinson guardhouse.

Even the two troopers outside showed their fear of the captive by jumping back from their posts of duty. The sole contribution they made to the immediate recapture of the fleeing man was to shout after him, 'Kill him! Kill him! Don't let him get away!'

As the desperate fugitive reached the outer courtyard, his own friends, not wanting to see him shot down by the soldiers now massing to block his flight, seized Crazy Horse in a spontaneous act of protective custody.

It was Little Big Man, a very muscular brave, who took him from behind, pinning him by both elbows drawn behind the back, and crying, 'Wait, Ta Sunke! Do not do this thing!'

But Crazy Horse had seen the iron bars inside the 'little house.' He knew at last that the terrible story of sending him to that hot place in faraway Florida from whence no Indian returned was not a falsehood made up by his Indian enemies to force him into a killing breakaway from Fort Robinson. The warchief was seeing no friends in that instant. His mind was, as the Sioux said of such rages, 'beyond itself.' Twisting with a smothered cry, he plunged his blade into Little Big Man. The

23

loyal brave fell aside, spurting blood. It was then that Swift Bear and a dozen of the Brûlè friendlies took hold of him and forced him to subside. In their movement they made a circle about him instinctively.

Captain Kennington, rushing up hysterically, slashed with his saber at the members of the circle, shouting, 'Stab him! Kill the son of a bitch!'

The Indians tightened their wall around their friend. But now Crazy Horse was lunging and surging to be free again. He knew, if his red brothers did not, what the soldiers and their captain intended for him. The white men were also beyond their own minds. In vain did the Brûlè call for Ta Sunke Witko to quit fighting, to let them protect him. He burst away from them and, in seeming confusion, rushed back toward the guardhouse.

Some Indians later contended this action was not as it appeared. The warchief, these witnesses said, was trying to 'get around the little house,' to put it between himself and the soldiers, so that they might not begin firing their rifles at him. Whichever way lay the truth, freedom for Crazy Horse did not wait in either direction. The two troopers of his guard detail, desperate to repair their cowardice in letting the prisoner get by them, trapped him now against the closed door of the guardhouse. One of them, the one on the chief's left side, struck for the Indian's vitals. Missing, he jammed his bayonet so deeply into the planking of the door that he could not wrench it free. Crazy Horse, seeing this, turned to leap past that soldier and so win free. As he did so, he turned his side and back to the second trooper who drove his bayonet twice into the warchief. Each time, the blade came away showing a bright scarlet in the courtyard lamplight.

Crazy Horse staggered to the wall of the guardhouse, remaining upright against its bloodied support. Swift Bear and some of the Brûlè came again now to his aid, but the warchief gestured them away.

'Can't you see that they are killing me?' he asked them. 'Let me alone. Let me go.'

The others still made as if to put their hands on him, to help him. As they did so, Crazy Horse straightened and stood away from the guardhouse wall. He spoke beyond the Brûlé, to all the Indians now coming up through the night. His voice made all of them weep in their memories of it.

'Let me go, my friends,' he said. 'You have got me hurt enough.'

The words were soft, pleading. But the Brûlé, to a man, drew back away from the leader of the Oglala Bad Face people. 'They sneaked away,' one old Sioux remembered it, 'like coyotes and jackals from the presence of the king wolf.'

The warchief turned slowly, then, and began to walk. One step. Two steps. Three. And that was all; he slid without a further sound into the dirt of the courtyard, white buckskin shirt and leggins already dark with the running out of his life.

The Indians broke into a milling uproar. Here was the white man at his old tricks. Arrange a peace talk and, while the tongue of friendship wagged, slip the steel into the red man's back. Brûlé friendlies, Miniconjou, Sans Arc reliables, and hostile Oglala, alike, hooted, screamed, and war whooped. Ta Sunke Witko's worst enemies among the Indians felt their hearts now turn bad for the white brother. Cold murder had not been in the bargain of their taking of the warchief. Homicide was a crime virtually unknown to the Indian. That an armed man would stab an unarmed man in the back while that helpless one was not permitted to strike in defense or, worse, was trying to get away, not even knowing the names or the faces of his assassins, this passed the level of Siouan belief.

But it had happened.

The warchief was on the ground. More soldiers with more rifles and more bayonets were rushing all around. Crazy Horse's friends, those who had tried in their ways to save him, were quickly melting into the crowd and away into the night. The hour of the Sioux was done. The power of their war leader was running out with his blood into the dirt yonder. Run, Sioux, run. You were become as a rabbit

26

that had been a wolf.

But one Indian, Touch-the-Clouds, gathered courage enough not to flee. He ran to the body of Crazy Horse and bent down to shelter it. 'Let me take him to the lodges of my people!' he cried brokenly to the menacing soldiers. 'You have already killed him here. Let him die in peace with the Indians, his own people.'

'Carry him into the O.D.'s office,' denied Captain Kennington. 'You get out,' he ordered Touch-the-Clouds. 'All of you get out!' he yelled at the remaining Indians. 'Clear this yard,' he shouted at the troopers. 'Come on, come on. Pick him up and get him inside!'

Touch-the-Clouds was defiant. He had decided to die and be with Ta Sunke Witko.

'I will not go,' he told Kennington, 'except that I go where my friend goes. You may shoot me, but I will stay with him.'

The officer of the day must have known that he would indeed be required to shoot this Indian or to let him remain with Crazy Horse, for he spoke quickly, under his breath, to Touch-the-Clouds.

'You may stay if you give up your gun.'

Touch-the-Clouds stood up. He gave his weapon to the captain. 'You are many. I am only one,' he said. 'You may not trust me, but I will trust you. Now make a way for the warchief.'

With the words, the tall brave knelt again

27

and picked up the softly moaning Crazy Horse. He held the smaller man's huddled body against him as tenderly as a child's. He went slowly toward the lamplight of the office. Behind him came only two other Indians. They were bent of form, shambling in their gaits: the aged, infirm, bewildered parents of the fallen warchief. No one stopped them.

Within minutes the camp was dark. Armed guards and Indian police roamed the shadows. Only the dim light in the O.D.'s office flickered uncertainly. The door opened, outlining the departing form of the post surgeon.

'He's dying.' The surgeon spoke back into the office. 'There is nothing I can do for him. The bayonet punctured both kidneys. Good night, sir.'

'Good night, sir,' echoed Kennington, and the door closed.

Inside the detention room, just beyond the cubbyhole of the O.D.'s office, came a low sound of Indian praying.

To ke ya inapa nun we
To ke ya inapa nun we
He wakan yan inapa nun we
He wakan yan inapa nun we
Kola he ya ce e-e-e yo . . .

It was the two old people praying in the old way. Their son Crazy Horse could scarcely hear them. They continued to chant the sacred

28

words, crouched with their faces to the wall, heads covered with their blankets. The prayer sounded like the crying of wounded animals.

The warchief lay on the bare floor, only a rumpled piling of worn army blankets beneath him. His dark copper skin was a gray color. The lips were already blue. By his side was the friend of his youth, Touch-the-Clouds, watching, waiting, weeping within.

The warchief opened his eyes.

'Give me your hand,' he said to Touch-the-Clouds.

The tall warrior did so. The clasp seemed to ease the suffering of Ta Sunke Witko. 'It is good, brother,' he nodded weakly. 'I am ready now. I do not blame them for what they have done to me.'

Touch-the-Clouds grimaced bitterly. 'Yes,' he said. 'They are only white men.'

Crazy Horse did not appear to hear him. He was struggling to marshal his mind, to give over to his friend a vital message for his old adviser, Crowfoot, at Spotted Tail. When he had composed this trust, he gave it to Touch-the-Clouds, making him swear to deliver it with his own lips. 'I will do it, Ta Sunke,' he said, tears thickening his deep voice. 'And what shall I tell the people?'

He felt the cold fingers tighten on his hand.

'My brother,' murmured Crazy Horse, 'I am bad hurt. Tell the people—' His jaws clamped together, trying to hold back the surge of bright blood from his mouth, but they could not. When the scarlet flow had slackened, he held up his hand, eyes closed.

'Tell the people it is no use to depend on me anymore,' he whispered.

They were the last words he spoke.

Ta Sunke Witko, Crazy Horse, warchief of the Oglala Bad Face band, Fox Dreamer, Keeper of the Sacred Pipe, Spearhead of the Fox Lodge Soldiers, First Warrior of the Seven Council Fires of the Sioux Nation, was dead.

The time: crowding midnight, September 5, 1877.

His age, only the moon before, thirty-three years.

His epitaph, given by Touch-the-Clouds emerging from the office of the officer of the day: 'It is good. He has looked for death, and it has come to him.'

Then, softly, unheard by any white man, 'Now he is with the wind.'

CHAPTER FIVE

Beginning from the very first, from the time of Lewis and Clark, no war had been made on the white man by the Nez Perce Indians, the Slit Nose people. In their lovely mountain valley homelands of the Blue and the Bitterroot ranges of central Idaho, northeastern Oregon, and south-eastern Washington, the Nez Perce

30

welcomed the pale-eyed brother. They even took up the religion of Jesus Christ and sent their children to the mission schools of Marcus Whitman and others, so that they might be taught the ways of the new settlers and thus live at peace with them.

It was not to be.

With the 1840s and the advent of heavy wagon traffic out the Oregon Road into their country, the Nez Perce learned too late what the Sioux and the Cheyenne were to know before them: Where the white man moved in, he never moved out.

The Nez Perce lands were among the choicest in the great Northwest. Moreover, in the valley of the Wallowa, where dwelled their quiet leader Tuekakas and his small sons Heinmot Tooyalakekt and Ollikut, lay the best of all these rich pastures. When, in the later period of the 1860s, the booted and bearded gold hunters discovered that the meadows and mountains of the Wallowa also held the precious yellow metal, the days of the Nez Perce were numbered.

At this same time Chief Tuekakas, who had embraced the white man's religion and renamed himself Joseph, tore up the Bible he once treasured and vowed an end of his friendship to the spoilers of his homeland. This was in 1863. By 1871, Joseph, growing old, his eyesight failing, called to him his eldest son Heinmot and gave him instructions for the care

31

of their people in the hard years that the old man clearly saw ahead.

'My son,' he said, 'my body is returning to my mother earth, and my spirit is going very soon to see the Great Spirit Chief. When I am gone, think of your country. You are the chief of these people. They look to you to guide them. Always remember that your father never sold his country. You must stop your ears whenever you are asked to sign a treaty selling your home. A few more years and the white man will be all around you. They have their eyes on this land. My son, never forget my dying words. This country holds your father's body. Never sell the bones of your father and mother.'

Heinmot Tooyalakekt took the old man's hand and promised it would be as he asked. When Heinmot left the lodge, the soul of Tuekakas was departed and a new Joseph strode forth to lead his people. When they buried the old chief, the young Joseph said, with rare Indian emotion, 'We bury him in this beautiful valley of the winding waters. I love this land more than all the rest of the world. The white man shall not have it. The bones of my father belong here.'

But in far Washington the will of another people, the Pale Eyes, prevailed. The Wallowa was thrown open to white settlement, and the tragedy of Joseph and the Nez Perce was thus guaranteed; the war was made inevitable even though young Joseph did all that he might to keep his people on the path of peace. Others of the Nez Perce chiefs—old White Bird; old Toohoolhoolzote; Ollikut, Joseph's own fierce younger brother; Looking Glass; Two Moons; and Yellow Wolf—all knew that war must come. They were making ready for it even as Joseph talked for peace with General Oliver O. 'One Hand' Howard, commander of the area.

When General Howard, a one-armed veteran of the Civil War and a tough fighter, heard of the revolt brewing among the Nez Perce, he accused Joseph of two-faced talking and ordered him to round up and bring into the army's control at Lapwai agency all of the Nez Perce horses and cattle. This was of course impossible at that time of the year, when all the streams were in full flood and the animals would have to be swum over Snake River. Nonetheless, Joseph ordered it done. When his people saw thousands of their finest horses drowned and saw the bloated bodies of hundreds and hundreds of their fat cattle and tiny calves bobbing down the roaring torrent of the engorged Snake, they could stand no more of the Pale Eye's cruelty. That night the drums of war began to thump in camps from the Imnaha to the Clearwater.

Gathering what was left of their livestock, the Nez Perce started on the long, fighting road that would take them from their sheltered homelands across the brutal rocks of the Lolo

Trail into Idaho and Montana, striking for Canada and for sanctuary with the Sioux brother there.

Joseph, a graduate of the school at Lapwai and a Christian for twenty-five years, wept in his heart. But his dark face showed no tear. He would go with his people. He would lead them on the last war trail. He would do this because the only peace they would ever find, now, must be in another land.

It was in the latter part of June, 1877, while Crazy Horse still lived and conspired to break out and fight his own way to the same freedom with Sitting Bull and the Hunkpapa in the Land of the Grandmother, that the Nez Perces' final decision was taken.

Two great battles had already been fought with the troops of One Hand Howard seeking to force the Nez Perce to 'come in with all their animals,' as ordered. These were in White Bird Canyon and at the Clearwater. Both were total victories for the desperately retreating red warriors. But, once beyond the Clearwater, no way to freedom remained but over the terrible rocks of the Lolo Trail into Idaho. It was, then, either surrender there, or leave the homelands forever.

'*Taz alago, aihits palojami!*' cried Joseph dramatically, ending the war council on the Clearwater, 'good-bye, oh dear fair land!'

In the wind-drive of that black and rainy night the Nez Perce fled again; this time there could be no turning back. Joseph was leaving the bones of his father, but he had sold neither those bones nor the beloved land in which they lay. Now he would do as Crazy Horse would do. He would die to ride free. Wherever his own bones might fall, or wherever lie buried, they would never be sold or surrendered to the white man.

Doomed to be outnumbered eight to one by the soldiers of four field armies converging upon them, the Nez Perce struck out toward their destiny, to a place as yet as unknown to them as well as to the troopers of One Hand Howard, Red Nose Gibbon, Colonel Samuel Sturgis, or Bear Coat Miles. The name of that rendezvous where fate awaited them was, in their own tongue of the Wallowa, Tsanim Alikos Pah, Place of the Manure Fires, taken from the great supplies of buffalo-chip fuel abounding there. The white man would have another name for that place, the name remembered in infamy by all Indians.

It was the Bear Paws.

Takasayogot, the telegraph—that strange soldier machine of the little sparks that talked across rivers and over entire mountains through the open sky—is what killed the Nez Perce. The Slit Nose people thought that by their bloody fighting and terrible sacrifice of marching from Big Hole to Camas Meadow to Canyon Creek to Cow Island and the Missouri River—last barrier to Canada and freedom—

35

they had done the necessary work of slowing down One Hand Howard in his relentless pursuit. The people of Joseph, the pitiful few and wounded survivors of the fifteen-hundred-mile exodus from the Wallowa homelands, made themselves believe that they had only to watch out for One Hand Howard, now many safe miles behind them—at least two, three days hard ride—and all would be well. Had they not at last reached the wide waters of Seloselo Wejanwais, the Painted Water, the great Missouri River? Could they not rest now and do a little buffalo hunting against the last run for the border into the Land of the Grandmother? Surely they had gained time enough for this.

' Lean Elk, the 'trail leader' since Big Hole and Camas Meadow, shook his head in denial of the query.

It was the twenty-third day of the September moon. The weather was turning. Northward across the Seloselo the clouds lay black and low and ugly. A sudden biting cold spat sleet with a rising wind. '*Uetu saikiza*,' said Lean Elk to Joseph, 'I don't like this weather. We had best keep the people moving. I say go on over the river and keep going. What do you say?'

Joseph was given no chance to reply. Old soldier Looking Glass was before him.

'Listen,' said the premier warrior. 'Look at the people. They are cold and wet and hungry. Do we have food? Yes, a little camas-root bread, moldy with the damp. Some bad tea. The flesh of horses dead along our trail. Do you know, on the other hand, what awaits us on that big island there in the river? The one they call Cow Island? Listen again. On that island the big boats from down the Seloselo dump their loads of supplies of everything for the white man in this north country. Even for the redcoats up there in Canada. Yes, and if you will look over there now, in this failing light and through the rain, you will see the stacks of those supplies. Do you look now and see? We must have the food and blankets that are over there. We cannot go on. We must eat and rest and then get in enough fresh buffalo meat to make it to Canada. There is time. One Hand is far behind.'

In vain did Lean Elk rail at this optimism.

'Curse you!' he cried at the old chief. 'Will you never understand that we face other soldiers than those of One Hand? We have already fought Red Nose Gibbon at Big Hole and that eagle chief Sturgis with the Seventh Cavalry at Canyon Creek. You know there will be others. We must push on. This is madness to wait here. We have only to force on now to Milk River and we are free. Speak, Heinmot!' he appealed to Joseph. 'Do not permit this tragedy. This old fool Looking Glass is senile now.'

But Joseph looked into the faces of his starving people and he could not do it. 'There is

37

time,' he said. 'Let us cross over to the island and put something in our bellies.'

Lean Elk was not yet done. Standing with those few unbending fighters who agreed with him for forcing on, he made one last reminder of something all had forgotten.

Did the people remember, he asked the assemblage gathered about Joseph and Looking Glass, the messenger whom Joseph had dispatched to the Sioux brother after the terrible loss of lives and of horses run off by Red Nose Gibbon at Big Hole? That messenger who bore to Ta Sunke Witko, the Crazy Horse of the Bad Face Oglala, the plea of his Nez Perce brother Joseph for Crazy Horse to leave the reservation with all Sioux men and horses he might command and come to meet Joseph and the Slit Nose people to help them win the way to Canada? And did the people not recall, Lean Elk demanded, how that Nez Perce messenger, whose name was Fire Rifle, did reach far-off Red Cloud agency and the Sioux at Fort Robinson, Nebraska? And how Fire Rifle did then return accompanied by a fellow messenger, a Sioux brother called Long Fox, who bore back to his Nez Perce cousins the assurance that Crazy Horse heard their call for help and was coming? Had all the people so soon forgotten the great hope stirred when the Sioux rider came to them on the march with this promise from Crazy Horse? Did none of Lean Elk's listeners care to think back on all of this?

Aha! They did. It was admitted then. Most remembered, most now were thinking back. Good.

What then had been the meeting place agreed to? What famed Indian crossing ford of the Painted Water had been chosen by both bands as a meeting site, where Sioux would join Nez Perce in the long war trail from the Wallowa to the Land of the Grandmother?

Aha, yes. Lean Elk saw them all nodding now. He saw their straining, sudden looks over at the island. Well, damn them all, did they see any Sioux waiting for them over there?

The men with Joseph and Looking Glass began to shift about uneasily. Some began to say they did not care for this situation. The Sioux should have been there.

Lean Elk pressed the opening. 'If there are no Sioux on the island,' he said, 'where are they? I don't see any of them, anywhere. I think they have been defeated. Maybe even all of them are dead. They have had many weeks to meet us here, and they have not come. That's a bad sign, my brothers. It makes this a bad place.'

He paused, staring at them. Lean Elk was a French halfbreed, a very sinister-looking man, one of the great fighters. The people respected him, some say they feared him more, but all listened when he spoke.

'My brothers!' he implored them finally.

39

'Keep going!'

But Joseph, ever the politician, sensed that Lean Elk's words of continued sacrifice were not working. The people wanted to stop. Accordingly, he denied that the Sioux absence was anything but a delay. They would come. Meanwhile, their tardiness gave the people a reason to camp and wait for their Oglala friends, a happy outlook.

It was decided.

The Nez Perce crossed over to Cow Island, capturing it from its tiny garrison of twelve soldiers without one shot. That night the warming fires leaped high. The people ate and were snug in new blankets, and in their dreams they saw no more soldiers, no more sorrow.

＊ Ahead the clouds still hung dark. There was bad weather brewing up on Milk River. It looked especially threatening over the Bear Paw Mountains where Lean Elk had said they would cross the Milk and go for Canada, after they had made their big hunt for the winter's supply of fat cow. Yet what was a little early snow to people who had just come thirteen hundred miles through three armies of United States soldiers? Who now were within four sleeps of the Land of the Grandmother, into which no American soldier could follow them?

Eeh! let it snow.

In their Nez Perce hearts it was sunshine and fair sky.

One Hand Howard? Red Nose Gibbon?

40

Slow Fighter Sturgis? They were all far, far behind. In front there was nothing but Milk River and fat cow and Canada. *Taz, taz,* kick up the ponies. Laugh again. Sing out loud. Chant the old brave songs of the Wallowa. Be happy. Don't look back. Tomorrow is the only day that counts.

*   *   *

But One Hand Howard had not slowed his pursuit because of heroic Nez Perce marching. He had slowed down because of a talk he made across the *takasayogot* with Bear Coat Miles at Fort Keogh on the seventeenth sun of that September moon, thus days before the Nez Perce even made their fight with Sturgis on Canyon Creek!

Said One Hand Howard, on the telegraph to Bear Coat Miles:

'I am going to go slow after these Indians. I know them. When I slow down, they will slow down. The distance from your camp to Cow Island, where we think they will cross the Missouri, is less than it is the way they will travel it from Canyon Creek. You should be able to catch them before they cross the river, if you are ready to go at once. Are you ready? Can you do it?'

Answered Bear Coat to One Hand:

'I am ready; I can do it.'

Nelson Miles was not a big talker like

Custer, but he was the same breed of Indian chaser. He knew, as Yellowhair had known before him, that the way to get a star on his coat instead of an eagle was to count big coup in Indian country.

Only the winter before, he had missed his main chance by letting Sitting Bull and Gall, with the remnant of their Hunkpapa people, slip away from him. He had not even gotten his fair share of the credit for forcing in Crazy Horse and the Oglala. How would Mackenzie and Crook possibly have handled the warchief of the Bad Faces without Nelson Miles sitting down there on the Yellowstone keeping the Sioux from coming south? But that was all bad water gone downstream. Right now he remained a colonel hungering to be a general like Oliver O. Howard. If he could only capture Joseph and the Nez Perce, it would make the eastern papers, and the public would forget that Sitting Bull had made him look foolish. It would get him his star, and then some. Especially if he could bring it off alone, before Howard had a chance to come up and take over the glory.

Miles moved, and he moved fast.

Howard's message came at sundown. Before midnight Bear Coat had his men put into boats and rowed over the Yellowstone. By earliest light, with six hundred soldiers of the Second and Seventh cavalries and the Fifth Infantry, with even the foot soldiers mounted up and riding, and with thirty of the finest Sioux and Cheyenne scouts prowling out front to cut for sign like wolves running a blood track, he began his drive to take the unwary Nez Perce from the rear right flank and without warning, cutting them off south of the Missouri River.

He came to the mouth of Musselshell River, a distance of one hundred twenty-five miles, crows-flight, in time to see the steamer *Benton* slipping downstream. The captain told him he had seen no Nez Perces up the river. There had been no sign of them or any other Indians when he had left Cow Island that same morning.

Miles was extremely pleased.

He could see his general's star glittering in the rain mist, as the *Benton* swept on down the river and went out of sight around a long bend. Calling to his red scouts, he waved them on along the south bank of the Missouri. Firm jaw clamped, he told his officers, 'Well, we've got them now. They are not yet at Cow Island crossing.'

But they had gone only a short way upstream when there bobbed into view a small mackinaw boat tumbling down the fast set of the current below Cow Island. In the bullboat were three white men who had used the heavy rain to slip away when they saw the Indians putting their Appaloosa war ponies into the shallows of the crossing above. What? they cried to Miles. No Indians up there at the island? My God, there were more of the red

43

bastards up there right then than the three of them had seen in seven years of trading on the upper Missouri. Of course it was Joseph and the 'Neppercies.' Who in the hell else did he expect it would be up there this time of year? Sitting Bull?

Nelson Miles's jaw clamped harder still.

What a merciless bit of foul luck. To have the murdering devils right in his hand and have to let them get comfortably away while he could do nothing but sit on the wrong, south side of the river and curse his stupidity for letting the *Benton* steam on by no more than a matter of minutes ago!

If there were only some way to stop the steamer.

She was only around the far bend, still so close they could see her woodsmoke rolling above the low hills. Yet she might as well have been clean down to Fort Union at the Yellowstone. No rider could catch her now. No cavalry horse of mortal breed could reach that rolling smoke before it trailed away to nothing down the Seloselo Wejanwais.

Miles was beaten. The people of Joseph had come ahead of him to Cow Island. He was trapped on the south bank and he would stay a colonel because he could not stop the steamer *Benton* from going on down the Painted Water.

But there was a young lieutenant with Bear Coat who was not so easily defeated. His name was Biddle. If it is white history, honor his

44

name. If it is Indian history, curse it forever. But remember it in all fairness. It was Biddle who stopped the *Benton*.

'Colonel,' he said quietly, 'if you will bring up the twelve-pound fieldpiece and explode it against that high yellow bluff down there where you see the *Benton*'s smoke, the captain will know something is wrong up here and will turn about and come back to see what it is.'

So that is the way white man's history is written. Three cannonballs, exploding into a dirt cliff far down a mighty river, were all it required to bring the steamer back to Miles's encampment. By that night the *Benton* had put Bear Coat and all of his men and all of his horses on the north bank of the Painted Water.

Shivering dawn saw the column from Fort Keogh mounted and moving northwest into the snow clouds roiling over the rugged line of peaks they could see stretching beyond the badlands through which they presently struggled.

'What mountains are those?' asked Miles of the officer who rode with him at column's head.

The officer, a short, fat major, reached into the pocket of his issue greatcoat and spread a wrinkled, rain-limp map on his saddle horn. He scowled at the document a long moment, squinting hard. The rain was freezing now on a rising wind. Snowflakes, cold as the blue-ice gut of the Arctic, were sifting with the sleet.

45

The officer nodded, refolded the map, returned it to his pocket.

'The Bear Paws,' he said.

CHAPTER SIX

The old Indian stood in the blowing cold just outside the office-infirmary of Dr McGillycuddy at Spotted Tail agency. He was waiting to be invited in. He did not ask or plead to be seen. It was accordingly day's end before the busy doctor chanced finally to glance out and see him.

'That old fellow out there,' he said to his orderly, 'how long has he been waiting?'

The orderly peered out. 'Oh, that's old Crowfoot,' he said. 'He's been hanging around most of the day. He don't want nothing, sir.'

McGillycuddy frowned quickly. 'He must want something.'

'Oh, sure. He's got a sick squaw. Which of them ain't, sir?' The orderly gestured defensively. 'I told him if the squaw ain't better to come back in a week. You know what I mean, sir. If I don't weed them out for you, there wouldn't be nothing but sick Injuns lined up out yonder. And Major Lee, sir, he says they're not to pester you. He says if we don't watch you, you'll have every sick Sioux in the Department of the Dakotas down here to Spotted Tail.'

'So I've heard, Maggart. They're blaming me for Crazy Horse trying to bring his woman here. Isn't that it?'

'He didn't just try, sir; she's here.'

'Oh? Why wasn't I informed?'

'Major told me to tell you, sir. I forgot.'

McGillycuddy arose from his desk. 'Maggart,' he said, 'suppose Crazy Horse's wife had been General Bradley's wife. Would you have forgotten to mention she wanted to see me?'

'That ain't fair, sir!' Trooper Maggart was indignant. 'You're comparing a squaw to a white woman. And a general's wife, too!'

'Maggart,' said the agency physician, 'don't you know that Crazy Horse's squaw is the wife of a far greater general than Bradley, or Crook, or any we've got out here?'

'No sir, I don't.'

'Yes, well, never mind.' McGillycuddy's tone was weary. 'Ask that old Indian out there to come in now. Get his woman's name, the one that's sick.'

Trooper Maggart brightened. 'Oh, it ain't old Crowfoot's woman, sir,' he said. 'It's Crazy Horse's. She's the old man's granddaughter, he says. Name's Black Blanket. Comes out Tasina Sapewin in Sioux, sir.'

'Oh, my God,' said McGillycuddy, and he picked up his medical bag and reached for his army greatcoat.

When they were inside the lodge of Tasina

47

Sapewin, McGillycuddy asked Crowfoot to lay some more sticks on the fire to provide a better light for his examination. But the doctor was only trying to draw the stricken woman's eyes from his face. He did not wish her to read his thoughts. He had heard the wracking cough and gagging expectorations as he approached the lodge. Inside, he could smell tuberculosis. The place reeked of the foul sputum of the disease. Barring the miracle of spontaneous remission, the woman was done.

He made a cursory examination nonetheless. He then instructed Maggart, who served as his interpreter, to inform Crowfoot that he was leaving some laudanum pills to ease the woman's suffering, and he would return to see her. 'Be careful,' he admonished the orderly. 'Do not frighten them.'

But Maggart did not get to speak to Crowfoot.

The oldster surprised both white men by answering for himself directly and in good English.

'*Waste*, soldier doctor,' he said, 'it is a good thing.'

He pronounced the Sioux word '*wash-tay*,' and, when she heard it, the squaw smiled wanly up at the agency physician and murmured, '*Ha-ho, hohe. Zunta. Owotanla woyuonihan.*'

'She calls you brother,' Crowfoot told McGillycuddy. 'She says you are truthful and she respects you deeply.'

48

McGillycuddy knelt on the earthen floor beside the rude buffalo-robe pallet. Across from him, he was conscious of the hostile stare of the younger squaw, Twilight. Ignoring the young girl, he took the sick woman's hands in his and pressed them compassionately. 'The medicine will help you,' he told her in English, Crowfoot translating. 'Only take it as I shall direct the grandfather—three pills in each day—and you will feel its power. Do not be afraid.'

McGillycuddy stood up and the wife of the warchief lay back gratefully. The old man, Crowfoot, then indicated he wanted to speak with the soldier doctor 'one man to the other.' Would the doctor please send the trooper to wait outside?

Bidden to retreat, Maggart grumbled about the safety of leaving his superior with a crazy old medicine priest and a wild young squaw who carried a knife just in the way she looked at a white man. McGillycuddy's reply was, 'Get the hell outside,' and the reluctant trooper departed.

For a moment the only sound remaining was the hoarse breathing of Tasina Sapewin. Then Crowfoot spoke.

In the darkness of the past night, he said, a friend of Crazy Horse's had come down from Red Cloud agency to tell what happened there, and to bear a final word from Crazy Horse to his family at Spotted Tail. That word had been for all of them to look after themselves. The soldier doctor would of course know what the warchief really meant by that message.

'What I want to know of you,' the old man concluded, 'is if this woman is able to travel? I ask it in trust.'

Ahh! thought McGillycuddy. Maggart had been right. A single white man was no match for this red cunning.

The old rascal and his younger granddaughter were going to run for it. He was asking if he might entrust the older sister to the care of Dr McGillycuddy, the prescription so written as to include the good doctor's silence and even assistance in the flight to the extent of covering up for the two miscreants long enough to give them a good start.

McGillycuddy had to laugh.

The idea appealed to both his humanitarian sense of justice and his Celtic fey streak.

'Go ahead, I am listening,' he told the old man.

Crowfoot nodded and made the sign of indebtedness. It would be the best thing, he suggested, for the doctor to order Tasina taken into the small sickhouse where the doctor himself lived and worked. That way the soldiers and the Indian police and spies would not have to worry about where Crowfoot and Twilight might be, since they had Tasina Sapewin where they could watch her all day long. But here McGillycuddy interrupted.

50

'On the other hand,' he pointed out dryly, 'the soldiers and the others would know where you and the younger sister were not—and that would be where you should be every day, visiting the sick sister.'

It was Crowfoot's turn to think, ahh! and to see that this soldier doctor was indeed a *hohe*, a brother, as Tasina had called him. He grinned and patted McGillycuddy's hand.

'Go ahead,' he winked. 'Now *I* am listening.'

The agency physician opened his medical bag and took from it a small blue glass bottle of pills. They were for the woman Tasina, a supply for three days, he told Crowfoot. That would be specifically tonight and then two more days following. Tomorrow and the next day he, McGillycuddy, would come and see the woman, and no one else with him. Neither the trooper outside nor any other soldier would visit the lodge. The doctor did this occasionally with very sick patients. Did Crowfoot understand?

'You should have been an Indian!' said Crowfoot, admiringly. 'You think just like a Sioux.'

'Well,' said McGillycuddy, 'what do you say?'

Rare emotion lit the seamed leather of the old medicine priest's face. He reached across the tipi fire and took the white man's hand. He wrung it happily with both of his hands. 'I say good-bye, soldier doctor,' he said. '*Waste!*'

51

McGillycuddy closed his bag, straightened. He said no more to the old man but bent and went out of the lodge and did not look back. In his mind was peace and in his heart contentment. To him, as to Crowfoot, it was '*wash-tay*.'

He was a doctor, not a soldier or policeman.

CHAPTER SEVEN

Crowfoot scarcely waited for the doctor and his orderly to be gone, then he called Twilight to him and told her to make her preparations. He explained that the kindly physician had given them more than the small bottle of pills for Tasina. He had provided them with a promise of two days beyond this night to get away from Spotted Tail agency. They must not delay.

To this, the young squaw nodded vigorous agreement. She demonstrated, however, subsequent indecision about leaving her elder sister, demanding to know why Tasina might not go away from the agency as she had come to it, on the travois?

'We cannot take her where we go,' was Crowfoot's only answer. 'Hurry and arrange the things for our journey.' He ducked out the flaps to return in a few minutes with his old mule and the travois. They loaded the dragpole conveyance swiftly. 'Come on, girl,' he urged, joining Twilight within the emptied lodge. 'We must be on the trail.'

Tasina Sapewin, the ill one, lay fitfully asleep with the first dosage of the white man's potent drug given her by Crowfoot. Twilight, kneeling by her side, made certain to place the bottle of pills in the sick woman's hand, then looked up at Crowfoot. She had already spoken her farewells to the older sister a score of times in her heart and mind. Yet now that the real time was here, she did not have any words.

'It does not matter,' called her grandfather softly. 'She cannot hear you. Say anything and be quick. If that old travois mule brays or even snorts good and loud, someone will come looking to see what we do here at this late hour outside a sick lodge.'

Twilight nodded and made a sign to him. She leaned over and kissed Tasina in the white man's way. Her sister would know when she awakened that they had gone. And she would know why. It was a sad thing they could not tell her where they were going, that they could not say the goodbyes out loud while she was awake. But sick ones could not be trusted. They traveled outside themselves with the fever of their disease. They might speak at the wrong time and before the wrong people. Old Crowfoot had been right in this. Twilight knew it. She was of the old breed herself, even though of so few winters. She was smart and mean and shy as the bitch-wolf, and as ruthless. So her last parting was made with a brush of her lips, unfelt by her sister, and then she was at the entryflaps with the old man, and they were outside and had laced the flaps and the old one was motioning her to get into the travois.

Twilight shook her small head, the oval face defiant.

'One of the poles might scrape over a rock,' she whispered, 'or make a noise in gravel. The snow is not yet deep enough on the ground to muffle the sounds of the poles. Go on, lead out. I will follow the travois, watching rearward.' Her hand slid into the heavy winter coat she wore. Crowfoot could see the knife blade. 'If anyone comes up behind us,' the young squaw said, 'they will find they have taken the wrong trail.'

'I believe it,' said the grandfather. 'You are the true sister of the warchief, more his blood than his own sister.'

'Lead out,' repeated the slim girl. '*Hopo, hookahey—!*'

The old man took the halter of the mule. 'My friend,' he muttered, 'place your feet with the greatest care, but do not delay.' The ancient travois animal, as though he comprehended the instructions, snuffled quietly and pushed off through the thickening snowfall. He went as carefully as if treading quicksand or threading the lip of a mountain chasm. In minutes they were beyond the cluster of lodges and had cut away from the road to Red Cloud

54

agency and Fort Robinson and were into the near, low hills, north and west of the Brûlè agency at Spotted Tail. They saw no scout, no red police, no white soldier, and none saw them. Presently, just over the second hill, Twilight came wading the snows up beside the grandfather, puffing from the climb.

'Where do we go?' she asked the old man, breath regained.

'To the place where the warchief was going when they killed him,' he answered. 'Have no fear, H'tayetu. *Hopo!*'

'*Hookahey*,' the slim girl nodded. 'I fear nothing.'

The old man only grunted, spoke in Sioux to the backhumped mule, and set out down the second hill holding onto a travois pole. The young girl waited, looking back toward Spotted Tail and the lodge of Tasina Sapewin.

'I will make the white man remember you, poor sister,' she promised aloud, the beautiful face suddenly no longer so beautiful. 'And he will remember us, too.'

Then she was gone on down the hill after Crowfoot and the mule. Their direction bore away from both Spotted Tail and Red Cloud agencies and from the hundreds of soldiers of General L. P. Bradley at Fort Robinson. They were only one slight girl of sixteen or seventeen summers, one very old man of at least seventy winters, and one spavined, polegalled bonepile of a travois mule, but the white man would remember them. Twilight had said her vows on that.

CHAPTER EIGHT

Maggart came up to the lodge cautiously. Outside it, he crouched hidden behind a small growth of scrub. Dark as it now was, he could still see the twin wavering tracks of the travois poles and the round dots of the mule's hoofprints leading away to the northwest. The tracks were filling so rapidly with the new snow that they would have been covered within another ten minutes. Whoever had gone that way had done so only moments before his arrival.

He left the cover of the brush and came to listen intently against the cowhides of the lodge. He could hear nothing inside. Not even the fire crackled or popped or hissed. The squaw, if she yet lived, was in drugged stupor or coma. Damn.

Going to the front of the lodge, he found the flaps laced from the outside. My God, had they all gone? Had that old fool of a medicine man dragged that dying creature out into this weather? If he had, why? Maggart suddenly knew one thing for certain. He had been right about something being wrong here. Had he also been right in fearing it was something involving him? Or, rather, something involving the security of his plan for an early out from the service, and a long, prosperous 'over the hill' to Canada?

Had he also thus been a hundred and ten percent correct in his hunch to bring along his moneybelt with its weight of gold coin, the color he had insisted on receiving from his outlaw confederates as the payoff for his 'inside' services at Fort Robinson?

That last big question would depend on what he found in the Sioux lodge. For he understood now that he must go under the sideskins and risk whatever waited within. To unlace the entryflaps would never do. Maggart had been in Indian country long enough to know that you never disturbed the way the red man left his camps. That was the automatic mistake that labeled your visit that of a white man. Taking a final look around, the orderly went into the snow and wriggled under the pegged-down buffalo hides between lodgepoles.

Inside, he had to wait for his eyes to adjust to the gloom. The fire was smoking, giving no light but a feeble glow the size of two spread hands. When he could see well enough, he made out the sick woman lying where he had last seen her on the pallet of bull robes. The lodge had been gutted of Indian 'furniture,' including everything that would go into a travois and serve on the trail to support red life in the North Plains at that harsh time of the year, and on the Indian run.

'The stinking bastards!' hissed Maggart, anger blotting out caution. At once, the slight form beyond the fireglow stirred. 'What?' it asked in the Oglala dialect. 'Who is that? Who comes? Grandfather? Little sister?'

Tasina had started up to one elbow. But the few words exhausted her and she fell back again, moaning softly.

Maggart was very careful again. 'An old friend,' he called out. 'Sent by Crowfoot and Twilight. They have gone and I am to watch over you for them.' His own accents matched the squaw's skillfully. The voice itself was high for an Indian male, but the slurring that made '*wash-tays*' out of the *wastes*, and 'tashunkas' out of the Ta Sunkes, was perfect in its Siouan mimicry. 'Do you hear me, Tasina?'

The dark head stirred on the pallet, nodding assent.

Maggart looked about and found one old and rotted buffalo robe left behind by the fugitives. He shrouded himself in this, to look like the Oglala he claimed to be, and went to sit beside the moribund squaw.

'Now listen,' he said, 'this is very important. They forgot to tell me *where* they were going. You understand?'

Again Tasina Sapewin nodded perceptively.

'Good. Now then, try hard to remember. Where did they go? I must know this. Something has happened. I must go after them and warn them. Do you still hear me, Tasina?'

'Yes, yes; it is so cold. Won't you please put two or three—good, dry—sticks on the little fire?'

Maggart did not want to do that, did not want any new light shed on his Oglala disguise. But he could see that the woman was partly aware and he knew, as well, that the risk must be taken. He put the wood on the embers and blew on the smoky base to create more smoke than flame. Then he was back at the squaw, hovering over her in the rotted robe, looking like Yunke Lo, like death himself, in the flickering, foul-odored light of the sick lodge.

'Now you must understand, my sister. Crowfoot and Twilight have fled, a bad thing surely. The soldiers have gone after them. They will put them in the same prison where Ta Sunke died, and they will send them to Florida, to the Hot Place, where they will die. Don't you want to save them? Don't you want to tell me where they went? If you tell me, I can find them and warn them in time. No white soldier can travel through snow weather like an Indian friend can. I will find them before the soldiers do, but you must tell me where to look for them. All right, Tasina? *Shacun winyan wan aipi?* Don't you want an Indian to rescue them?'

Again the squaw's head moved weakly. 'Yes, yes—I do.'

'Then, tell me. Tell me now!'

59

The woman's lips moved and Maggart had to lean very nearly down to her face to hear what words were framed. There were lapses and gaps in the trail of what she told him, but the sense of it came through, and the hackles of the listening trooper's original fear for himself arose within him.

Tasina Sapewin did not say that in truth she knew where Crowfoot and her young sister may have fled. None had told her this, she informed Maggart. Or if they had, she, in her illness, did not remember it. But she did know where she would have gone in their same places. It was where the warchief had told them all he planned to go; it was where he had intended to get the horses to mount his breakout from Fort Robinson and the agencies.

Here, Tasina went into a paroxysm of coughing, and the agonized soldier believed the Sioux woman would die before telling him that vital destination. He had heard the rumor that Crazy Horse and his wild followers had figured a way to get horses. Now this Indian confirmation of the fact made him cold all over. For Maggart knew where the only horses within reach of Fort Robinson were being held—were being secretly held—and he knew why those horses were where they were. It was not for Sioux use, either tame or wild, that those animals were collected and harbored out there in the hills toward the home country of the Oglala. It was for white men's profit. And one of those white men was trooper W. O. Maggart, Ninth Infantry, Spotted Tail Agency, Nebraska.

He raised the woman up and got her lungs momentarily opened, and she was able, presently, to continue. The remainder of the story did nothing to banish the fear now chilling her visitor.

Indeed, he waited only until he was certain, listening as a man will whose life is threatened, that he and the Oglala squaw were talking of the same secret herd of stolen Oglala horses. Then he acted. His options had run out. If Tasina Sapewin lived long enough, or became lucid enough to repeat this story of the stolen herd to someone else—say, to Dr McGillycuddy—soldiers would indeed be out looking for old Crowfoot and his granddaughter *and* the 'ghost horses of the northwest hills.'

More than that: If Crazy Horse, damn his memory, had trusted a tame Indian like his wife Tasina with the knowledge of the supposedly hidden herd, God alone could know how many other Indians, including spies of the white man, also knew of the horses or at least knew of the story about them.

Well, there was one way to silence the squaw.

Maggart roused the woman again, asking her where she had put the medicine pills the white soldier doctor had left for her use. Tasina understood him. A thin hand came from beneath the robe, the infirmary bottle clenched within shrunken fingers. 'Little sister gave them to me,' she murmured. 'I remember now. She said she would be back, but I must take the pills for myself if she were delayed.'

'Yes,' nodded Maggart. 'Yes. Here.'

He spilled a handful of the opium pellets into his palm, forcing them into the squaw's mouth and holding the tin cup of water by the pallet's side to her lips. 'Drink deep,' he said. 'Swallow hard.'

When she had obeyed him, he emptied the remainder of the pills into his hand, put the empty bottle in the squaw's hand, and placed that hand back beneath the buffalo robe. The woman objected to taking so many pills but Maggart insisted and she was too ill to argue. The final swallowing done, she fell back on her pallet, the objects in her failing vision aswim and blurring. At the very last the straining eyes fastened on her visitor's face. The shroud of his disguise had fallen away, revealing the betrayer's true identity. Too late, Maggart reached to replace the rotted robe about his head.

'*Wicowicasa sni,*' the Indian woman said, 'You have lied to me. You are no red man. You are the *wasicun*, the white man, the one who helps the soldier doctor.'

Maggart nodded, threw aside the foul robe,

stood up.

'*Owatonla,*' he answered her, 'your words are straight.'

Tasina Sapewin did not reply. Neither did she see Maggart roll beneath the sideskins of the lodge, back out into the night.

The wife of the warchief was beyond the world.

CHAPTER NINE

'Ride the son of a bitch!' the first man yelled. 'Put them cartwheels in his goddamn ears!'

The Mexican youth to whom he shouted laughed and swung his hat and scratched with his Chihuahua rowels as high along the squalling horse's neck as he could reach. 'Not quite the ears!' he shouted back in Spanish. 'Why don't you show me how to do it?'

The first man had to delay his reply while the wild mount he himself bestrode jolted the earth in a series of stiff-legged jumps. When the animal stopped jumping and went into a flurry of sunfishing, its rider yelled back. 'It ain't the Anglo style, Frank. We do it businesslike. Watch close. Heeyahhh!'

With the shout, he put his spurs to their shanks into the forequarters of his mount. The brute squealed in pain, the blood showering like rain from the cruel incisions.

'Christ!' announced a third man, also

63

rocketing about the cleared breaking area atop a green bronco. 'Way you get to the ears, big man, is cut the poor goddamn horse off at the withers. Looky here at my pony. He ain't even nicked.'

'He ain't broke, neither!' cursed the white rider.

'Hell he ain't!' glared the Negro breaker, guiding his mount through a surrendering spate of buck-jumps to a quivering halt. He slid off the beaten animal, walked three steps away from it, not looking back. The mustang, as if bewildered, turned and followed after him like a whipped dog. 'Leave me see you pile off that bastard of yours and have him to foller you home,' the black rider challenged.

Here, the Mexican youth, having his own mount under control, cautioned the angry Negro. 'Don't push him, Blue. We damn near got this thing brung off.' Texas-born, El Paso-reared, his Anglo speech was as natural to him as soft Spanish. 'This is the last of them.'

The black rider relaxed. He checked his pony to stand beside that of his companion. 'Yeah, that's so,' he admitted. 'These here is the last three to be busted. I'd lost track.'

'I ain't,' said the Mexican. 'All me and you got to do now is keep old Con happy. Then we split the granddaddy pot and everybody dies rich.' For a moment they watched the third rider still fighting his sunfisher, but slowing him now. 'What's your final herd count, *hombre*?'

The black rider pulled off his hat, dug a crumpled tally sheet from inside its sweatband. He frowned over the scrawl of arithmetic, then said, 'Four hundred head, give or take a dozen lame.'

The Mexican youth glanced over to where the big third rider was bringing his bleeding horse literally to its knees in a last stumble of exhaustion. 'Yeah,' he said softly. 'God's name, we *will* be rich. I can't believe it even yet.'

Across the arena, the tall rider was stepping off the beautiful four-year-old chestnut he had just final-topped. The valiant gelding stood shaking, slender neck outflung, tongue protruded in a slather of pink froth, gasping to breathe.

'The bastard,' said the black man. 'That pore little chestnut ain't never going to bring five cents over to the fort. He's done broke his windpipe to puckerhole. Goddamn him.'

'*Cuidado, amigo*,' said the Mexican. 'Here he comes.'

Brushing the blood-flecked saliva from himself, the tall rider bowlegged his way over to where they stood. Eyeing his companions, he spoke with the dangerous man's deceptive quietness. 'I hate to see them blow like that,' he said.

The Negro breaker scowled, answered nothing. The Mexican youth shrugged, 'We all do, *jefe*.'

The tall man spat into the ground. 'Don't give me any of them "chief" cow chips, Frank,' he advised. 'We're divvying dead even. You know that.' He pushed past them toward the spiral of woodsmoke marking their campsite at timber's edge. 'Come on. Let's go see what Cookie's got wrangled up for our supper.'

'Skookum chuck, like always,' said the Mexican youngster. 'Thank God his cooking ain't as addled as him.' He moved off after the other, motioning the Negro rider to do likewise. But Blue Slattery was a southern black. Bred and born, but unbroken, to slavery, he was a fiercely proud man, resentful still of what his people had suffered. He raised his voice with the defiant jut of his jaw.

'I ain't hongry,' he said and stood unmoving.

The tall leader understood it was a challenge. Stopping, he turned slowly about. He spread his bowed legs, hand brushing his revolver's butt.

'You'll eat,' he said. Then, easily, 'Won't you, Blue?'

'When I want,' nodded the black man. He had no gun nearer than his Winchester at the camp. He knew that Con Jenkins might shoot him where he stood. Yet he stood there.

'Compañeros,' said Francisco Gavilan. 'This ain't nothing. Let it pass. We're almost home.'

'Yeah,' Con Jenkins nodded. 'No need to

66

push, Blue.'

The name came from Slattery's dark color. It was a Mississippi term which he disliked, as he disliked nigger. But white men had called him both for as long as memory served. The Mexican was right; he had better stand down. Be smart. Remember how far they had come with this Con Jenkins job.

The big herd was finally broken and ready for delivery to Fort Robinson as remounts for the cavalry troops. There would be more money paid them than Blue Slattery had ever seen or ever imagined there to be in all the world. And it was waiting for them just to the east, over the line in Nebraska, yonder. All he and the Mexican had to do was take a few more days of Con's roostering, while their 'inside man' over at the fort made his final dicker with the purchasing agent. Why, God, it would be crazy to buck Con now.

After they got their money, Blue and the Mexican kid had only to beat the coming winter south. It would be a life of kings, Gavilan had promised. Safe in old Mexico with all that American money? Why, man, they would be free as birds, the Mexican youth had told him. With never a care for the color of a black man's skin, or for the murder warrants out for both of them there in Wyoming Territory. *Ai Chihuahua!* as Francisco Gavilan always said: Don't argue with the Anglos.

Blue Slattery let the fight go out of his wide

shoulders, loosened the thick muscles of his arms and legs.

'Sure enough,' he nodded to the white outlaw, 'I ain't et since sunup. I plumb forgot.'

'You damned near did,' warned the lantern-jawed Jenkins, and he turned and led the way to the supperfire.

CHAPTER TEN

An old man, a young girl, and a pack-scarred mule would not seem the likely instruments of a larger Indian history. Many a Sioux before them had fled alone or with but a single companion rather than endure the captive despair of agency life. Some had reached Canada. More of them had found their freedom in death along the trail. But the flight of Crowfoot, Twilight, and the mule Itunkasan Luta, Red Weasel, was to become a folk thing of red pride to rank only below the defeat of Crook on the Rosebud and the killing of Yellowhair Custer on the banks of the Greasy Grass.

Tragedies of loss in the Siouan memory were all too many. Defeats of the white man were things more rare than albino buffalo and kept treaties. The journey of the three comrades the Sioux would come to call Tahunsa Yamini, 'the Three Cousins,' was such a defeat of the *wasicun*. It was more remarkable in the end

68

because the white man never learned its secret. And no wonder. The red men themselves did not understand the full audacity of the thing until long winters past its happening. Only then, when it was too late to appear in the white man's history books, did the Oglala skin painters enter it into tribal record. Their tardiness clouded the record. Indians do not print history books. Red earth and ocher symbols fade and bleach away. By the time the story was recorded, every schoolboy knew how the victory had gone and to which side, at Tsanim Alikos Pah, the Place of the Manure Fires, up toward Milk River and the Bear Paw Mountains on the way to the Land of the Grandmother.

It remained a certainty, also, that the elderly medicine priest and his handsome granddaughter, fleeing Fort Robinson, Nebraska, that night of the blowing snows, in September, 1877, held no real conception of their fated roles. True Indians, their primary concern that first night out was for a little hot food and for survival of the Wyoming cold. They were burrowed in beneath a cutbank that warded off the freezing wind. Their fire was small, made of dry wood that had been piled in the travois for the journey. The mule was with them snug under the shelving bank, eating what they were eating, a bit of parched corn and some buffalo tallow. All were safe for the hour, their spirits good.

When the snow water had boiled and the few crushed beans of their coffee were steeped in it a sufficient time, they drank in turns directly from the small battered pot. They had none of the treasured *can hanpi*, white juice of the wood, white sugar. But they smacked their lips and grunted in Oglalan and told one another of their good luck to this place. Soon, however, Crowfoot began to frown. He dug out his stone pipe and loaded it from his pouch of *kinnikinnic*, the awesome Indian tobacco made with the dried bark of the red willow and, white users insisted, equal parts of loco weed, bear gall, and buffalo chips. Lighting up with an ember, he traded the pipe back and forth with his granddaughter for a half a dozen ceremonial puffs, took it finally to himself, and he was ready.

'Girl,' he said with great seriousness, 'I must now tell you of the dream of Crazy Horse. I could not divulge it before. There were too many bad Indians at Spotted Tail and Red Cloud. They had sold their ears to the soldier chiefs. Listen to this.'

Twilight would recall, the old man began, that about one moon after the Oglala arrived at Red Cloud agency and Fort Robinson, a rumor spread that their Nez Perce brothers were at war with the soldiers out in their Wallowa country. The tale was that the Slit Nose chief Joseph had tried the *wasicun*'s road and found it rocky. When the white man stole

70

his land, Joseph struck his lodges in the night and fled for Canada, precisely as Sitting Bull had done.

At first it was not known that this story was true. But soon the Indian spies among the Cheyenne scouts of the Sioux agencies were hearing it from their soldier chiefs. Indeed, Joseph had led the Nez Perce people out of their homeland. Emissaries had come from Sitting Bull up in Canada inviting the Slit Noses to come and live with the Hunkpapa and the Red River Mixed Bloods. Already, the Nez Perces had won three notable battles from some of the greatest soldier chiefs. One Hand Howard had been badly defeated at the Clearwater and, before that, in White Bird Canyon. Red Nose Gibbon, a strong fighter, had killed many Indians at the Big Hole, a tragic thing for the Nez Perces. But the Slit Noses had rallied and escaped to Camas Meadow where they routed the pursuing troops of Gibbon, the eagle chief.

When Crazy Horse heard of these Indian victories, he called the Sioux leaders to secret council, exhorting them to follow the Nez Perce example.

What had become of the once-feared and mighty Sioux? he challenged the scowling chiefs. Would his old war trail comrades among the Sans Arc, the Brûlé, the Wahpeton, and the Miniconjou bands continue to cower on the reservation while Joseph and the Slit Noses were dying on their march to freedom? Come, my chiefs! he shouted. Who will ride with Crazy Horse to join our Slit Nose brothers in the field and fight with them up into the Land of the Grandmother?

Hopo! Hookahey! Who was ready to bring in the war ponies, paint the faces, and escape into the night to go and fight to be free? What, no one? Ah, for shame. *Wicowicasa sni!* But listen, do not turn away.

Had the chiefs not heard that Bear Coat Miles was marching north to cut off Joseph before he reached Canada? Did they not remember it was this same Bear Coat Miles who had lured Sitting Bull and the Hunkpapa cousins into his camp down on the Yellowstone and tried to kill them in a trap? Were the Oglala and all the other bands going to sit like squaws and turn away from their warchief's eyes? Or were they going to get their horses and say goodbye to their women? Go now. Do it!

But still the men did not move.

The horses, they pointed out to Crazy Horse, were the big problem with all of his grand talk. The warchief was bad-dreaming of the old days. Their Sioux horses, all of their good buffalo runners and soldier-fighting stock had been surrendered or stolen from them coming into Fort Robinson. All they had left were blind mules and windbroken packmares. What kind of a war journey might be ridden on such bonepiles? No. The fighters were not squaws who would turn away from Ta Sunke's eyes, but he was going to have to show them where all these wonderful war ponies were before they would vote the long stick and go with him to fight with Joseph and the Slit Noses against Bear Coat Miles and One Hand Howard. *Wagh!* It was easy for Ta Sunke to call them women and for him to grunt and roar like a boar grizzly in the rut. But he was no better than any of them without a war horse. So let that be the end of it. There were no horses and there would be no war. *Wonunicun*, they were sorry.

At first it seemed the warchief would strike the trusted friends and onetime great fighters who spoke thus to him. Then Crazy Horse calmed himself. Taking council with old Crowfoot, he asked the men to pledge to him their sacred honors that they would divulge nothing of what he was now compelled to tell them.

Had they heard, he asked them, the shadow story creeping in the night from lodge to lodge, whispering to the people that Crazy Horse had actually received a messenger from Joseph, chief of all the Nez Perces? Well, it was no shadow story. The name of the messenger was Fire Rifle. He had come in secret to Red Cloud agency and there spoken with Crazy Horse, pleading for men and horses to come and join

Joseph. A Sioux messenger, Long Fox, had been named to ride back with Fire Rifle, finding the Nez Perce column on the march and carrying to its leaders Crazy Horse's agreement to meet the Slit Nose brothers at Cow Island, where the old Indian crossing went over the Mini Sosi, the big Mud Water, the Missouri River.

*   *   *

Here, old Crowfoot interrupted his tale to suck the cold spittle out of his pipe. He packed in a second load of *kinnikinnic*, picked a coal from the fire bed with his bare hand, and settled it in the pipe's stone bowl.

The girl said nothing, waiting for him to continue.

'Now,' he said, puffing the smoke, 'here is how it went from there.'

The warchief, Crowfoot told Tasina, asked his men to trust him. To wait, to listen, to put their lives in his leadership, as they always had. He *knew* where the horses were that they must have. He could not tell them where these animals were, however, for fear that the spies at Red Cloud and Spotted Tail would hear of it and tell the soldiers.

Have I ever lied to you? Crazy Horse cried to them.

But the chiefs were getting up and going away.

They knew he did not have those horses. They understood the animals thundered only across the prairies of his fevered mind. Too bad, too. It was an eloquent thing Crazy Horse had said. It would be a splendid thing to fight at the side of the Slit Nose brother out there in Montana somewhere beyond the Greasy Grass where Yellowhair Custer had fallen. But it was coming into September soon. It would take two weeks of hard riding just to get up there in that Missouri River country again. And the cold was growing in the nights. No, it was of no use to be crazy like Ta Sunke. He would only get them all killed with himself.

Now of course if he really *did* know where those good war horses might be found, that was something else.

But they all knew where those horses were.

In Ta Sunke's crazy head.

*   *   *   *

'The only trouble with that,' concluded old Crowfoot, knocking out his pipe, 'is that Ta Sunke was not crazy in his head: He *did* know where those horses were.'

Twilight frowned, thinking the grandfather was also medicine dreaming about those good fighting ponies.

But she did not wish to hurt the old man.

'Yes,' she said gently. 'And where was that?'

Crowfoot narrowed his eyes until they were

slitted like a snake's.

'Where you and I are going, girl,' he said, and he would say no more.

Three hours later, with first light of the new day, they were repacked and traveling onward. As before, the mule Red Weasel knew the way unbidden. With dusk they had come another twenty miles. Just ahead loomed a shrouded ridge.

'The horses are there,' pointed the old man. 'Just over those rocks where the clouds hang low. There is a pass up there. You can't see it and neither can I. But old Weasel knows it is there. It will let us down into a lovely high meadow. That's where they are hidden. That's where the white devils hold the warchief's horses.'

It was the first the girl had heard of any 'white devils.' She repeated the term curiously, and Crowfoot nodded.

'Yes, I said devils. You'll see.'

'Perhaps,' shivered the girl, eyeing the cloud bank. 'If we stop talking and start climbing. That's a rough looking trail up there, Grandfather.'

'Yes,' said the old man. 'But there's time. You will get to see the warchief's horses.'

'And the white devils?' The girl was not teasing her grandfather. Her slant black eyes burned in the thickening gloom. 'Will there be time, also, to see them?'

'Yes,' said the old man. 'Go ahead, Weasel.

If you don't mind, I'll hang onto your tail.' He seized the paintbrush bristle of the pack animal's tail and the mule plunged ahead up the steep rise, towing the weary oldster behind him. After both of them came Twilight. She moved as if she were not tired now, eagerly and with a hunter's concentration. She wanted to see those Oglala horses, yes. But she wanted to see another thing even more. It was the white devils who guarded them. The white devils who had stolen those war ponies from her fierce brother-in-law, Ta Sunke Witko, Crazy Horse.

The slim red hand crept beneath her ragged winter robe to close about the haft of the long skinning knife belted there.

'I am coming, *wasicun*,' she whispered. 'Be ready.'

CHAPTER ELEVEN

It was a good supper of boiled grouse stew with yellow saleratus biscuits for sopping the rich gravy. The coffee, hissing hot and thick with sugar, sat just right with the gift of the *Habana* cigars handed round by a plainly contrite Con Jenkins. Where Con had gotten the rare smokes none of his comrades could imagine. But the fact that he had thought to share them was duly noted and sighed over in relief. Their gunfighter commander in chief was not the man whom even experienced outlaws such as themselves would care to anger on purpose. Moreover, Con Jenkins was not the leader in this thing only by virtue of his quick Colt. He had a teeming and fertile owlhoot mind that was known from the Hole-in-the-Wall to Robbers' Roost. 'It was a genuine Con Jenkins' had become bandit jargon for a job that went off superbly. That a man of his changeable temper and self-evident physical menace could also charm a whiskey drummer out of his sample case or divest a lady schoolmarm of her virtue, without either party squawking much less seeking formal complaint, was just one of those oddities of nature that defied classification. Like the grizzly bear that could grin a man to death or the bull elk in rut that bugled soprano, Con Jenkins simply refused to fit the pattern. The same man who had brutally ridden the little chestnut to a gasping froth was the one now handing out four-bit cigars.

Nor were the expensive smokes the end of it. Even while his comrades were lighting up and dragging to deepest cavern of grateful lung the wonderful light-blue aroma of the *Habanas*, Con was rummaging in his possibles sack and coming up with another, even more sacred treasure of the isolated owlhoot. It was a full half-gallon jug of beautiful white corn whiskey cooked off and charcoaled in far Kentucky, the 'pure thing,' and no mixture of boat varnish and kerosene 'shook up in Cheyenne' for the

Indian trade. How their headman had kept that crown jewel stashed for the four months of the great Oglala herd-breaking job was one too many for his fellows. Even when you began to think you knew Con, he would deal you three ladies and sit there himself with a set of deuces. He was *mas loco*, that's all.

'*Jefe*,' the young Mexican now said with a grin, 'you never cease to surprise a man. *Santa!*'

'Remember it, Frank,' said Con Jenkins, the slate-gray eyes suddenly as cold as the spit of the sleet.

'*Mas segura*,' nodded the dark-skinned boy. '*Gracias*.'

'Sure,' said Con, uncorking the jug and handing it to the youth. 'Drink up.'

Gavilan tipped the brown-glazed clay container and drank from it. The Negro breaker, Blue Slattery, did the same. When the jug came back to Jenkins he did not drink but called over to the fire, 'Hey, Cookie, come and get it.'

The camp cook, Beckwourth, a pockmarked breed of certain Indian and uncertain other blood, slunk around the fire to obey. He was a middle-aged man much used by whiskey and venereal disease and he had a hacking cough. The gang used him because he knew Indians and because he could not talk. A dozen years before, the Crows had caught him lying up with a chief's woman without the husband's

79

consent. Out of respect for the miscreant's famous father, old mountain man Jim Beckwourth, the Indians had not killed him or banished him forever from the tribe—the usual penalty for unasked adultery. They had merely double-slit his tongue. Henceforth, when he tried to speak, it sounded a gibberish that a Barbary ape might understand but that no handsome married squaw would be likely to accept in blandishment. The Indians, as those white men who truly knew them well understood, had a way with such judgments.

Now Beckwourth, coming to slouch hangdoggedly before Con Jenkins, mewed something in his private language and reached out for the jug. Jenkins gave it to him. When he took the jug back from the cook, he wiped off its mouth with a grimace.

'Here's to us,' he said, holding up the jug. 'Four into twenty-four goes six thousand each. I always knowed there was money in livestock.' He tipped the vessel and drank heavily. 'All right,' he said, smacking his lips appreciatively, 'where was we?'

Gavilan shrugged. 'Wherever you say, Con. *Digalo.*'

Before the dirty-faced outlaw leader could 'tell it,' however, his comrades saw the pale eyes narrow, the lank body go taut. 'Company coming,' Con rasped. 'Watch it.'

Blue Slattery, who could see like an Apache, rolled dark orbs in the direction of Con's nod.

'Christ, that ain't company,' he grinned. 'It's the Maggot.'

The Negro rider proved correct. When they had pulled the blue-lipped horseman from the saddle, knocked the snowcake off him, and oiled his tongue with four fingers of Louisville lightning, he was indeed trooper W. O. Maggart, all the way from Spotted Tail agency, bearing bad tidings.

'Such as what?' said Con, too quietly, when the soldier had blurted out the nature of his ride. 'Go over it real careful, now. Get it right the first time through.'

'Talk slow,' said Blue. 'I ain't got a fast brain.'

Even the friendly face of young Gavilan, the optimistic Chihuahuan, seemed suddenly blank.

'Yeah,' he breathed. 'Don't make no stumbles.'

The soldier from Spotted Tail did as he was bidden, the details of his story falling into a silence broken only by the wind in the bull pines and the snapping of the fire's coals.

He, Maggart, had deserted. He was throwing in with the gang for real. Reason? Simple. Deadly simple.

The army's Indian scout force at Red Cloud agency, or rather those chosen members of it on trooper Maggart's payroll, had suddenly come to demanding more 'shut mouth' money from the turncoat soldier. These demands

81

could not be met because Con and his gang could furnish Maggart no more hard money and, even if they could, things at Fort Robinson were getting too risky. The army was certain to learn soon from *some* of Maggart's paid-off agency Indians that the big remount herd they were expecting was in fact composed of animals stolen months earlier from the surrendering Oglala and not made up of 'incoming California horses' being driven all the way from the Golden State's Sacramento Valley by hard-working American drovers in legitimate venture.

Now, the nervous soldier continued, when the purchasing officer at Robinson discovered the real origin of those horses, it would be the finish for all of them. Maggart would be shot or sentenced to life in stockade. The remainder of the gang, if and when apprehended, would speedily be provided the standard justice for horse thieves the West over, that is, swung by the gullet until they stopped kicking.

Con Jenkins's cunning, in taking only the bays and blacks and grays and chestnuts and such solid colors as the cavalry would accept, was still smooth doings. Even more professional had been Jenkins's idea to stop the incoming Sioux herds well out along the trail, riding into the column in those trooper uniforms 'borrowed' from the supply depot by Maggart himself, and telling the stupid red apes that they represented General Bradley

82

and would cut out certain animals for the use of the commanding officer and the pony-soldier garrison at Fort Robinson. The ruse had been particularly effective because the poor damned fool Indians had done all the cutting-out work and the gathering into a held herd, while the bogus soldiers had been able to sit by and ogle the young squaws and even, Maggart had later heard from the Sioux complaints to the command at the fort, fornicated with the best of the young women right on the gathering ground. All that the make-believe troopers had done was thank the Oglala drive guards and haze off the solid-colored horses.

It had been without question the most brazen and the biggest single horse thievery of all frontier time. And Con Jenkins had been using its masquerading trooper techniques on band after band of the incoming hostiles. The officers at Robinson, hearing the Sioux claims of white soldiers taking away their best stock, had quite naturally assumed that the 'red bastards' were lying through their broad-jawed teeth. What was happening was that the chiefs of the various incoming bands, knowing their herds would be taken by the army at Fort Robinson, were simply stopping a safe ways out and 'creaming' their animals to hold back the best stock. This top-cut stuff was no doubt then driven off in a dozen different directions to rendezvous somewhere no white man went, or, if he did, did not return from.

'Come on, man,' interrupted Blue Slattery, 'you ain't telling us nothing. We know how we made this gather. And how you sold the Californy bushway to the cavalry yonder to Robinson. Now you telling us we're going to have to *eat* these here four hundred head?'

Maggart was spooked now; he could feel their eyes on him.

If they hurried, he said, there should still be time to get the big herd cashed out. But, after that, the game was closed up. They would all have to clear out and stay cleared out. Any of them caught in Nebraska, once the identity of the counterfeit horses was found out, would get the rope.

That was precisely why he, Maggart, had stolen the best horse in the army stable, put a dummy in his bunk, brought along his loaded moneybelt, and ridden the picked horse wind-broke to reach his pals in a day and a night.

'Wait a minute,' Blue said, scowling. 'All you done told us so far is we got to rustle our butts and run this bunch of cayuses into the fort before this snow gets much thicker. I don't see where that adds up to you deserting and stealing no horse and highlining it out here in the black of a bad night.' The scar-faced Negro seized the soldier by the lapels of his overcoat, lifted him a foot off the ground. 'Maggot,' he nodded, 'you ain't coming clean with us.'

'Maggart, Maggart,' corrected the trooper

angrily. 'Put me down, you black bastard.'

'Yeah, put him down.' It was the dry voice of Con Jenkins. 'You already got his *huevos* shrunk up to the size of rabbit berries.'

'*Pues, yo no se,*' grinned the young Gavilan. 'I am beginning to wonder, *jefe*, if he ever had any *huevos* at all.'

'Shut up, Frank,' advised Jenkins. Blue Slattery had put Maggart's boots back into the light snow, and the leader merely flicked his pale eyes in the soldier's direction. 'Go ahead on, Mister Cavalryman,' he said. 'What else?'

'Ain't cavalry, goddamn it,' whimpered Maggart. 'How many times I got to tell you dumb sons of bitches, it's infantry. The Ninth Infantry.'

'That,' said Blue Slattery, in his deep bass, 'ain't what we're waiting for you to tell us.'

'I was getting to it, goddamn you. I was.'

Con Jenkins moved between the men. 'Before you do,' he said, 'leave me show you something. Magpie,' he called to the mutilated Beckwourth, 'get over here.' He had used the Absaroka, or Crow name, for the bastard son of old Jim Beckwourth. It was taken from the harsh chattering of the camp nuisance bird, and from the fact, too, that the Indians often slit the tongues of magpies in an effort to make them speak in human tongues. Now Beckwourth, whose given name was Charley, crept up, and Jenkins nodded. 'Say something to our soldier-boy friend from Fort Robinson,

85

Charley. He don't talk too clear and we want him to hear how his palaver is going to improve when we fork his licker like the Absaroka done yourn.'

Beckwourth frowned, forcing his damaged mind to match the injury of his tongue so that he might please these dangerous men for whom he cooked and kept camp. The result was a mewling slobber intelligible to nothing human. Trooper Maggart shivered, but not from the cut of the wind.

'It's the Injuns I was going to tell you about,' he chattered. 'They're what brung me out here.'

'What Injuns?' It was Blue Slattery again.

The soldier told of his drugging of Crazy Horse's sick wife after the woman had told him of the horse herd in the hills that her murdered husband had planned to use to mount his Oglala Bad Faces in their break out from Fort Robinson and their run for Canada. Maggart was sure he had given Crazy Horse's wife enough opium to kill a dozen squaws, sick or well, and they did not need to worry about her blabbing to anybody. But there were two other Indians he had come to warn them about. And these two for certain could spring the trap on all of them.

'They ain't your mill-run agency Injuns, understand?' he frowned. 'One of them is sister-in-law to Crazy Hoss hisself. Other's her old grandpaw. Gal is a white-hater like Crazy

86

Hoss. Old man's smart as a cross fox, but he ain't a killer. He was Crazy Hoss's tribal adviser. You know, chief medicine man. Name's Crowfoot, and him and the young squaw's coming hell-bent for High Meadow and our hosses, right now. They aim to get them, and us with them, I reckon. All for old Crazy Hoss.'

Con Jenkins twisted his lips. 'You saying some ragged-ass old man and a kid-snip of a girl what have run off from the reservation are, for serious, intending to lift this here herd of ours?' The pale eyes slitted, pinning Maggart. 'What was it you said? In memory of Crazy Hoss? You're the one's crazy, if you think we're swallering that.'

'Well, think about it,' the trooper answered. 'If you was these two blood kin of Crazy Hoss's, and the soldiers had just plainly murdered your people's hero chief who had a plan to join up with old Joseph and the Neppercies if only the Sioux could get back the hosses stole from the Oglaly when they surrendered, and you knowed where them stole hosses was, what the hell would you do for the warchief's memory?'

Jenkins and his fellow horse thieves considered the question. Shortly, they decided the old medicine man and his white-hating granddaughter could indeed become a menace to the herd being held in the remote rock-walled meadow above the breaking ground.

All the pair had to do was *find* the meadow. Then they could go gather a passel of their unsurrendered Indian friends—the hills of the Wyoming-Nebraska line were crawling with such red renegades—and steal back the herd; a patently unfair and grossly treacherous thing to do.

Con Jenkins, Blue Slattery, and Frank Gavilan had not the least interest in Chief Joseph and the fleeing Nez Perce. As far as they were concerned, the Sioux from Spotted Tail could join Joseph, Geronimo, Quanah Parker, Sitting Bull, or any other redskin hostile there was. But not, by God, with *these* horses! Four hundred ready-to-ride replacement mounts at sixty dollars per head? Twenty-four thousand dollars in government gold coin? To hunker idly by and let an investment like that go under on account of two runaway relatives of the murdered Crazy Horse?

'All right,' said Con. 'We'll deliver them tomorrow.'

'Bright and early,' agreed Blue Slattery. 'No other way.'

'*De seguro*,' said young Gavilan. 'No way whatever.'

'Well,' grunted Con, reaching for the whiskey jug, 'I reckon we just run out of problems.'

'What about me?' asked Maggart incautiously.

Jenkins lowered the jug.

'You going to be a problem, soldier boy?' he said.

The Spotted Tail infantryman drew back. With obsequious tone and gesture he hastened to assure his hard-eyed comrades that the thought was the fartherest imaginable. 'What I meant to say was,' he gulped, 'what do you want me to do?'

'Oh,' said Con understandingly. 'Well, for openers you can hand over your moneybelt to Gavilan. Since you're throwing in with us, full tilt, there ain't no reason for you to tote more'n your share of the load.'

'Wait!' cried Maggart desperately. But Con Jenkins didn't wait. The long-barreled Colt appeared. Its bore, looking big enough to Maggart to 'chamber a cue ball,' stared at the shrinking area of his navel. Con drew back the hammer.

'Now,' he said, 'you got maybe the time it takes a fart to fade away in a high wind. Unhook.'

Maggart quakingly unbuckled the moneybelt. It slid to the hard earth by the fire. Blue Slattery reached with his carbine barrel, hooked the belt, passed it across the flames to the Mexican youth.

'Four piles,' said Con Jenkins to Gavilan. 'Even shares.' He paused, spelling it out. 'Me, you, Blue, and Old Ben up yonder guarding the herd.'

It was too much for Maggart's small heart.

Or for his even smaller brain. 'What about me?' he blurted again, without realizing what the asking of it might mean. But it was Con Jenkins's night to be generous.

'Oh, yeah,' he said. 'You.' He paused to lower the hammer on the Colt, return it to holster. 'You run along up to the meadow and relieve old Ben on herdguard. He ain't et all day. And soldier boy,' he specified, as Maggart turned to find his ridden-out mount, 'if you come up short one head on our tally tomorrow morning, I will finish drilling that .44-calibre minedrift through your belly button. You *comprende*?'

The Spotted Tail trooper only bobbed his head and continued going for his horse. It would be a hell of a cold and lonely vigil up there in the high meadow. But it was better than dying here by the fire, warm and pleasant with his good friends.

When Maggart was gone, Francisco Gavilan resumed counting out the four piles from the moneybelt their hard cash had filled for their inside man at Fort Robinson. At the fire, Con and Blue Slattery traded back and forth on the jug. If they were happy men, they did not show it. They kept at the jug until it was empty.

CHAPTER TWELVE

Nearly five hundred crow-flight miles to the northwest of High Meadow, Wyoming, Montana's Bear Paw Mountains reared up in lonely isolation from the grasslands abutting them. The grass itself ran to the horizon on all sides. Upon the flanks of the range, good timber stood. From the crests of the serrated peaks sprang several fine streams of the mountain water dear to the Nez Perce heart. South of the upthrusts, the plain stretched to the roughland brakes of the great Missouri. Northward the buffalo pasture reached away to Canada, no hindrance on its gentle swells save for the shallow, easy channel of Milk River.

The Nez Perce people knew of the best place to camp up there, Tsanim Alikos Pah, the Place of the Manure Fires, on Tipyahlanah, Eagle Creek. The Slit Noses had visited it since time out of tribal memory to hunt the shaggy bulls and curly cows. Along Eagle Creek there was always enough scrubby tree growth to provide dead wood for fire starting and to serve for wind shelter, a matter of life and death in that land of extreme cold and killer snows.

There was a certain thickly grassed natural depression in the prairie along Eagle Creek where the Nez Perce traditionally made their base camp for the running of the winter's fat cow. This broad hollow lay thirty feet below the surrounding plain on the south of its circle, from where the land fell away to the Missouri. On its northern side the circle of the hollow was less deep, perhaps twenty feet below the level of the plain.

The place made a snug and happy camp for people who believed they were safe from enemy pursuit and who, on their way to freedom in the Land of the Grandmother, wished to make a rest halt and to hunt the buffalo.

* The endless ocean of grass that swept as far as an Indian eye might reach pastured uncountable thousands of antelope and curly cows in all seasons. Here, too, the deer ran with the Wapiti, the noble elk, in common herds as thick as geese. Tsanim Alikos Pah, 'the Place,' was the ideal haven to lay in meat, to gird the people with hot hump ribs and warm sleeping robes and new hides for the lodges against the final march for Milk River and the protection of the redcoat soldiers of the Land of the Grandmother. Eagle Creek sang a happy song for the Indian brother going to live in red freedom and peace with their old enemies and new friends, the Hunkpapa Sioux of Sitting Bull.

It was toward this storied retreat that the proud Asotin chief, Looking Glass, now guided the joyous Nez Perce.

Looking Glass did not hurry the people. Time was taken at his order to cull the entire horse herd for the coming last march to the border. The Nez Perce were certain the soldiers of One Hand Howard were far behind. It was an easier thing to cull the herd before they got to the meat camp up at the Place. Of course it lost time to do this work upon the trail. But time was no longer their enemy.

Looking Glass, who some were later to claim had died at Big Hole, in the attack by Red Nose Gibbon, was one of the five principal fighters of the band. The others were Joseph's young brother Ollikut, the two very old chiefs White Bird and Toohoolhoolzote, Two Moons, and the celebrated hater of the white man, Yellow Wolf. But the stubborn Asotin held the imaginations of all the people. He was *the* soldier of them all.

Joseph, on the other hand, was never the great warrior white man's history would make of him. He, like his counterpart among the Sioux, Sitting Bull, was the spiritual leader of his people. He provided the final word of advice, wisdom, camp discipline, and order on the march. War was left to those who had made its practice their entire lives. Such among the Sioux as Crazy Horse, Gall, Hump, Walking Hawk, and White Bull. And such, among the Nez Perce as the five named, and then the others like Wottolen, Naked Head, Hahtalekin, Black Eagle, and Band-of-Geese.

Joseph remained the peacemaker, the mediator.

Lean Elk, that wise pessimist whose ignored advice not to delay at Big Hole would have spared the gruesome slaughter there and who later argued against the long stop at Cow Island, had since been deposed as march leader by Joseph. The power to guide the people had been returned to Looking Glass, who had been responsible for the near-fatal halt at Big Hole. Now, as always with soldiers, the fierce Asotin made assumptions of victory already earned, and the people cheered Looking Glass and were of his mind in the matter.

As for Joseph, he was uneasy in his weary breast. He felt deep within his Indian instincts that the people ought not to tarry. He wondered sleeplessly if Lean Elk were not right. If they should not press on for Milk River, not even stopping to hunt at Tsanim Alikos Pah. Yet Joseph also understood that the people wanted to stop there. They wanted to believe what Looking Glass said, not what Lean Elk insisted upon. At the last, as the column of the march wended down upon the old place, he gave in, calling Lean Elk to him.

'Do not divide the people anymore,' he said. 'Do not continue to agitate them and cause them fear. Let them be. Let them feel happy. Listen to Looking Glass. It will be all right. We have the time now. Let the people go on selecting the horses. We will come to the Place soon enough.'

Lean Elk, his old friend, said not a word. He only went away, darkness in his heart.

The moving culling of the horse herd continued. The lame and worn mounts were taken from the line of march. Each of these animals was cut on the foot and ankle in a particular Nez Perce way. The wounding would make the horses useless to soldiers who might want them for fresh mounts. At the same time, it was done with a secret skill so that the cutting would not spoil the lovely things for later Indian use after the soldiers had gone away. A great deal of dawdling was done over this process, as the Slit Nose people loved their horses very much and took great care with each horse selected to be left behind. At the end of the work, the remaining herd counted thirteen hundred head, each animal now fit for any duty required of it. But the hours of the September sun had slipped away. And the people had still not reached Tsanim Alikos Pah, and Tipyahlanah, Eagle Creek, camp.

True, hunters were sent ahead of the main column so that the great hunt might begin before the big number of the moving tribe came up to frighten away the game. These hunters had also the greatest luck in many seasons. For two glorious days of running the buffalo they brought down the brutes by the score. Nothing like it had been known in Nez Perce memory. When the main column came up and the women took the robes and saw to the butchering of the meat, the camp was piled high with curly hides and stacks of fat tenderloins, hearts, livers, tongues, and fresh hump ribs. The grateful people, their lodges pitched in Eagle Creek hollow, gorged themselves.

It seemed they could not get enough. They ate and slept, ate and slept again. After the first wonderful hours, no true guard was mounted. And why should there be? The last of the rearward scouts had ridden in with the word that One Hand Howard had not even reached the big Painted Water yet, much less come to Cow Island crossing.

What was that? The Sioux? Had they yet appeared down there on their way to help the Nez Perce brother? Well, no, in fact they had not. But what of that, anyway?

Eisin! Liloin! Uegeleitimt. Tiet, tiet!

Let there be happiness, joy, words of merriment, and loud laughter at the jokes of relief and gratitude.

Looking Glass had said it; the people believed him. Why worry about the tardy Sioux brother and those extra horses? Who needed them anymore?

Listen to Aleemyah Tatkaneen, old Looking Glass. They had won. They could smell the snows of Canada on that night's increasing wind. Forget the Sioux. The Nez Perce were free!

96

CHAPTER THIRTEEN

Along about dusk, herdguard Ben Childress built up the small warming fire. He was supposed to have gotten relief at sunset, but he knew Con Jenkins and he stayed on the job. Freezing or starving was a better way to go than with a bullet in the belly. That damned Con. Him and his answer for everything—the gun.

Well, Ben might not be the brightest pup in the litter. Still, he understood the owlhoot rule. You had one honcho in the bunch and what he said, you did. So Ben would wait.

A mean, sleety snow stung his face and hands. The herdguard stirred the last of his coffee into the tin can of boiling water hung over the fire. After his java, he would hole up in the dog tent. Con wouldn't mind that. Not in such weather. But he had best not fall asleep.

Ben took the steaming coffee tin from the fire, poured himself a cup. Ahh! That smelled grand.

'You betcha,' he said aloud to his tethered and saddled horse. 'You can have all the whiskey and women there is. I'll take a hot cup of the bitter black any old foul weather night in Wyoming, or wherever. There ain't no liquor and no human female 'twixt here and Green River can compare to a good cup of coffee.'

The horse had nothing to add to this and the wind blew harder, whirling the snow like white buckshot. Ben Childress shivered and stopped talking to the night and the saddle mount. There was something more than the wind and the bonechill wrong with this camp and this darkness. It got to a man. Made his neck-bristles lift. God, but he wished old Con would hurry up and send Gavilan or Blue Slattery up to relieve him. He could never remember being so cold and so lonely.

* * *

The old man and the granddaughter came up into the notch of the pass over into High Meadow. Crowfoot was wheezing and puffing. The prowling wind tore at them like a rabid coyote.

'Wait a moment,' the oldster pleaded. 'Step in behind this rock. We can see the meadow from here.'

Twilight went with him into the wind-shelter of the boulder. Red Weasel, the mule, followed them unbidden. The Indians peered into the drive of the snow, squinting the flakes from their eyelashes.

Late as the light had grown, the young eyes of the squaw made out the distant, stolen herd. To Crowfoot's eyes, the animals were only faraway shadows, and shadows of shadows. But the smell of them came to him on the rise of

98

the wind, and he inhaled with a joyousness he had not felt in four moons. 'Our ponies,' he said, seizing the girl's arm emotionally.

'Yes,' she murmured. 'Yes.'

They stood a moment, knowing the feeling that only nomad horse people can know for the sight and the smell and the sounds of a grazing herd at day's end.

'Tell me how you see them,' the old man said. 'Are they fat? Well? Has the grass been good to them?'

'*Owanyeke*,' the girl said. 'All is good to the eye down there. *Waste, waste.*'

'Ah, I wish that I could see them.' Crowfoot sighed, wiped an eye that watered not of the wind. 'Listen, girl, wait for me here a moment. I want to relieve myself.'

Twilight was looking across the horses below. In the far rocks, she saw the flicker of the newly lit small fire. It would be the camp of the herdsmen, she thought, and the hatred for the white man arose again within her. They had stolen those beautiful horses from her people. They had made the warchief look bad to the soldiers. Those white devils down there had hurt Twilight's people when those people could not fight back. That was a blood debt.

'Listen to me!' snapped the old man. 'Do I talk to the wind up here? I said I had to go make water. You know an Indian can't defile the trail.'

'Oh, what? All right, grandfather. I hear

99

you. Go on. I'll keep watch.'

'Keep watch of that damned old mule, too,' complained Crowfoot. 'He is liable to get the wind of those Sioux ponies and get away from you. Remember, he is old friends with those horses,' he admonished. 'If he starts braying down the trail ahead of us, well, just hold onto him.'

But H'tayetu, Twilight, the sister of the wife of the warchief, was not going to let the old mule get away from her. Even as the old man grumbled his way off into the rocks, her slim hand had tightened on the frayed lead-rope. The moment Crowfoot was out of sight, she vaulted to the pack beast's back, undid the travois poles, let them drop. They made a sound falling and old Crowfoot called from the rocks guardedly, 'Eh? What was that? I heard a sound. What was it, girl? Do you say that you are all right out there? I am coming, never fear.'

When he had groped his way back to the trail, he believed for one breath that he had found the wrong boulder. Then he noted Red Weasel's droppings—the Sioux ban on soiling the trail applied not to packmules—and understood this was the same place he had left his granddaughter.

'Girl,' he asked the silent rocks about, 'would you play a game? Come on, there's no time for this. We must be going.' The rocks gave no answer. Only the wind tore at his threadbare blanket. He moved around the boulder, almost falling over the abandoned travois pack and dragpoles. He caught himself by his outstretched hands on nearby rock outcrops. 'Goddamn,' he exploded in plain English, 'I will have her buttock skin for this.'

But he was only talking.

The girl and the mule were gone, and Crowfoot knew, or feared he knew, where they had gone, and why.

He picked up the travois poles, one in each hand. Going downhill now, he could drag the pack by himself. Maybe the fool girl would come to her better mind before reaching the small fire over there across the meadow and bring back the mule to help him. In no event, though, was Crowfoot going to leave their camp gear behind. The old man could smell the bad weather coming in from the Shining Mountains. They would need the clothing and the shelter-hides and the scant food in the travois. Let Twilight follow her hatred to the fire of the white man. Crowfoot would pray for her but meanwhile keep pulling on the travois poles.

At least one Sioux was not going to freeze or starve in those low Wyoming hills.

*   *   *

The young squaw got down off Red Weasel. Wrapping his muzzle with a rawhide thong so that he could not bray, she tied him in the

101

heavy brush of the thicket behind the white man's fire. Going forward, she found enough snow piling on the ground to make her approach soundless as that of a spiritwoman. Just beyond reach of the fire's circle of light, she held up to watch the herdsman and scout the rude camp for any of his fellows. As she did so, she began to discard her under clothing, all that she wore beneath the old robe.

There was no extra gear, saddle or otherwise, in the area to indicate a companion. The main encampment of the white devils must be where the grandfather had said it would be, on down below the meadow. At the thought, the young Sioux girl's eyes narrowed. The man at the fire was alone and he was white. The rest of it came as naturally to her wild nature as the instinct to cut a lone bull's hock tendon comes to the she-wolf.

When, next instant, Ben Childress heard a scraping of snow-laden boughs and looked up across his fire, it was no wonder that he sucked in and bit off his breath and stared dumbfounded at the beautiful child of the snowy waste who stood there with her great dark eyes on him.

'Great God Almighty,' he said, coming to his feet. Then, belatedly, and glad to see any fellow human on such a bitter night. '*Hohahe*, welcome to my tipi, little sister. Come along in, old Ben won't bite you.'

The young squaw watched him. She stood

like a doe, one foot planted, one slightly raised, apparently ready either to bolt or to come on. Childress was honestly confused.

Simple Ben had never seen a figure like that on a red Indian before in his life. Nor had he seen one like it to recall just then on any white sister. The light of the fire wasn't much, but it was enough to show a man that, underneath the cling of the old calfskin robe, this child stood naked as the day God made her.

Ben could see the big breasts thrusting to be free of the otter-fur trim of the loosened robe. And, as he gawked, the Sioux girl shifted her weight, bringing down the poised rear foot. The movement opened the robe below its leather belt. Deliberate as the exposure was, the girl blushed, murmuring an apology. It was not an intended thing, she lied to the stricken herdguard. Her people were poor. Everything had been taken from them by the Pale Eyes. She had nothing else to wear.

Swaying, she came around the fire.

Ben actually backed away, overpowered by the nearness of her. But the burning dark eyes caught him and held him in a trap. Ben was a rough man, untutored with women. His was not a vicious, much less a violent nature, but he was helpless now.

'Jesus God,' he breathed. 'Oh, Jesus God Almighty.'

She smiled at him, nodding, waiting. Ben stammered something else, thickly, and the

103

Indian girl nodded again, yes, and loosed the belt and let the calfskin robe fall open.

Beneath it, her body glowed like burnished copper, and the impact on the herdsman's senses nearly choked him. But when he reached clumsily to take the young squaw, she laughed and stepped away, motioning toward the dog tent in the rocks.

It was language old and plain to any man. Ben replied to its pulse-thumping invitation with a mindless, happy lust.

Yet when they reached the little tent and slunk beneath it, Twilight's hatred failed her. The thing that had seemed so easy in its planning, even up to the moment of coming to the white man's fire naked beneath her outer-robe, was not so clear to her now. She still held the knife there beneath the robe. Its blade was still honed for the life of the white devil she had trapped into the little tent. But the heart of the young Sioux woman was no longer bad with anger.

The reason was the man himself. Awkward Ben Childress was being oddly gentle with her. It was as though, older than she and not a handsome man, he actually knew gratitude. He could speak her tongue well and he was saying small decent things to her in Oglalan, stroking her almost wonderingly, seeming unbelievably to be in some fear of her, or at very least holding a strange and startling respect for her, red squaw that she was.

It unnerved Twilight. Of a sudden she knew she did not want to kill this white man. She wanted only to escape from the assignation she had brought him to. But any refusal she made now would be perilous for her, not for the *wasicun*, for suddenly she knew she had tempted him too far. His hands had become demanding, the gentleness gone from their touch. He was pulling her to him, Sioux love-talk forgotten, only the lust she had deliberately aroused within him blinding his mind and tongue. But she could not accept him now. She must stop him. Must make him understand what had changed.

With fierce young strength she twisted free of Ben Childress and pushed herself into the farthest corner of the tent. She held up to him the palm of one hand in the prairie sign-language gesture to wait, and with the other hand she brought forth the unsheathed knife with which previously she had planned to murder him. It was her Indian intention, by showing him the blade, to then cast it aside and disclaim its original mission, asking that he let her but go free and not follow her.

But the horse guard had heard a hundred frontier campfire stories of such hidden blades and their use by Sioux and Cheyenne and Arapaho women in their blanketings with the white brother. The sight of the bared knife gleaming in the tent's darkness made only one Plains Indian sign for him. He did not read the other meaning of the young squaw's upraised palm or hear the soft beginning of her words to explain. He saw only the bared blade, and he thought only natural white man's thoughts seeing it in an Indian hand: The red bitch had meant to kill him.

'Ah, goddamn you—!' he grimaced, and he lunged to pinion her arm and twist the knife from her hand.

But Twilight writhed aside and the twist of the knife did not go where Ben Childress wanted it to go, harmlessly from the fingers of the beautiful Sioux child he still intended to bed. The young squaw was strong. She held fast to the weapon's haft. And, in the fall of their struggling bodies, its long steel went unguided into Ben Childress.

The herdguard sank back groping at the mortal wound she had given him. He stared at Twilight as though the thing that had happened to him could not be.

The girl crouched beyond him looking down at the knife still in her hand. She had, even if by chance, unwantingly killed her first *wasicun*. That was her enemy dying there. The enemy that had murdered the warchief, denied life-saving medicine to sister Tasina, stolen the Oglala horses when the Indians were helpless, and, yes, shamed the Bad Face women before their own men. This was the white devil. He deserved to die even though it was not his real blood there on her hands.

106

But she looked at those hands again and there was blood on them and it was real blood.

'*Wicowicasa sni*,' she whispered, 'it was wrong.'

Ben Childress appeared to hear her. His eyes did not open, but a hand, large, calloused, much broken by a life with horses, stirred and reached forth. It touched Twilight, lingered a moment, fell away.

'*Wonunicun*,' it seemed to say to the girl, 'I am sorry.'

Uttering a single low sobbing cry, Twilight fled the small tent.

CHAPTER FOURTEEN

When old Crowfoot came cursing up out of the snowstorm to the camp of the herdguard, his granddaughter was drinking the *wasicun*'s coffee and examining the slick, smooth action of his fine Winchester carbine.

'*He-hau*, well, well,' the old man greeted her. 'What is that you have there? How did you come by it?'

Twilight held up the beautiful weapon so prized by every horseback Indian of the short-grass plains.

'It's a gift for you, grandfather. From the *wasicun*.'

Crowfoot dropped the travois poles, came around the fire, Indian suspicions at once aroused.

'Where is the *wasicun*?' he demanded. His granddaughter only motioned toward the dog tent and did not look up. The old man was suddenly afraid. 'You say he is still in there? And you sit out here playing with his lovely small rifle?' he asked.

Now Twilight raised her glance to him.

'*Katella*,' she said, low-voiced, gesturing toward the tent.

'What! He's dead?'

'I killed him,' the girl said. 'It was an accident.'

'Wakan protect us!' gasped the old Sioux. 'You are the warchief's child.'

Twilight compressed her lips. 'I have always thought so,' she said. 'I am his child and never was his sister-in-law.'

'Bah!' growled Crowfoot. 'You know I don't like to hear that damned old campwives' lie. Crazy Horse had no children. And your sister was his true wife. Don't you think I know about all these things?'

'I think you do, yes,' the girl accused him. 'But you don't want me to know.'

Crowfoot dismissed it. 'Be quiet,' he said. 'Stay here. I am going to look at the *wasicun*.' He was back from the tent in a moment, frowning and shaking his head. 'That's a deep wound,' he said. 'You cut the bottom of the heart. How did you get so much steel into a big man like that one?'

108

The girl shook her head. 'I let him think I would be his,' she said. 'More was not required.'

'Ah, Jesus Christ,' the old man muttered. A look almost of despair crossed the weathered face. 'Of course more was not required. It never has been. But that *wasicun* did not mean to harm you. He was only sitting here watching these ponies. You did not know him. He did not know you. Yet you offered him your body and then when he desired your offering you put your knife into him. Why?'

Twilight turned away from him, but Crowfoot had seen the sadness of the face touched by the fire's light.

'I told you,' she said, voice almost inaudible, 'it was an accident. I tried not to do it in the last moment but the knife twisted the wrong way.'

Crowfoot stared at her, withered lips compressed.

'If this be so,' he said, 'Wakan Tanka will forgive you. But it was a wrong thing that you did to him in the beginning. It was an evil thing. *Wicowicasa sni*, H'tayetu.'

'Yes, I said that to him,' the girl murmured.

'*Ih!* I hope he heard you.'

'He did hear me. I know he did. He reached and touched me with his hand.'

'And died, eh?'

'Yes.'

The old man nodded. 'Well,' he said, 'we are Sioux. We do not lie to one another. We cannot

109

change this thing, and we must go on.' He was thinking, worrying, casting ahead. 'We are but two against whatever number there is of these thieves,' he continued. 'And they will be coming soon to learn what keeps their friend in the little tent over there.' He swept the campsite with a gnarled hand. 'We better move up into those trees and wait for them. You know, set a *wickmunke* for them, a trap. What do you think?'

The girl was not sure. She looked about uneasily.

'I don't know. The warchief never waited; he always attacked. Perhaps we should go down where those thieves are right now. Can you find the trail down in this heavy darkness, grandfather?'

'Of course, of course. There is but a single trail down out of this meadow. You know, we Oglala are well acquainted with this place. We used to bring our own stolen herds here to fatten and be safe after a hard war trail of stealing them.'

'You say but one trail *down*,' Twilight was quick to ask, 'is there then a second trail? One that leads not downward but upward out of this meadow?'

'Yes, there was once. But we closed it off with rocks many winters ago. It was a secret way of our Bad Face band to be used only if no other escape remained for hard-pressed warrior or stolen herd.' Crowfoot looked off

110

through the night and over the unseen hundreds of Sioux horses gathered in the darkened meadow. 'It's still a secret of our band,' he said. 'That was what the warchief was depending on. He was going to use the old secret trail to get our horses out of here, away from the white man.' He paused sadly. 'Alas, that is all no good anymore.'

Twilight, thinking her own thoughts, did not hear his words of defeat. Her mind was on that old secret trail. And her Sioux heart was leaping within her.

'Come on, grandfather,' she said excitedly. 'Help get the dead one's food and other camp things loaded into our travois. I will ride the *wasicun*'s saddled horse. You ride the mule. I will give the *wasicun*'s horse his head and he will lead us naturally to the camp below. What do you say to that plan?'

The old man had to be pleased. It was a good plan, much better than his own. Of a surety the saddled animal would know the trail down to the main camp and would guide them there much more safely than Crowfoot and Red Weasel stumbling about in the dark and snow.

'I say, *hopo, hookahey*!' he cried. 'Lead on, granddaughter. You are a true Bad Face.'

CHAPTER FIFTEEN

Trooper Maggart put his horse along the darkening trail to the holding meadow. The animal, worn from the two-day ride from Spotted Tail agency, stumbled and hung back. Its instincts told it that this was a time to be finding good shelter, in out of the quickly changing weather the animal could scent upon the rising northwest wind. But its rider cursed and kicked the wise beast upward along the narrow trail to High Meadow. It was this commotion of his, together with his mount's snorting and backing in response to the abuse, that provided the warning to the downcoming riders; that, and the scent of the icy wind coming to them from the Spotted Tail trooper and his horse.

Suddenly, Maggart felt himself going forward over his mount's neck. He managed to stay in the saddle, but, when he had regained his seat and gotten his halted animal's head up, he found himself being stared at by two sinisterly muffled figures blocking the trail upward.

He immediately understood these travelers were not friends. The forward rider was unarmed but the second one had a Winchester short rifle trained on Maggart's chest. '*Hohahe,*' grunted old Crowfoot. 'What the hell are *you* doing away over here in the far hills, medicine soldier? Did you lose your way from the agency?'

Maggart could not believe that in such light he would be recognized so unfailingly. But, at the same time, he was relieved. If that were the old Sioux medicine priest speaking, the slighter forward rider had to be his shapely granddaughter. Trooper Maggart was no combat soldier, but he was armed with a .44 Colt service revolver and a Springfield carbine and he did not think one old man and one young girl would try his weapons unduly.

He shrugged and made the greeting sign, speaking in Sioux fluently to disarm them. But when his hand moved to ease inside his winter coat to find the revolver's walnut butt, the old warrior told him quietly that if the hand came out with anything but 'the little bag of smoking tobacco,' he was one dead soldier.

Fortunately for trooper Maggart, he did have his sack of cigarette tobacco and book of rice papers under the coat.

'Sure,' he said, tossing over the makings to the girl. He was trying to startle her, to make her get in the old man's line of fire. But the young squaw snared the sack and the papers in mid-air and without an instant's awkwardness, and the old man said warningly, 'Be careful. This child will cut out your liver.'

'All right,' nodded Maggart. 'What do you want of me?' Again the smile, the shrug. 'I have nothing.'

Here, the Sioux girl broke in to say that he must take them for fools. The only explanation for him being here was that he was the soldier-friend of the thieves who had stolen the Oglala horses. That being the truth, what they would want of him was only his life.

'Didn't I tell you?' cried old Crowfoot. 'This one is for blood. She means it. Only I can protect you.'

Maggart was beginning to think of some things.

These Indians were desperate, he knew. They were not friendlies but hostiles of the meanest stripe. It was true they might murder him. But, more than that, had they already murdered some other white man before him? They were coming down the High Meadow trail. You did not get on that trail except out of the meadow.

What had happened to Ben Childress up there?

The girl had passed the tobacco and paper to Crowfoot, who had made two cigarettes and lit them with a thumbnail-scratched sulphur match. He now handed one to Twilight. She sucked in on it and exhaled the blue smoke into the chill air. So did her grandfather with his cigarette.

'Listen,' said Maggart. 'What of the herdguard?'

'Hmmm, yes,' said Crowfoot, 'what of him?'

114

'Did you see him up there?'

'Yes, we both saw him. There was no trouble.'

'I don't believe you.' Maggart thought he had found the loophole. 'Let's ride back up there and see.'

'You want to see that herdguard, medicine soldier?'

'Yes. I think you're lying.'

'I don't think you want to see him,' denied the old man. 'Why are you afraid? Why do you keep looking around? I won't let harm come to you. We can talk.'

'We can talk better up there at the herdguard's camp,' pressed the Spotted Tail soldier. 'Besides, if I don't relieve him soon, the others down there in the breaking camp will become suspicious. That herdguard is supposed to go back down there for his supper.'

The old man stared hard at him.

Finally, he said, 'All right. Come on. If you really want to see the herdguard, we will show you we do not lie. We were there and we talked to him and he made no trouble. He is still waiting up there.'

Maggart hesitated now. 'Are there any more people with you?' he asked. 'You know I cannot see beyond you in this snow.'

'We are alone.' Crowfoot waved in candid admission. 'But not so alone as you are,' he added pointedly.

115

The soldier understood this. He shivered and said quickly, 'Let's go,' and they turned their horses about. Maggart rode in the middle, behind the girl, ahead of the old man and the short black rifle. In only a few moments, they had come back to the High Meadow herdguard camp. The little fire was still burning, the coffee tin still smoking in the embers of its bed. Over in the shelter of the rocks, the army tent seemed snug and flap-tied for the night. Crowfoot pointed to the small structure.

'When we left, he was in there,' he told Maggart.

'Childress—' The soldier called the guard's name uncertainly and without result. Only the wind whistled in reply.

'He has gone to sleep,' said the old medicine priest.

'That's funny,' frowned Maggart. 'With no supper?'

'Go and see for yourself,' said Crowfoot.

Given no real choice, the soldier got down off his horse and went to the tent's entrance. He untied the flap, bent down, and peered within. 'Childress?' he repeated. Then, straightening, pale as the snow that whirled in at the opened flap, he faced the Oglalas.

'You two,' he said. 'You did it.'

Twilight's hand reached inside the calfskin robe, reappeared with the skinning knife.

'Get in the tent with your friend,' advised old

116

Crowfoot behind the girl. He motioned with cocked rifle. 'You will be warmer sleeping together.'

Maggart backed as far against the tent as he could. 'I ain't going in there,' he said.

The Indians exchanged glances. Twilight slid off her mount and moved in on the trooper. But Maggart had the cunning of a cur dog. He growled and slunk away. When the girl then feinted so as to strike him with the knife, he simply ran squalling for mercy.

Old Crowfoot stared in disbelief, then called off the young squaw.

'Wait,' he shouted after Maggart. 'I don't care to shoot you and I don't want you to run any farther away.'

Maggart glanced back and saw Crowfoot aiming the Winchester at him. He halted, but returned the old Indian's shout. 'By God,' he yelled, 'I am damned if I will wait here to be carved up by that crazy squaw!' Seeing Crowfoot hesitate, he sensed an advantage. Switching to Sioux, he warned, 'I would say, also, that you and the girl should not wait either. When those thieves down there come up here to see where their herdguard is, and when they see *where* he is, you know they will kill you. You first, old man, then the girl after they have used her.'

Twilight turned to Crowfoot. 'Will you shoot him or must I finish him for you?'

'No, wait,' said the old man irritably. 'We

117

can't just shoot him. They will hear the reports down below. That will wake them up and they won't be in their blankets as your plan requires.'

The young squaw had not thought of that. 'All right,' she said. 'But if you are not going to let me knife him and you refuse to shoot him, how *do* we take his life?'

Maggart did not wait for the old man's answer.

'Listen,' he called to them. 'Why does anyone have to die at all? I will go with you and help you drive the herd wherever you wish to take it. You know that having a white man with you could be very important on the trail. Suppose you met a cavalry patrol?'

Crowfoot scratched his head. 'To be truthful,' he admitted, 'we had not planned to meet any cavalry patrols. But you are right, we might meet one.'

'Yes, and if you do we can tell them it is my herd and you two Indians are driving it for me.'

Maggart waited anxiously. Down by the fire the two Oglalas gestured and disputed. The girl remained intense and the soldier guessed she was still arguing to kill him. Well, if the game went that way, they had some shock coming to them. He would offer to lay down his Springfield rifle but would keep his powerful service revolver hidden under his winter coat. He wasn't really that much of a white fool to leave *all* of his guns in the rocks. The furtive

118

eyes squinted, watching the Indians. By God, the man who couldn't win that sort of a poker game, with a Colt army revolver for a hideout ace, would need to be one hell of a lot slower in his head than W. O. Maggart.

All right, he had the Indians sandbagged, but he was still in a damned bad place with Con Jenkins and the others. They were desperate men and the Spotted Tail soldier knew that, having taken his money, they would now—at their professional convenience—take his life, as well. They would have to. He, Maggart, had been a fool not to have seen that way back. But it had been the money as always. He had not wanted to lose his main cut of the herd. Trooper Maggart knew his sums. He could divide twenty-four thousand by four or five as accurately as the next horse thief.

But right now, it was Sioux showdown he was playing.

'Friends,' he called down in Oglalan to the still undecided Indians, 'I am coming out. Look. I put down my rifle in peace. I leave it up here in the open where you can see it. I want to come down to the fire and shake hands on our agreement. What do you say, old warrior?'

'Agreement, medicine soldier?'

'Yes, you know; to help you and the girl drive the horses out of here.'

Crowfoot frowned over the offer a moment longer, then waved the trooper down from the rocks without consulting Twilight. 'This is a thing for men to decide,' he told the girl gruffly. 'You keep quiet. And, here, give me that knife of yours. Make some more coffee. Where did you put that sack of smokes?'

Twilight reluctantly surrendered the knife, found the tobacco and papers for the old man, saying nothing. The deserter and her grandfather began their talk about the Oglala horses. Maggart was persuasive. A good Indian-talker. It was not long before Crowfoot was brought to believe that joining their forces was the prudent solution. If the Indians did not accept the soldier deserter as an accomplice, then they must kill him. Conversely, if they did accept him as a partner in stealing the Oglala herd, he could be of real and valuable service to them. One remaining thing puzzled Crowfoot.

'Why is it that you want to go with us all of a sudden?' he asked. 'Why do you not stay with your friends down below there?'

Maggart was impressively sober with his answer. First, he said, they must understand that he, Maggart, had been the 'agent' inside the fort for the outlaws who had stolen the horses. Maggart it was who talked the army into buying the Sioux herd as California horses. But the problem for Maggart had arisen from just this position. The Indian scouts at Fort Robinson had found out about the stolen herd being Oglala horses. They had demanded shut-mouth money from Maggart. He had paid them, then they had held out for more, blackmailing him. They had thus forced him to desert in fear of being caught by the army.

'What more is there to tell you?' the trooper concluded. 'Those outlaw thieves down there turned on me. They took my moneybelt and sent me up here to relieve the guard. They do not fool me. They mean to murder me in their own time. So I am here ready to help you. I do it to save my own life.'

Crowfoot nodded thoughtfully. This was Indian logic. He understood it. A man would do anything to preserve his own hide, even join up with two red Indians. Had their positions been reversed, Crowfoot would have tried to make precisely the same partnership with the soldier.

'Perhaps you are right,' he conceded, 'but how can you be certain you want to help us? You haven't even heard our plan yet.'

'*Waste*,' said Maggart, with improving confidence, 'good. Go ahead and tell it to me.'

CHAPTER SIXTEEN

'Well,' Crowfoot began, 'it was only a small plan you must realize. Nothing exceptional. We were just going to wait until all your friends down there were asleep, then go from blanket to blanket opening their throats, Sioux manner. One person smothers the mouth, the

121

other person makes the cut.' The old man drew his hand across withered gullet. 'That's why we Sioux are called the "Throat Cutters" by the other Indians. You see?'

Maggart swallowed stickingly, dry of spittle.

'Of course,' Crowfoot amplified helpfully, 'one person can do the entire thing, one hand to clamp the mouth, one to slice the throat. It's just that with two persons the art is greater. Much less messy.'

'My God,' said Maggart. 'Murdered in their blankets? Throat by throat?'

'You don't like the plan, medicine soldier?'

'No,' Maggart winced. 'Not hardly. Listen, old friend Crowfoot. Hear me carefully. I haven't told you all that I know about plans either. I mean about the plan of those thieves down below. Everything has been changed. They are taking these horses of yours out of High Meadow with first light tomorrow. There is no time for you to carry out your blanket plan. And no safety in it regardless. They keep a sentry all hours of the dark. The one on duty now is the *chancero*, the Mexican young man. His name means Hawk in their language. You know how a hawk sleeps, Crowfoot. With both its eyes wide open. Of course you remember that.'

Crowfoot scowled and nodded, yes. It sounded like a true thing anyway. A Mexican hawk might very well sleep in that open-eyed manner.

122

'That's not all,' Maggart rushed on. 'Do you know the other man down there is no white man. He's a black buffaloman, a Negro. They're very dangerous. And do you know their camp keeper's name? Well, it's Crazy Charley, old Jim Beckwourth's bastard son. You want to try and creep into a camp with him watching you? Why, that *sunsunla*, that wrong-brained donkey, they say he can hear a field mouse break wind in a thunderstorm.'

Crowfoot scowled harder than ever.

'Well,' he demanded of the silent Twilight, 'what do you think we should do? You see, it's just as I told you. That's no band of white devils down there. There is but one *wasicun* among them. I don't know—'

'They stole our horses,' insisted Twilight, scowling even harder than her grandfather, 'and this one here, this medicine soldier, he is the worst of them all. He sold our horses to the soldiers. He did not tell the soldier doctor when my sister Tasina lay dying at Spotted Tail. I say go ahead with the plan. Begin it right here.'

'How is that?' asked the grandfather. 'In what manner do you mean?'

'Our manner, the Sioux way. By slitting his throat.'

Crowfoot shook his head hurriedly. He held up the skinning knife. 'You can't decide everything with this,' he said sternly. 'It's a good thing I took it from you. No,' he said, sliding the knife into his own belt. 'We will do it

123

my way.' He turned again to Maggart. 'All right,' he said. 'You help us drive the horses out of here and we won't kill you. But we are not entire fools. What assurance do we have that you won't try to kill us?'

Maggart could scarcely conceal his pleasure. He had read these simpletons like a child's primer.

'I put my gun on the ground up there.' He pointed to the Springfield rifle. 'I came to the fire with both hands open. Does a man give away his gun if he means to shoot somebody?'

'No,' broke in Twilight softly. She had picked up the Winchester carbine. Its muzzle was aimed at the soldier point-blank across the tiny coffee fire. 'A man does not give away his gun when he is going to shoot somebody. Stand up, deserter soldier. Open your coat.' She cocked the Winchester's hammer. The metallic *clink* was loud in the stillness. 'Do it now,' she said.

Maggart understood that his life was suspended.

He arose very carefully from where he had been seated talking with the old medicine priest. Beyond pursing weathered lips in speculative curiosity, Crowfoot did not move.

'Deserter soldier,' Twilight said, 'put up your hands. Grandfather, open his coat for him.' The old man got up stiffly as Maggart took a step back and elevated his arms. Crowfoot unbuttoned the coat and spread it

124

wide. Both Indians saw the big Colt stuffed in the soldier's trouser tops. 'Take the gun, grandfather,' Twilight directed.

Trooper Maggart knew where he was then. If that old devil got his Colt, the game was over. It was play his hole card then and there, or save it for eternity.

When Crowfoot reached for the weapon's walnut handle, the trooper seized the old man's arm and whirled the slight body of Twilight's grandfather in front of his own and so that Twilight could not fire without hitting Crowfoot.

'Goddamn you,' he snarled at the Indian girl. 'You make one more clink with that rifle hammer and your grandfather will be as dead as a gutted buffalo. Old man,' he jabbed him hard with the muzzle of the Colt, 'move over by the girl. If you stumble, I fire.'

Crowfoot only nodded and edged around the fire to stand beside Twilight. Maggart followed in stride behind him. When they came up to the young squaw, the soldier lashed out at her with the long barrel of the revolver without warning. Twilight tried to avoid the weapon but did so only partially. It struck her a grazing, numbing blow on the side of head and face. Staggering, she went down. Crowfoot cried out in hurt.

'Ah,' said the old man, ever so softly. 'You should not have done that.'

Maggart did not hear him. He was picking

up the fallen Winchester, thrusting the big Colt back into his waistband, turning for his saddled horse.

'Don't follow me, you old fool,' he warned Crowfoot, 'or you'll get worse.'

The old Indian nodded. He waited until Maggart, backing the first twenty feet, turned to look for his mount. In that moment the knife of Twilight was in the aged warrior's hand. The throwing motion perhaps was not smooth. The hurt that it gave the arthritic joints of the arm and shoulder came audibly past clenched teeth. But the ten-inch skinning blade flew like a fletched arrow to its mark. Trooper W. O. Maggart heard the throwing grunt and knew in the terror of his heart what came behind him. He tried to turn, tried to spin and bring the Colt into play. He was too late and forever too late.

The Sioux knife took him in the broad flat between the shoulder blades, rupturing the dorsal vertebrae and the cord they sheathed.

Maggart did not feel the rocky snow into which he fell facedown.

All sign that the two Sioux saw as they came to stand over him was the reflex twitching of his outflung hands, gripping spasmodically at the snow.

'See,' said Crowfoot quietly. 'Still grasping.'

Twilight did not answer. She reached down and got the Colt and the Winchester, putting the revolver in her leather belt, handing the short rifle to Crowfoot. 'I'll get the other one,' she said, and she went up into the rocks and picked up the Springfield where the soldier had left it. It was a 'trap door' model—one of the new ones. The kind that had gotten Yellowhair Custer's men killed up on the Greasy Grass because the shells stuck in it when it became hot with firing. But it was a soldier gun and Twilight was an Indian, and she brought it back to Crowfoot as a trophy of war.

Her pride was met with an unexpected grimness.

'Done as an Oglala,' the old man said, accepting the weapon. 'But do not stand so haughty. We have made a very bad mistake. The plan is no good now.'

'What?' Twilight glanced quickly about. 'I see no mistake. You're growing afraid again. I am not. Come on. I don't fear sungrinners or black buffalomen any more than white men. When they are rolled in a blanket, they are all the same.'

'Look about you again,' ordered the old man. 'Do you see the soldier's fine horse?'

Twilight grew pale. 'The horse!' she cried. 'It is gone. The soldier's horse has run off.'

'Yes,' said Crowfoot bitterly. 'While we played this simpleton's game of watching the body twitch, the horse got away. Now how long do you think those thieves down there will stay rolled up in their blankets for you, once they see this riderless horse come pounding

127

back down the trail from High Meadow? Eh? What is your quick answer to that problem, knifewoman?'

Twilight fought the question in her mind, bending it this way and the other, but it would not arrange itself to satisfy the old man's hard-eyed query. In despair, she turned to the spirit world. 'What would *he* have done, grandfather?'

'The warchief? You mean the warchief?'

'Yes, yes.'

'Well, he was a religious man of deepest feelings. He would have prayed of course.'

'Do you know a prayer, grandfather?'

'Yes. One.'

'How does it begin?'

'It begins, "*Tunka sila le iyahpe ya yo*, Father receive my humble offering." You want to pray it with me?'

'No, you're the medicine priest. Pray hard though.'

Crowfoot raised both arms to the blackness overhead. He had not gotten more than well into the old chant when the Sioux gods replied to his appeal. A strong air current swirled open a hole in the deep clouds above the meadow, revealing clear sky and sparkling starlight above. The grassland was illuminated briefly. They could see the entire meadow from rimrock to rimrock, including at least three hundred of the four hundred Oglala horses peacefully on graze. And they saw one thing else. A lone animal standing on a wooded point not fifty paces from the coffee fire. It was an ancient freckled white mare, and Crowfoot knew her at once from the old days.

More importantly, the mare remembered him.

When he whistled to her, she whickered back, then commenced to neigh excitedly to the herd in glad announcement to gather up, to come in on the high lope, that the Indian masters had returned and all would be loved as pets again.

'Wakan Tanka be praised,' sighed Crowfoot. 'We have starlight to see by and, by it, we have found the old bellwether she-horse, Speckledbird.'

'*He-hau*, yes,' agreed Twilight, 'and by it we have found one other gift-thing, too.'

'Eh, girl?' said Crowfoot, puzzling it. 'What the hell is that?'

The girl laughed excitedly.

'It's an old Oglala Bad Face medicine priest who knows the ancient way up out of this meadow over the high country,' she answered. 'Come on, grandfather; we're taking these horses of ours home—the high way!'

CHAPTER SEVENTEEN

It was September 29, 1877, in the camp of the Nez Perce at the Bear Paws, south of Milk

River. After the good weather of the buffalo kill, the clouds were coming down once more. The wind rose, stalking the lodges, howling dolefully. A sleety mist replaced the rain. Ice stiffened the lodgeskins and made the stacks of fresh hides rattle in the wind. As the day faded, it began to snow up along the ridges.

In the hollow where the lodges stood, the freezing rain continued. Now and again a flurry of snow made the ground gray. Until dusk, conditions did not alter. The people grew uneasy. In this great open land of the *moosmoos illahee*, the buffalo country, the threat of the White Wolf—the arctic storm— prowled constantly. At ten o'clock that night, the wind switched. It went into the northeast, snow-lair of the very worst weather.

In his lodge Allemyah Tatkaneen, whom the white man would call Looking Glass, heard the drum of the lodgeskins change. Arising, he went outside. The moment he 'smelled the wind,' he summoned a council of the leaders.

The business was soon enough agreed. The pleasant days at Tsanim Alikos Pah would now be memory. The scent of Yauz Imekes, the Big Cold, was in the air. Winter was coming early. The White Wolf was howling for all who would tarry and be hunted down.

It was the time to pack the lodges and make the last two rides for the new home beyond Milk River.

The meeting was closed by Joseph with a

prayer to Hunyewat, the Nez Perce Great Spirit Chief.

*   *   *

The following morning, September 30, the camp on Tipyahlanah (Eagle) Creek—some argue it was called Snake Creek—came astir with first light. The rain had stopped, but the wind cried eerily among the lodges, warning the people to be gone from that place of the buffalo-chip fires.

Joseph had arisen before dawn to go out and inspect the horse herd. With him went his twelve-year-old daughter by his older woman, Heyoom Yoyikt. The child's name was Kapkap Ponmi, Noise of Running Feet. She had unusual gaiety and was Joseph's pet. Also with the chief were a young warrior of noted eyesight and a tall girl-squaw whose gift was that of being an extremely skilled rider.

Joseph said nothing of any apprehension.

The child, Running Feet, sensed nothing; she shared Joseph's love of fine livestock and thought her father was concerned only with inspecting the herd.

The horses were being held east of Eagle Creek, across the stream from the camp hollow. The morning had turned ever more raw and cold. Every animal stood with its back humped, rump swung to the north wind. Some family pets among them raised heads and whickered, glad to see human friends on such a foul day. The herd appeared to feel the changing weather, being restive to move. They crowded the visitors anxiously.

The scout and the tall squaw dropped behind Joseph and his chattering daughter. The young couple were also talking. But suddenly the girl touched the scout with an alerting hand. '*Tayiaksa*,' she said in a low voice, 'I don't like this. See what horses Joseph selects yonder.'

Her companion looked ahead, scowling. 'I don't like it either,' he said.

An Indian faced with a war march will choose different mounts than he will on a day when the band will be moving peacefully or when a buffalo run is planned. The horses Joseph had neck-roped out of the herd were not peaceful movers or buffalo runners. They were his premier mounts: Ebenezer, his war horse, and Ebenezer's half-brother Joshua, the Sunday or show-off horse of the Nez Perce chief. Together, they were simply the best and swiftest in the herd.

The young couple waited in anxiety for Joseph to come up to them with the animals. When he had done so, the scout spoke bluntly. '*Taz meimi*, good morning again, my father. But what are you doing with those two horses for only a trail march?'

Joseph smiled his beloved brief smile, indicating by a handsign to the young scout

that he would speak with him a little apart
from the women. 'Don't look so surprised at
that,' he winked to Running Feet and the tall
squaw. 'You know very well that men speak of
many things you women would laugh at and
make us to feel thus small in your eyes.
Elaptauksa, excuse us one moment.'

The young squaw knew now, surely, that
something was wrong. But she was, as Joseph,
a creature whose heart beat for others. She
merely nodded and put her arms about the
shoulders of Joseph's daughter.

When the two men were out of hearing of the
women, Joseph spoke with quick intensity to
his scout.

'Do not question me but do precisely what I
tell you,' he said. 'I want you to take these two
horses of mine. The woman will ride Ebenezer,
who is a step more slow than Joshua. You will
take Joshua for your own horse. Running Feet
and I will walk back to camp as we came out of
it, alarming no one. You and the woman, as a
young brave and a handsome girl, can ride out
with no one thinking anything of it. *Mizisa*,
warrior, do you understand all this?'

The scout, trying not to look fearful, felt the
chill of the question. He shook his head, not
quite certain. 'What has gone wrong, father?'
he asked.

Joseph turned away so that the watching
woman and the child could not read his lips. 'I
was awakened in the night with a stone upon
133

my heart,' he said. 'Our God was speaking to me and I was cold with sweat in my warm bed. He said to me, "Heinmot, go you out and gather in your two best horses and do with them as you know you must do." I answered him, "Father, do but show me the trail that I may lead my people in safety upon it. I shall get up the horses as you bid me, but show me the trail; *Inehmuze*, Father, I petition it!"'

'And he showed you the trail ahead?' said the uneasy scout.

'No.' Joseph shook his head. 'He showed me the trail behind. It was very dark but I could see along it.'

'What did you see back there?'

'Soldiers. But no more talking now. It will be for you and your great young eyes to go and see what is really back there. Are you ready?'

'Yes, father. What must I do?'

Joseph touched his shoulder. 'You and the girl take the horses on a guarded pace. Don't run them but don't walk them either. Go straight to the high rim of the buffalo pasture where it drops off to the Painted Water. That is a far country you can see from there.

'Now if you see something moving along our trail, send back the girl on Ebenezer. Do not wait to be sure it is soldiers—it might be our Sioux brothers coming at last—but send the girl waving the slow blanket, to tell us to get ready to move.

'You yourself stay where you are after you

send her. Then, if you see that it *is* soldiers coming, you leap on Joshua and drive him at all his speed back to camp waving the fast blanket, to tell us to prepare to fight.'

He took the young brave by both arms. 'You ride for all the people,' he said. 'Remember it.'

The scout touched his brow with the tips of his left-hand fingers, the gesture of acceptance with highest respect.

'*Taz alago*, Heinmot,' he murmured, 'farewell.'

Joseph stood and watched him go striding back to the tall young squaw, and he watched them still as they mounted and rode away, southward, from the herd. He watched them until his small daughter Running Feet came up and took his hand, speaking to him. Then he broke his eyes from the riders he had sent upon his people's destiny, recovering as from a journey to another world.

'Eh?' he said, surprised. 'Oh, it's you, little rabbit.' He gripped the trusting hand in his dark fingers. 'Why, then, come along, *miaz*. Let us go and see what your mother Heyoom has in the breakfast pot.'

CHAPTER EIGHTEEN

When Maggart failed to report for duty the morning following Dr McGillycuddy's visit to see the ailing wife of Crazy Horse, the post physician sent to learn what the trouble might be. Being informed that his orderly had stolen a company horse and was gone over the hill, McGillycuddy told the new man, Corporal Sweeney, to watch the infirmary until he returned.

'I've a very sick woman to see,' he told the soldier.

Celt that he was, McGillycuddy was suffering premonitions. There might not necessarily be any connection between the old medicine priest and the granddaughter jumping the reservation with his blessing, and his medical orderly going A.W.O.L., but if there was, the softhearted doctor was somewhat in the middle of the affair.

Hence the scowl as he pushed through the morning cold toward the lodge of Tasina Sapewin. And hence the forming curse when he was close enough to the lodge to sense its unnatural quiet. And to note, as well, the undisturbed outside lacing of its entryflaps.

'Damn it,' he said softly.

He stood a moment. He ought to have come sooner. If anything were amiss with his patient, it would be a plague on his professional conscience. But that blasted Maggart had chosen to run off at the very time when he could have been sent over to check on Mrs Crazy Horse, despite McGillycuddy's promise to come himself and *not* send Maggart. A doctor never could keep up with his promises.

136

It was a medical fact bearing no prejudice, red or white.

Ah, well, in you go, Little Beard, he told himself, employing one of his Sioux names. He took scalpel from black bag, incised the entryflap cleanly. Going inside, he found the stench as high as that of battlefield surgery. But once he saw the corpselike stillness of the abandoned squaw and anxiously dug past the dried vomit that glazed the woman's face and chest, he discovered, to his amazement, that she still lived.

Moreover, she was conscious and able to take medication.

He worked with her, giving restoratives, chafing limbs, talking to her continually in an effort to break through. Yet, in reply to his querying, the woman was able only to bring out from beneath her fouled pallet the emptied bottle of opium pills and to gesture toward the flaps of the lodge, indicating a connection between the vanished pills and the departed members of her family, McGillycuddy surmised. In addition, all he could get from her was a motion of raising the bottle to her mouth and lifting it up as if to empty it. He could not determine if this meant merely that the pills were gone because she had taken them as directed, one at a time and properly, or if she had swallowed them all at once in an attempt to either get well at once or to pass into her ancestral Land of the Shadows quickly. Or if, finally, some other hand than her own had forced the medication upon her.

At the point of summoning stretcher bearers from the post, McGillycuddy was accosted from the entryway by a friendly small Indian boy of about ten years inquiring if the warchief's woman were dead yet. The boy spoke excellent English and was plainly a product of the agency's struggling educational program. He was, as well, rather bright and forward. McGillycuddy thought to invite him in, reclose the flaps, and employ the grinning youngster as interpreter.

Within a minute, the matter of the diagnosis, or, at any rate, the etiology of the dried vomit, was solved. The entire bottle's contents had, in fact, been forced down the poor creature's throat.

But no, it had not been her grandfather, old Crowfoot, or her young sister Twilight who had done this wrongful thing to Tasina. The soldier doctor must not seek them out to punish. Should he wish, instead, to believe a simple Indian, then he must be told the truth. It had been his own servant, the medicine soldier Maggart, who had made her take all of the pills.

As to the vomit, Tasina apologized.

Shortly after Maggart had departed, she had become fiercely ill and sick all over herself.

'Aye,' nodded McGillycuddy. 'Therefore saving your life very certainly for the day, and I must say, although I understand it not at all, that it would seem you are better in every way.'

He patted the boy on the shoulder. 'Tell Mrs Crazy Horse that the soldier doctor thinks she is going to get well now. She has no fever and her lungs are clearing.'

McGillycuddy waited while the youth talked to Tasina.

Tears welled in the woman's eyes, spilled down her wasted cheeks.

'She says to say to you that her gods thank you,' the boy chirped. 'But myself, I think it was your pills, soldier doctor. When I get sick I want you to come and see me with a bottle of those pills. Right now,' added the boy, 'I will trade you my dog sled outside there for only part of a bottle of them. I know many sick Indians, old ones and children, who would like to get well. Is it a trade, soldier doctor? That's a very good sled.'

McGillycuddy glanced out the flaps.

'Aye,' he said. 'So it is. I'll tell you what I'll do, boy. You help me haul this woman over to the sickhouse on your sled, and I will give you a whole bottle of much bigger pills than these. All right?'

Tuweni Oyuspi thought it over. His name meant Nobody Catches Him. It didn't mean he was fleet of foot, but lightning fast in his mind. Nobody got around Tuweni.

'Well,' he finally agreed, 'I'll do it because I like this woman. I felt sorry for her all the time

139

before you came to see her. Besides, she is the wife of the great warchief.'

'That's right,' said McGillycuddy softly. 'Come on, bring your sled closer. I'll carry her out.'

As they went through the new snow, both pulling Tasina Sapewin on Tuweni's little dog sled, the squaw pleaded with the physician not to report her vanished relatives. She explained that perhaps they had only gone up to Red Cloud. Surely they would be back. Crowfoot might merely have gone out into the hills to make a meditation over her health. He would be back, and with him her sister. Would the soldier doctor wait a little?

McGillycuddy's frown returned. He heaved a heavy sigh. It was not an easy thing making these Indians understand the way that the white man functioned.

'No,' he answered at last. 'You see, I must report that the soldier tried to kill you. He is a trooper of the army. The army will go after him and capture him. They will punish him for running away and also for what he did to you. He faces death either way.'

McGillycuddy sighed again. 'In the same manner,' he said, 'I must report the circumstances of your missing grandfather and young sister to the army. They will probably send Captain South and his Cheyenne scouts after them, because they are Indians. This you also know they must do. I am sorry about it.'

The post physician had spoken to the woman in English, with Tuweni waiting to translate. 'Be careful in the way you tell it to her,' he warned the boy. 'Don't upset her, but tell the truth.'

Tuweni did not lie to the woman on the sled. When he had finished relaying the doctor's words to Tasina, the wife of Crazy Horse burst at once into the mourning notes of the Katella song, the Oglala chant for the 'already dead.' McGillycuddy scowled at Tuweni and leaned once more into the towrope of the dog sled.

'Better for you, red sister,' he muttered unhappily, 'had you not vomited the medicine. Now, God alone knows what hell Captain South and his damned Cheyenne scouts will bring to your kin out there.'

McGillycuddy glanced off toward the snow-hidden, distant hills of Wyoming, and his small companion said pertly, 'What is that you said, soldier doctor?'

'Not one damned bit of your nosy business,' huffed McGillycuddy. 'Pull harder on your part of the rope. You talk too much and work too little.'

'I heard what you said,' the boy insisted cheerfully. Then, straining in honest effort to haul a little more of his share of the sled's burden, he added, 'I think I will try to go with Captain South and those Cutarm scouts of his. It must be great fun to chase Indians when you are on the soldiers' side.'

'Nonsense!' snorted McGillycuddy. 'You don't want to be on the soldiers' side. With those Cheyenne? Why, the Cheyenne hated Crazy Horse. They were the very ones to come in here and volunteer to help run him down.' The doctor paused, frowning. 'Don't you understand that Captain South's scouts are all Little Wolf's people?'

Tuweni nodded. He had an old face for a boy of but ten winters. There was now upon that face a look of cunning far removed from his few years.

'I know that,' he said. 'But what the soldier doctor doesn't understand is that maybe I would not be helping them.'

McGillycuddy glanced at the boy, amused.

'Are you saying you plan to make trouble now for Captain South's Indian scouts? A moment ago you were asking for half a bottle of pills and were going to go about making old people and children well again. And then you spoke of having fun chasing your fellow Sioux with the pony soldiers. You know something, friend Tuweni? I think you are a great *wowima haha*, a great big joker. Isn't that so?'

Tuweni looked up at him with sudden seriousness. 'No,' he said. 'I am *wablenica*, and very small.'

'*Wablenica?*'

'An orphan boy,' explained Tuweni. 'Very small one.'

'Ah.' The post physician understood the

world of loneliness. What such abandoned ones as this Tuweni needed was someone who cared. Someone who would offer more than empty words. He patted the Sioux boy's head.

'Listen,' he said. 'If you could have anything you wanted, right at this moment, what would it be?'

'A fine horse,' answered Tuweni Oyuspi quickly. 'Do you have one?'

As a matter of fact, McGillycuddy did have such an animal, his Kentucky-bred bay saddler named Lucifer out of respect for the beast's uncertain temperament. The canny doctor saw a chance to do good for all parties concerned— himself, the Indian boy, and the damnable Lucifer.

'Why,' he answered cheerily, 'yes, I do. Moreover, he is difficult to manage and I believe the stable soldiers would welcome anyone who might volunteer to care for him. Do you know of a person for the job, lad?'

'Hmmm,' said Tuweni, 'a small person perhaps.'

Dr McGillycuddy stopped short, properly startled. 'What!' he exclaimed. 'You mean you yourself would look after Lucifer? I warn you, now, he's dangerous. He's proud-cut, you know.'

'The best ones are,' nodded Tuweni sagaciously. 'Let me see him. I am very good with horses.'

'You accept then?' McGillycuddy was

143

genuinely delighted. 'You will get no pay, only food and a warm place to sleep. The stable work is not easy.'

'Let me see the horse,' repeated the Indian boy.

'Ah!' said McGillycuddy. 'You have a head as hard as any Celt. Aye, and a sharp wit with it. I suspect your Sioux grandmother may have gotten too near some bonnie fur-company factor on a visit to Red River.'

At the mention of Red River, he saw the orphaned boy's face light up. 'Did you know my grandmother was up there?' he said. 'I didn't tell you that, did I?'

Seeing that his small companion was so interested, McGillycuddy answered soberly. 'No one told me,' he said. 'I was joking with you. But you *do* have such a grandmother living up in Canada, eh lad?'

'Yes, up there on Red River. You know, up there in Canada where Sitting Bull went when he took his Hunkpapas out of our Oglala camp. That was when Crazy Horse decided we Oglala would come in and surrender at Fort Robinson.' The boy's features took on a cast that wrenched the post doctor's soft heart. 'I became separated from her in the confusion of the departure. I thought she was with us, but she went by mistake with Sitting Bull. Now I am *wablenica*, a poor orphan boy, as you can see. I have no one. And I will never see the grandmother again.'

144

No fool, despite vulnerable emotions, McGillycuddy eyed Tuweni closely.

'I suspect,' he said, 'that you have given the entire problem a great deal of thought. Further, I doubt very much that a young warrior of your determination would hesitate to go and find his grandmother in Canada, given the least proper chance.'

'What? What is that you say, soldier doctor?'

'I said, you rascally scamp, that I suspect you are just what I said you were, a great storyteller, a real *wowima haha*. I don't think you ever had a grandmother. I believe you sprang, fully grown, from the forehead of some Indian Juno who—' He broke off his words to once more pat the Oglala urchin on the head. 'Never mind,' he concluded. 'I appreciate your spirit. We will get on first-rate. Come on, pick up the sled's rope again. We must get this woman to the sickhouse. *Hopo!*'

They started on, but Tuweni was still frowning.

'Her name was Keya, the Turtle. My grandmother, I mean.'

'Oh?'

'Yes. She was hurt bad as a child. Made to walk wide and clumsy. The people thought she walked like a turtle. But I think Keya is a pretty name.'

'Indeed, aye, it is that. You really did have a grandmother, didn't you? I can tell your words are straight. You're not joking now.'

'She walked slow,' said the boy, 'but thought very fast. In that way, she told me, she could keep ahead of any Indian, though he might run like the antelope.'

'I can see,' laughed McGillycuddy, 'where Tuweni got his sly mind. Old grandmother must have been a caution!'

'Oh, yes, she was always very cautious.'

'No, that wasn't my meaning,' McGillycuddy began, then understood that the span between his English and that of the Oglala boy was unbridgeable beyond immediate or practical repair. 'I'm sorry about old Turtle,' he said. 'Perhaps one day you will see her again.'

Tuweni nodded suddenly. An inspiration had taken his agile imagination. He looked off to the west and north, toward the Wyoming line.

'Soldier doctor,' he said, 'do you believe what all the Indians are saying about old Crowfoot and Twilight?'

'That depends on what they're saying about them.'

'That they ran away to go and get those Oglala horses out in those hills over there. The ones the white man stole and hid there when we Oglala surrendered. And that Crowfoot and Twilight intend to take those Oglala horses up to join Chief Joseph and the Slit Noses running for Canada, where they will live with Sitting Bull and the Hunkpapa. *Ih*, that's what the

Indians are saying, soldier doctor. Now what do you say?'

McGillycuddy's brows drew down. He made a mental notation to add this newest rumor to the belated report of the flight of Twilight and Crowfoot that he would make to Major Jesse Lee upon return to the infirmary. Such an Indian story should be checked out even though it would seem, on the face of it, just another specimen of Sioux camp gossip.

'Well,' he answered the boy belatedly, 'I know nothing of this tale you tell me about the stolen Oglala horses. Oh, I've heard the rumor about it, of course. Who hasn't, who works with the Sioux, here? What I mean is, I know nothing myself of old Crowfoot and the girl being personally bound to carry out any such plan.'

He paused, and Tuweni eyed him sharply. 'Aha!' he said. 'So you have heard about that story, soldier doctor. I thought so. It must be true then. They've gone out there to get those Oglala horses.'

McGillycuddy frowned, shook his head. 'Listen, boy. Pull harder and don't talk so much.' The post physician pointed ahead. 'There's the infirmary. Come on, we've got to get this poor sick woman under cover.'

'Yes, thank you, soldier doctor.' The boy reached over and patted Dr McGillycuddy just as the doctor had patted him. 'I'm glad you found me and will let me live with your evil bay

147

horse. *Ha-ho*, may your lodgeskins never dry and rattle apart in the wind.'

'Ah!' smiled the doctor. 'Not only a liar and a tale-spinner, but a poet. I may adopt you myself.'

The white surgeon chuckled softly.

It warmed a man, deep down, to help any of these red people. But to be able to give one of their orphans of the wars a safe shelter and good honest work for the coming winter and, God knew, perhaps a permanent home at that, well, it simply made the heart glow.

By his side, the small Oglala boy was not smiling.

Neither did he share the anticipations of a warm winter with a full belly.

His thoughts were far to the west, and the north, and he was smelling the winds of Wyoming and of home.

He could not wait to see that very fine big bay horse of the soldier doctor.

CHAPTER NINETEEN

Crazy Charley had his blanket pulled over his head. He wore the article like a garment, not a piece of bedding. It was his little Indian home away from home. Inside that odorous shelter he was once more with the Absaroka, or the Bloods, or Piegans, or the Arapaho—far, far away from the white man's camp. It made him happy to huddle in his blanket thinking Indian thoughts. It also had its practical applications since it was, after all, an Indian habit.

When he was under his little blanket lodge, Charley could see things without it being apparent he was even looking.

He was seeing something right now.

It was the empty-saddled horse of the runaway trooper from Fort Robinson and Spotted Tail agency. The riderless animal came wearily in off the High Meadow trail toward the camp picket line. Here it joined the mounts of the gang. The other horses, all well-broken working stock, greeted the return one with a soft snuffle or two and went back to their tethered dozing. Maggart's horse wedged itself in among their warmth, gave a grunting sigh of relief, and dropped its own head in equine slumber.

Crazy Charley looked at once at Con and Blue motionless in whiskey-drugged sleep beyond the fire; then he looked at the serape-cocooned form of Francisco Gavilan dreaming dreams of warmer climes on the fire's near side. None of the men moved in response to the arrival of the cavalry horse.

Neither did Crazy Charley Beckwourth move. He should, of course, go at once to the fire and tell the men that the little soldier named Maggot had come onto some kind of bad trouble up the trail. The return of a riderless mount to any outlaw camp, or to any lawful frontier camp for that matter, was an alarm signal always. But Charley should have told them something else even before the horse came back: Ben Childress had not come down from the meadow for the supper that Charley had left warming in the Dutch oven by the fire. Indeed, young Gavilan had tried staying awake to talk with Ben and tell him about the changed plan and tomorrow's emergency measure to gather and drive out the herd. But with Con and Blue dead drunk and passed out, the Mexican youth had fallen asleep also, and Crazy Charley, left alone to watch the camp, had begun to suffer his 'feels' and to think those Indian thoughts. Long before the horse came back riderless, Charley Beckwourth had commenced to 'go hunchy.'

It was his Absaroka, his Crow blood, calling him.

In the wind he could smell the Big Snow. It was autumn, the Dust and Dirt Blowing Moon, the warning time which told all red nomads to find their winter camp; to get in their meat for the long cold; to snug-up the lodgeskins and the calfrobes and the trade blankets for that happy time of rest and Indian family living, all safe and warm in that good camp with wood and water and winter-browse for the dear horse herd.

Charley wondered where the Crows were winter camped this time. Was it on Bitter Creek? Was it in the Tensleep country? Wolf

Creek? Or way up on the Little Blue where Crazy Horse and the Oglala had been when Little Wolf and the Cheyenne survivors came seeking shelter after the terrible thing at Powder River camp?

No, the troubled camp cook decided. His mother's people would be nearer to their ancestral range. The tribe was getting smaller all the while. The camp these past winters would likely be in the heart of the homeland. In the mountain foothills somewhere. Ah, now Charley knew. It had come to him by his Indian feel. The Crow camp would be in the Gallatin country up at the Yellowstone headwaters and, precisely, it would be on the forks of the Sweetgrass below the Greycliff Hills.

Ah! Charley could see his red people in that wonderful camp. There since Indian time remembered, the Crows had snugged away the snow months until spring brought their good friends, the Nez Perce over the Bitterroots, up the East Gallatin, and down the Yellowstone to the Forks, to join the Absaroka brother in the annual buffalo hunt in Sioux country. This year, of course, the Nez Perce would not be coming. They were running for their lives from General One Hand Howard. But Charley's people, the Crows, would be there at the Forks.

A frown shadowed the vacant stare of Crazy Charley Beckwourth. Wait a moment. He could not go home any more. His Crow brothers up there had taken his tongue and nearly killed him. How could he forget that?

But he was homesick nonetheless. Charley wanted to live in a cowhide lodge that coming winter. He wanted to hear the children laugh at their snow games and their tipi work. Charley loved children. And they loved Charley. But where might he go that he would find a red welcome?

Then, frowning ever more as his poor damaged mind struggled to remember things—Indian things—Charley remembered something forgotten only moments before. It was the Nez Perces. They were going to Canada to live with the Sioux of Sitting Bull. Charley could go with them. They would not know of his trouble with their old friends the Absaroka. He would be welcomed by the Slit Noses. Many times he had been the best hunting guide the Crows had in their joint meat-taking with the Slit Noses. Yes! Joseph's people would remember Charley Beckwourth. They would let him in a lodge. Their children would be glad to see Charley again. Oh, how wonderful!

But the shadowed frown closed in once more.

The Forks of the Sweetgrass were many rides away. And the Nez Perce were last heard to be much north and west of that place, away up on Canyon Creek. Or was it going past Cow Island, even beyond the Canyon?

Either way, Charley needed a horse to ride. That spavined old Blackfoot mare he used to pack the camp gear of the outlaws would not last two days on a forcing trail. And if he did not go away from the outlaws on a good horse, they would catch him and kill him surely. Well, what a sad thing. To dream of home and almost to have gotten there. No matter. Charley had no horse of his own. He had better go and awaken the tall man who was the chief of the outlaws. Better awaken him and tell him about the Maggot's stout soldier horse that had just come back with an empty saddle.

Crazy Charley got to his feet. He started toward the fire to arouse Con Jenkins. Then he stopped short.

But wait. That horse with the empty saddle. The animal was tired, yes. But Charley had all night remaining in which to walk the tired horse by hand, resting him on the move. And Charley could carry over his shoulder a flour sack full of rolled oats stolen from the outlaws' supply of the grain for their work horses. Why, that stout horse was as good as being Charley's own horse. If Charley spirited him out of the camp right then, the outlaws would never even know the horse had come back without the Maggot on his back. Charley Beckwourth had never owned a good horse, much less a saddle of any kind. Who would give such treasures to a thing like him? Now, just a moment. What had he been thinking about just the second

153

before? Oh, yes. Having his own horse and riding out to find his Nez Perce friends and go live with the Indians in Canada, where they had never heard about that Absaroka woman and what had happened to Charley Beckwourth's tongue because of the bad thing she had made Charley do to her.

There was the horse, right over there. And he was a horse that did not belong to the outlaws. All right. Charley would take him. *Tamtaiza*, as his Slit Nose friends would say. He was declaring it; he was going to do it right out in the open, just like that.

The pockmarked mixed breed turned about and went soundlessly to the picket line. There he filled one flour sack with oats for the horse, another flour sack with food for himself. Five minutes from the time he first began to frown and to think of Indian things, Crazy Charley Beckwourth had stolen trooper Maggart's saddled cavalry horse and was gone into the timber of the breaking camp, homeward bound to the Land of the Absaroka—and beyond it to the lodges of his Nez Perce friends, where the children would laugh to see old Charley again and the winter would be good.

CHAPTER TWENTY

The old man went to the travois of Red Weasel and got his personal war bag. From this, to the

154

young squaw's astonishment, he produced a well-wrapped 'pony bell' of the musical variety used by the Plains Indians since Spanish times. 'We shall need to fasten this to the white mare with old Weasel's hackamore. It would sound prettier, and more like home to the others, were it hung from a regular bell collar. But then, it will do. Go catch up the speckled mare yonder. Hurry.'

Twilight mounted Ben Childress's rangy saddle horse and in minutes returned with the white bell mare on a lead-rope. '*Waste, waste,*' nodded Crowfoot. 'Here, pretty one, let me fasten this lovely tinkler with the hackamore upon you.' The white mare nuzzled him and made low, happy horsetalk to him. When the bell was in place and the old man released his hold on the hackamore, the freckled old she-horse bobbed her head and swung her neck, delighted to be, in fact, once more a bell mare. 'Now,' said Crowfoot to Twilight, 'you take her on the lead-rope and ride the fine horse of the dead man. Make only one reduced circle of the meadow.' With graceful Siouan handsigns, he painted in the tour he wished the granddaughter to take. 'Go to the rock outcrop, there, and around it to come back up the far side of the pasture. You will see that those Oglala horses, for all their white-man breaking, have not forgotten what a Sioux pony bell sounds like. They should fall in and follow you and Speckledbird like sheep or goats. All right? Are you ready?'

'Yes,' said the girl. 'What will you be doing?'

Crowfoot made a sign toward a place directly across the meadow. 'Do you see that notch up there in the rim?' he asked her. 'Not the big one that looks like a pass but the small sharp one to its left. You see it?'

'Yes, yes. Is that the old secret Indian road?'

'Yes. Lead the old mare and the herd for that point. When you come near the far rocks, you will see the trail begin. If you do not see it, let Speckledbird go her own way. She knows that place. Go now, girl. Weasel and I will be ahead of you up the Bad Face Pass trail. We have to get those rocks out of the way that were put there by the Indians to close the road.'

'You can do that?' Twilight frowned. 'You and that knock-kneed old mule of yours?'

'Eh, what? Goddamn, I am glad you reminded me.' Crowfoot came over to the side of her borrowed mount and removed the coiled lasso of Ben Childress. 'Yes,' he then said firmly. 'You see, I will rope those big stones all to come down at once. That is because I was there when we closed the road. All those big rocks will come down and go over the edge like a waterfall, if you know the key stone rock down in the center of the others to put your rope on and give a good hard pull, such as with a mule.'

Twilight turned Ben's sorrel.

'All right. Good-bye, grandfather. *Hopo!*'

156

'*Hookahey!*' answered the old man happily. 'Go at a trot, no slower. Make that pony bell jingle.'

The girl clucked to the sorrel and started out. Behind her, still slewing her neck and bobbing her bony old head delightedly, Speckledbird came along with a spirit forgotten these long months in enemy captivity. The bell danced beneath the chinstrap of the Indian hackamore. Its musical sound stirred deep memories in the young sister of Tasina Sapewin. She felt wild and free. Her heart beat like that of an animal getting away from the hunters. *Hopo, hookahey!*

As Twilight and the old white mare rode into the herd, it seemed seized with the same nostalgia, the same fierceness of that remembering called homesickness. By the dozens at first, then by the scores, the beautiful animals threw up slender heads and whickered their welcome to the familiar song of the pony bell. Even while Crowfoot watched from the embers of the dead white man's fire, nearly a hundred horses had begun to drift in upon the slim girl and the bony ancient mare.

'Aye,' nodded the old medicine priest of the Oglala Bad Face band. 'Thanks be to you, Wakan. But don't forget it was all my idea. Nobody would believe it when I said I was going to get the warchief's horses. Aha!'

He gave Red Weasel a slap on his dozing haunch.

'Come on, tattered ear,' he shouted. 'Wake up, wake up! Don't you want to go home?'

Itunkasan Luta, the old Red Weasel, answered with a brass-lunged, wheezing hee-haw. He wanted very much indeed to go home, and he remembered exactly the direction in which that beloved land lay. Without hesitation or guidance from Crowfoot, he set out on a jarring mule trot, straight across the lush grasses of High Meadow. It was as though he too could see that distant small V-shaped notch far above the hidden meadow. It was all that the puffing Crowfoot, following on foot behind the travois, could do to keep up with the old mule's pace. Finally, the old man was unable to hold the gait. With a desperate lunge, he leaped into the sling of the travois and rode with the baggage. Red Weasel never missed a stride. The only thing of a natural force greater than that of a white man's horse turned stableward was the unalterable course of a red man's mule pointed away from the bare dirt of the agency pastureland back out into the trackless ranges of the shaggy buffalo bulls and their curly cows in the Land of Wanbli K'leska, the Spotted Eagle.

Red Weasel was going home. He could have pulled ten Crowfoots in that rotten old cowhide and spruce-pole travois. Well, at least three of them.

'*Hopo! Hookahey!*' yelled the old man from the bowels of the lurching travois, as though sensing the thoughts of his rejuvenated servant. 'Hurry up! Hurry up! Once those ponies down there get this wind of home in their nostrils, they will run over us. Go on, old Itun, go on! The gods bless your eyes that see back through the years. Yes, and give me the strength in my hands to hang onto this goddamn travois one more bounce!'

Crowfoot threw back his head. From scrawny throat issued a wobbling and reedy war cry. Red Weasel · brayed raucous accompaniment. Moments later, the ragged brute had found the foot of the Bad Face Pass trail and all breath was required for the steep way upward.

CHAPTER TWENTY-ONE

Con Jenkins cursed in his sleep. Bad dreams were battling the rotgut fumes that snaked and coiled sourly through his fogged brain. But a dozen years of dozing on the owlhoot trail honed a man's instincts. Whiskey or no whiskey, the outlaw leader sat up blear-eyed, aroused by that inner bell that had always rung for him where it did not for ordinary men.

His pained gaze stabbed at the stillness of the horse camp. It was a couple of hours past midnight. Well, there was Gavilan, beyond the fire. Here, by him, lay Blue, sundering the preternatural silence with a staccato of snores seeming to shake the fire-dried earth. The picket line was quiet. Goddamn it, he still didn't like it. Something had awakened him. Best go and rouse out Crazy Charley. He could smell things a dog would miss.

Throbbing head and queasy stomach aside, Con made his way soundlessly over to Crazy Charley's bedding spot. It was past the picket line and thus out of sight until the gaunt outlaw rounded the roped horses.

Stopping short, Con stared at the empty place where Crazy Charley Beckwourth had kenneled himself for all the months they had been camped there. In that instant, Jenkins's mind cleared, the bloodshot eyes narrowed, the juices of danger squirted through his muscular body.

'Son of a bitch,' he said softly, and turned and long-strode his way back to the banked fire.

The first of his boots found the haunch of Francisco Gavilan, the second took Blue Slattery in the off-shin. Both men came up with guns in hand, rolling away from their sleeping spots on the rise.

'Hold it!' snarled Con Jenkins. 'Put away the artillery and start thinking. Charley's gone.'

Gavilan nodded, no whiskey fog to shroud eye or mind.

'So's Ben,' he said, 'providing he ever came down from up above.'

'Well, Christ,' said Blue. 'What's all the

commotion about? The Maggot ain't come back to say anything abouten Ben being missing, is he? Maybe old Ben he just decided to stay up yonder with the herd, after the Maggot told him we was driving with first light.' He shook his dark head. 'But that don't wash, does it? Man don't go to sleep on a empty belly with ptarmigan stew and yeller saleratus biscuits for gravy-sop waiting him downtrail.'

Con Jenkins was moving for his horse. Gavilan and Blue Slattery exchanged their usual looks behind Con's back, then followed the tall leader to the picket line. Saddling was done swiftly and with no more talk. They all knew something was wrong by this time. The only comment was by Blue, as he and Gavilan swung up. 'Looky yonder,' he said, pointing to the sky overhead. 'Wind's blowed a hole in the snow cloud.'

Con Jenkins, still on foot, squatted suddenly to stare at the ground and what the unexpected starlight revealed to his practiced eye.

'Frank,' he called. 'Come here.'

The Mexican, noted for his trailing eye, got down and came over quickly. He struck a match and, stooping, joined Jenkins.

'Yes,' he said, cupping the match and peering at the tracks and feeling them with fingertips. 'They're laying over our stock's sign. That's a government shoe; Maggart's horse for sure. The print ain't deep enough

161

neither. I'd say that animal come in with nobody on him.'

Con glanced over to Beckwourth's vacant bed spot.

'How'd the hoss go out?' he asked. 'Rode or unrode?'

Gavilan got up and followed the animal's tracks into the picket line, then found where they went away again.

'With somebody on him, *jefe.*'

Con and Blue Slattery traded hard glances, and the black outlaw said, 'Sure now, it was old Crazy Charley. Never figgered him for such a sharp horse trader. Got to say that Blackfoot packmare of his he swapped us for the Maggot's horse ain't that exciting, Con.'

The tall leader eyed him, but only said, 'Come on.'

'Whereaway?' asked the Negro rider, as his companions swung up and reined their mounts around. 'After Charley?'

'When a boar-pig grows milk!' snapped Con. 'Don't you get it, you dumb bastard? It's the Injuns. They've come for the horses. That's why the breed vamoosed.'

Blue still delayed. 'You mean them two kin of old Crazy Hoss's what the Maggot claimed was on their ways out here to lift the herd? You believe them bull chips?'

Con checked his mount. 'We been over that ground,' he said. 'The only bull chips about it was there being but two of them. Charley ain't

162

going to cut and run because of no old medicine man and a girl-squaw working alone.'

Young Gavilan agreed quickly. 'He's right, Blue. It's just like we figured when Maggart told us about them. Just what we feared, remember? They've gathered up a bunch of stray agency Injuns out of the hills on their way here. We got us a war party up yonder.'

They rode then for the High Meadow trail, spurring upward along it with outlaw caution not for the war party but the weather, which again had closed in tight and low. At the last, they were riding with their knees only, giving their mounts their heads. When they topped the rim, they dismounted, going the rest of the way into the camp on foot, guns at the ready, neck hairs bristling.

Gavilan briefly checked the dust of the campfire site. 'Lots of overtracks,' he said. 'Could be a couple or three, four walking on top of themselves. Could be a whole bunch. Injuns for certain, though. And Sioux.'

'Hell!' Blue Slattery laughed. 'You ain't telling me you can read Injun sign good enough to name the tribe. Maybe Crazyhead Charley could, for sure his father, old Mulatto Jim Beckwourth could, but you, Hawkman?'

'In Texas,' answered young Gavilan quietly, 'we got Indians you never heard of. Bad ones and then more bad ones. Mainly, though, we got the Comanche. The man who learns his

163

sign-reading on Comanche Indians, he don't require no other lessons to do his sums on Sioux or Cheyenne or Crow or Blackfoot or Shoshoni or Siwash.'

'Well spoke.' Con Jenkins grinned wolfishly.

His light eyes searched the camp, settled on the wind-whipped silhouette of Ben Childress's dog tent. Motioning for the others to flank him, he moved silently toward the little shelter. At the flap, motioning his flankers to step away from a line of fire from the tent, he ripped aside the canvas closure.

'*Santos!*' breathed Francisco Gavilan.

'Christ Jesus,' echoed Blue Slattery.

'One brisket-ripped, the other back-knifed,' said Con Jenkins. 'It's the Sioux for sure. Rake in the pot, Frank.'

'Thanks, *jefe.*' The young Mexican horse thief broke his stare from the bodies of Ben Childress and trooper Maggart where the Indians had put them together in the tent. 'We better move out. They may still be around.'

'No, Frank.' Con's voice was calm. 'We'll look to our herd, first. Spread out and walk natural.'

They started down out of the rocks, threading their way toward their waiting saddle mounts. Then the wind shifted once more. As they came up to the huddled animals, the meadow, only moments before entirely fog shrouded, lay clear before their startled eyes.

They felt that sight down into the last twist

164

of their insides. They could not even speak.

As far as their skilled eyes might see, rearing rock wall to rearing rock wall of historic High Meadow, no solitary cavalry-colored sixty-dollar Oglala gelding now grazed the secret grassland that had hidden the stolen herd of four hundred head. They were busted flat. Out of stock. The Sioux—some Sioux—had come in the black of the Wyoming night to take back that which was their own. Con Jenkins, Blue Slattery, and Francisco Gavilan, as Con now flatly announced, could stand there until their pizzles were old and bent, it would still add up to the same bitter sum: They were out twenty-four thousand dollars.

And perhaps more. Suppose, suggested young Gavilan, the Sioux *had* left a rear guard in the rocks of the herd camp? That guard could right then have its sights laid square away between their own shoulder blades. If the three of them wanted to continue to stand there toting up their losses for the summer, they could get themselves just as vanished as the Oglala remount herd.

'Right again, Frank,' gritted Con Jenkins. 'Ease back for the horses. Walk slow, talk loud. Blue, you give a good laugh on the way, like nothing was wrong. When we get among the horses, pile on and hit out for home camp.'

'Sure, sure,' said Blue, leading the way cheerfully. 'We ought to have gone after Charley like I said. That way, we would at least have got one horse back. Hahaha!'

Con Jenkins stared at him. The thin upper lip lifted in a mirthless smile. 'Don't josh yourselves, either of you,' he told them. 'Suck in your guts and gather your wind for a long run; we're going after that herd of ours, and just you remember it.'

They continued walking. Their mounts were only ten paces on. Neither Blue nor Frank Gavilan answered.

Con continued, deeply incensed, 'Them was *our* horses,' he grated. 'Stole full-legal and fair from nothing but a raggletail bunch of dumb-ass red Injuns. They're still our horses. We been siwashed by them damned agency Injuns and that don't wash ten cents to the pan with Con Jenkins, you hear me?'

Blue and Gavilan didn't even nod, but they heard him.

It was Blue Slattery who spoke as they came up to their waiting horses.

'Con,' he said, 'in this business you got to know when to quit. Me and Frank has turnt hunchy. We're peeling out whiles we still got our hair glued on.'

Con reached for his buckskin gelding.

'You reckon the Sioux will lay for us? That what's turnt you chicken-livered?'

'Some of them laid for old Ben and the Maggot,' said Blue Slattery.

'*Que tal!*' said young Gavilan. 'What a truth. *Santos!*'

166

'We'll vote it down to camp,' Con said. 'Leg up and lay out flat on the withers. We'll be in the fog yonder in six jumps. Let's go.'

The outlaws found saddle and made mount all in the same motion of spinning horses and driving them for the opening of the downtrail to lower camp. No shots followed them, and no Sioux whoops.

Somehow, the silence spurred them harder, even so.

CHAPTER TWENTY-TWO

Joseph's chosen scouts, the youthful warrior and the tall squaw, reached the rim of the great bowl of grassland that was Tsanim Alikos Pah, the Place of the Manure Fires. There, they reined in Ebenezer and Joshua. For a long moment both the scout and the young squaw scanned the fall of the land toward the distant Missouri River. Presently, the young man spoke.

'What do you make of it?' he asked the squaw, pointing to the hazy distance.

The girl squinted harder. 'I see nothing,' she answered. 'Neither where you point nor anywhere.'

'Try again. There to the south of that creek we rode along coming in from Cow Island. You see it?' The warrior scowled uneasily, watching the young squaw. 'You must see it.

Beyond that thin rash of brush that covers the last gullies of the stream. South and south.'

The girl shrugged, broke off straining to see. 'If you mean those shadows across the gullies,' she said, 'you are imagining things. That's four or five miles off. Not even you, with your famous eyes, can see pony soldiers that far away. Come on, warrior.'

' The youth shook shaggy head. He was still scowling. 'No. I am thinking of Joseph's bad dream. He saw pony soldiers to the south. So do I think I see them.' He paused, licking dark lips. 'Listen,' he concluded, 'you go on back right now. Tell Joseph his best scout sees shadows moving at five miles on the rear trail. That's all. Just tell him that.'

The girl turned Ebenezer. 'Do you want me to wave the slow blanket?'

She was asking about the Nez Perce first signal of distress. In the maneuver, the returning scout rode his horse in slow progressive circles waving his blanket precisely four times to each round of a circle. The sign meant for the camp to come on the alert but not yet to take final alarm. 'Get set but don't run yet,' is the way that they said it.

Now the young warrior told her, yes, that she must wave the slow blanket as she went back. Then, when she was returned, she must seek out Joseph where he would be helping the women load the travois animals at the horse herd and seeing that the old people and the

168

children all had mounts and were ready.

The young squaw smilingly reminded her companion that she well knew where famed Chief Joseph would be.

'That's where he always is,' she said. 'Seeing to the weak ones, to the women, especially. All of them think he is our finest chief. Trust Joseph, is what they say. They all love him.'

'They should tell it to the men!' answered the scout bitterly. 'But, no, they would rather listen to that fool Asotin, that Looking Glass. He is a devil. Go on now. *Koimmze*, hurry up! Those shadows back there are moving in on us.'

The girl rode out, then, on the beautiful Appaloosa horse of Heinmot Tooyalakekt, Thunder-on-the-Mountain, Joseph, chief of all the Nez Perces. Waving but once to the young warrior, she was gone.

Left alone on the windy ridge, the youth went back to his hand-shaded staring into the distances.

It was a difficult thing to see anything in the shift of the weather that last day of September, 1877. The constant blowing about of the clouds and resultant changing of the patterns they cast on the darkened ground made identification of specific objects at the distance, now something less than four miles, impossible even for this keenest eyed of Joseph's men. The clouds themselves had dropped so low in places that they literally hid the earth. The

169

scout blinked his dark eyes repeatedly, trying to clear them, trying to put a danger-name on those shadows he still believed were moving within the camouflage of the clouds.

Something in the order of sixty minutes, a full hour—remembering that a pressing cavalry force covers four miles even in the walk-trot over broken country—passed before a favoring alteration of wind currents pried up the cloud-bellies from off the prairie southward.

The young scout cursed in horror of what he saw.

Soldiers. Pony soldiers. Hundreds and hundreds of horse-mounted troops which were not those of General One Hand Howard. Those were cavalry troops and infantry troops all together, and they were formed in a long line that would enclose the camp south, east, and west, leaving only the north open for escape.

There was one saving mistake alone. The changing clouds with their dark underguts laid flat upon the grass had made seeing as difficult for the pony-soldier scouts as for Chief Joseph's young watchman on the rim. In result, the troops had been advancing almost parallel to the big meat-hunting camp in Eagle Creek's hollow and were still very nearly that original four miles out from the dismantled lodges of Joseph's people.

The scout spun fleet Joshua about. He was

the fastest Indian horse within the tribes. If any mount could bring warning to the Nez Perce in time, Joshua was that mount.

'*Koimmze!*' screamed the youth. 'Go!'

Joshua dug in and went away from there in great driving jumps. Even as he went the young scout saw the swords of the officers so far away. He saw those sabers flash in the brief rays of the sun that pierced the clouds. And he saw, as those bared steel 'long-knives' gleamed distantly, the entire line of the mounted enemy turn on its own right flank, correct its lateral direction, and move once more ahead, on the gallop, directly for the camp of the Nez Perce.

After that the rim of the grassy bowl of Tsanim Alikos Pah hid the soldiers from the racing scout's view. All he could do was to stand in his stirrups and wave the fast blanket about his head. The scarlet King George coverlet carried the warning of its bloodlike color in the weak September morning sun. But the young scout did not see any action in the camp in answer to his signal of final danger. Standing again in the iron stirrups of Joseph's saddle, the youth shouted at lungtop, '*Koimmze! Koimmze! Koimmze—!*' But still there showed among the Nez Perce camp-breakers no sign of fright or heed of danger.

Well, the people had one chance. That officer back there in command of all those soldiers had made another mistake. In the confusion of the cloud-broken sunlight that

171

lasted only so briefly, the officer had misjudged the remaining distance to the camp of the red men. No sane cavalry chief would order the full charge from four miles out! That officer had done this, and his horses would accordingly be so weary when they reached the brim of the Eagle Creek drainage that the Nez Perce could still get to their mounts and ride out from under the soldier guns.

But Hunyewat, the god of the Slit Nose people, was not in his sullen gray heaven that fatal morning.

When the scout beat his panting Appaloosa into the very center of the camp-breakers, no more than a scant one hundred Indian horses—of the thirteen hundred composing the band's herd—stood trail-ready, either saddle, pack, or travois poles in place.

At the ready were only the horses of Joseph and his immediate family and friends who believed in him over all. Joseph had seen the slow blanket of the young squaw and he had seen the fast blanket of the far-eyed warrior he had sent to the rim, and he had believed both blankets and had made his preparations, pleading all the while for the others, for all the people, to do likewise.

But it was Aleemyah Tatkaneen, old Looking Glass, again. It was the Asotin devil who would not believe the warning blankets of Joseph's young scouts and who, even as the warrior and Joshua pounded into the camp, was slowly walking his horse among the lodges and the loading ponies advising the people to take their time, not to hurry, to go as carefully as they needed.

'*Mimillu!* Idiot!' the young warrior raged at him. 'Turn your fool's eyes up to the south ridge! What is it you see up there, Asotin traitor? Nothing? What is it riding those soldier horses up there by the hundreds and the hundreds? Are those our friends, the Sioux of Sitting Bull, come down from Red River to welcome us? Coming from the south like that? Up from the Painted Water and Cow Island?'

The wild young brave spun Joshua around, rearing the lovely animal.

'All you people!' he yelled hoarsely. 'Look up there on the south ridge. Take plenty of time to look as Aleemyah advises you. Oh, no, don't hurry. There is plenty of time. Look! Look! Look! And *Ukeize!* God curse your ears that listened to Aleemyah Tatkaneen—!'

The scout was screeching in fury now and the scores of people hearing him broke off their labors and turned their eyes toward the ridge. A terrible sound of pain came from them in that moment of discovery.

On the ridge for its entire ragged length, from east to west along the high ground encircling the camp, uncountable hundreds of horse soldiers had suddenly appeared. Even as the cry went up among the Indian watchers below, the bugles blew along the blue-coated

173

line; and, whipped to them by the twisting wind, the Nez Perce heard the order that would kill them: 'Charge—!'

CHAPTER TWENTY-THREE

Con awakened with the melting sting of fresh snowflakes on his face. Coming up on an elbow, he shook his head like an angry bear caught short of a safe hole for hibernation. Goddamn it, what was this kind of a blue norther blizzard doing blowing up so early in the fall? Jesus. Now daylight would not mean a thing. They could huddle there in the breaking camp all they wanted, they weren't going to see the sun that day. Then the real meaning of the new snowfall came home to Con Jenkins. A big fresh fall like this one, if it held, would utterly blanket any sign in High Meadow as to how in Christ's name those bastardly Sioux had gotten the remount herd out of the secret pasture.

He shouted Blue and Gavilan awake. The two needed no lecture on the weather report. 'There may still be time, if we rustle our butts up there *mas pronto*,' Con said to them. 'Let's ramble.'

Once more they got to horse, once more charged up to High Meadow. At the dead fire of Ben Childress's camp, they paused to breathe their mounts and to make their

174

reckonings.

The obvious thing was to circle the meadow watching the snow for evidence of the herd's exit upward. But when Blue Slattery suggested this, Con shook him off. So did Francisco Gavilan.

'We got to do better than that,' the Mexican rider said with a frown.

'Sure as bear manure smells bad, we do,' agreed Con. 'A man don't win no main-chance pots without he hangs his bare butt over the fire.'

'What does that mean?' said Blue.

'Long shot,' answered Con. 'We've already paid our money, now we takes our chances. It's either that, or we push back from the table. We don't head that herd and get it on the drive for Robinson this coming day, we can forget our four-months' sweat.'

'You're believing the Maggot again,' Blue charged.

'Aren't you?' Con's gray eyes blazed. 'You all hot to think that goddamn Maggart up and went over the hill for the horseback ride?'

Gavilan broke in soberly. 'I'm wondering if we ain't already too late. Seems to me if the army's onto Maggart deserting and onto them two Oglala Sioux jumping the reservation to go after Crazy Horse's pony herd, we ought maybe to turn square around, right here, and ride the hell away from Wyoming.'

Con Jenkins shook his head. He was not yet

angry, even though his wolfish eyes were alight and the muscles were working along his jaw. 'We don't know all that,' he said. 'How do we know they're going to hook Maggart up with our horses, right off the bat? As for them stupid redskins, where's the army going to connect one old medicine man and a girl-squaw running off into the hills with a remount herd of Californy horses all the way from Sacramento Valley?'

'Well—' Blue Slattery began. But Con cut him off.

'There's only the three of us left now. We're talking about eight thousand dollars apiece.'

The other two were human, after all. It was an awesome sum of money. And like Con said, if you wanted to clean the table you sure as hell had to see the last raise. Young Gavilan gave the answer quickly.

'All right. What you got in mind for the ante?'

Con explained that Blue would go to the right while Frank circled to the left, aiming to meet on the far side of the basin. Meanwhile he, Con, would spur straight out across the meadow and wait for them over there.

'Got you,' nodded Gavilan. 'Head out, Blue. I'll see you yonder at the foot of the big rock spill.'

'That's the place,' growled Con. 'I'll take a line square on it. Dig out!'

The three horsemen kicked their mounts

176

into a high lope and were almost instantly lost to sight of one another. Con could not see the big slide across the pasture, but he had the instincts of the hunter and, when his horse had cantered and quick-trotted the four miles of the meadow's span, the outlaw leader was not surprised to find himself within two hundred yards of the talus fan spilling down from the rim of the western wall.

'Whoa-up,' he called softly to the horse. 'We're here.' Then, as the animal quieted and stood blowing out, 'Christ Jesus. Talk about outhouse luck—!'

Whirling the horse, Con Jenkins cupped his hands, threw back his head, and sent a high-pitched rebel yell out across High Meadow. Almost immediately, the cry was picked up and answered by Blue and Gavilan, starting on their respective eight- to ten-mile tours of the valley's walls. Both abandoned their circling routes to drive directly cross-meadow, homing on Con's yell. Within minutes they had found their leader and were sitting their panting horses staring at what had caused Con to shatter the quiet of High Meadow at five in the morning: the thousand-hoofed passage-sign of the Oglala herd leading upward over the treacherous surface of the talus spill.

'God Almighty!' breathed Con Jenkins. 'Come on.'

He put his own horse digging and slipping up the precipitous grade of the ancient trail out of High Meadow. But, behind him, neither Blue Slattery nor Francisco Gavilan stirred spur or lifted rein to follow. Furious, the outlaw leader slid his mount back downslope to confront them. 'Goddamn you,' he said. 'Don't you *never* hold back on Con Jenkins.' The Colt .44 appeared in his hand. 'Come on.'

Young Gavilan advised him to go ahead and shoot. There was no chance, the Mexican said, that he or Blue Slattery were going to head up that rockslide and broken-cliff trail in the teeth of a building blue norther blizzard. Not for damned certain, the dark-faced youth added. 'Me and Blue, we come from warm country,' he said quietly. 'Happen old Blue agrees, we ain't going to winter-in up here. Blue?'

The Negro rider nodded. He was as afraid of Con's gun as any man of normal intellect would be. But Blue Slattery had lived with fear all his life. It was in his bones. Yet so was the cold of the alien Wyoming country in his bones, and the black rider was suddenly sick to his south-born heart of it.

'Go ahead and shoot,' he told Con Jenkins.

Con eyed him but did not fire. 'Happen this means the two of you are cutting out on me,' he answered. 'Say your piece and be damned. Whereaway you bound?'

'Home,' said Gavilan and laid it out for him.

The Mexican youth and the big Negro had talked it up and down last night after getting back from High Meadow and the Sioux horse

178

theft. For them, the entire idea of the California horses had gone mushy. Fort Robinson had come to look more like the hangman's noose than the jackpot payoff. The gamble that they could still sell the Oglala horses for Sacramento stock trailed clean to Nebraska was all at once gone to clabber. Eight thousand dollars was a mort of cash money, sure. But not enough for a man's life kicked out at the end of a rope.

'Blue,' said the Mexican rider out of the side of his mouth, 'start backing your horse. Go wide of me as I back mine. He can't make the cross-shot.'

The outlaws began sidling their mounts rearward and away from Con Jenkins. They guided the highly trained animals with knee pressures, hands free to use weapons.

Con never opened his mouth. He only slid the big Colt back into its frozen leather, beaten. Just before the end of it, he shook his head and spoke to them. Startled, they heard more of sadness than of malice or threat in his low voice. 'Boys,' he said, 'you're wrong; *them's still our horses.*'

He waved to them in the Plains Indian sign for 'safe trails' and turned his own horse away once more up the icy grade of the rockslide, following the fading hoofprints of the Oglala horses into the high pass and into Indian history.

CHAPTER TWENTY-FOUR

Crowfoot grunted and struggled and managed, all out of breath and a bit dizzy, to get the lasso rope he had taken from the dead white man fastened securely about the archstone of the dam of boulders built across the upper trail by the Sioux in former years. '*Hi-hunh*,' he puffed at Red Weasel. 'Go ahead, give it a pull.'

He had the mule in a small side gully so that the animal would not be struck by the release of the jam of boulders. Hence, when Red Weasel gave his answering grunt and laid into the stout lasso, the keystone came slamming neatly out, and the entire blockade of big rocks went tumbling harmlessly over the edge of the cliff. Nothing remained to obstruct the flight from High Meadow save some minor rubble, and the thing had been brought off without a piece of gravel so much as nicking the old man or his ancient mule.

'*Woyuonihan*,' chortled Crowfoot, 'I salute you, old devil. *Wonunicun*, I apologize for all the ill and mean thoughts I've held for you.'

The old man broke off to look with sudden alarm back down the trail toward High Meadow.

'Eh?' he cried. 'What's that rumble? Is that ponies running? Yes, it is, and they are coming

180

this way. Why, Jesus Christ, it must be our Oglala herd. The damned girl has gotten them all together—'

Again he broke off to point down the trail.

'Look there, Weasel! It's the old bell mare who leads them. My old friend Speckledbird. See, there the she-horse comes now, bringing our ponies up here. Hear the pony bell. Isn't that a pretty sound? You know what it's saying in the wind, Weasel? Home!'

The mule, not caring for the pony-bell music, swung ragged ears downtrail and snorted anxiously. It made no animal sense to stand in that trail and be run over—or pushed off the cliff—by four hundred head of Sioux horses pointed toward the buffalo pastures of their birth. With a second snort, Red Weasel plunged back up into the safety of the side gully. Crowfoot seized the tail of the vanishing travois mule and was thus towed free of the trail himself. Next instant, the liberated Oglala herd was pounding past the hiding place. All Crowfoot could do was huddle there and pray, stifled by the acrid stench of horse excrement made liquid by excitement, as the hundreds of the beautiful ponies of his people crowded up the ancient trail toward the V-notch pass above.

It required nearly an hour for the entire herd, slowed by the constantly narrowing track, to clear the gully's outlet. Before they had done so, it came on to snow, then to blow

181

fiercely. By the time the last of the horses had passed the old man's sanctuary, he was frozen numb with the cold. He could not find voice to call out to Twilight when she came up the trail riding the fine tall horse of the *wasicun* herdguard and vigorously crying on the stragglers of the herd. His best effort was a hoarse croak which carried scarcely to his own ears. He could not even get the willful Red Weasel to bray his usual raucous greeting and so alert the girl to come in and find him, where the old mule had dragged him away from the trail.

So, in fear and enfeebled silence, Crowfoot watched Twilight go on by and saw the last of the ponies round the turn of the cliff and disappear. How long he crouched in the gully, alive only because the side declivity was out of the wind, old Crowfoot could never afterward say. He thought it might have been four or five hours—from the midnight time of the herd's passing to the hour before sunrise. In any event, he did recall the circumstances that terminated his wait.

They were begun by the neighing of a strange horse.

This sound came from below on the trail and Red Weasel perversely and at once answered this unknown comrade. Only a mule would do such a deliberately mean thing to its master and Crowfoot had enough ire and fire left in him to curse Weasel wickedly.

Indeed, so aroused was the old man by the stone-headedness of his travois mule braying happily to an utter stranger that he managed to stagger to his feet and fetch the Weasel a 'somewhat kick' in the left hock. The old mule never noticed the attention but slid down out of the side gully to meet the approaching horse. Crowfoot followed as best he could. Even a poison-spirited mule was better than no company at all. Besides, the old brute's hairy belly provided the animal warmth that spelled life or death in that arctic cold at the blizzard's heart.

In the trail, the new horse came to a dragging halt, nose and nose with Red Weasel.

Crowfoot, peering hard, made out the form of an unhorsed rider, a booted foot hung in the onside stirrup of the saddled mount. The man lay motionless in the snow, either dead or, as the Sioux said, *telanunwela*, dead yet alive—unconscious.

The old medicine priest could hear a faint heartbeat when he pressed a frostbitten ear to the chest of the white rider.

'Damn to hell,' Crowfoot said. 'You cannot leave a man to die in a cold like this one. Now what must I do with him? Ah, yes, all right, I will do it. I will if I am able.' He patted Red Weasel. 'Perhaps it will balance against the wrong thing the granddaughter did to the other *wasicun*,' he suggested to the old pack animal. 'But we won't say a thing about that to

183

her, eh?'

After much tugging, he got the tall white man into the travois and lashed securely there under a buffalo robe. Then he mounted the white man's horse and ordered Red Weasel ahead. The mule obeyed and the horse followed the travois sensibly enough.

'You see,' the old man called to Red Weasel, 'the *wasicun* must have fallen off his horse back down the trail somewhere and struck his head. There is a very big cut, almost to the skullbone. I don't know why we saved him. He's going to die of the cold anyway. But at least it won't be our fault. *Hopo*, pull harder.'

Red Weasel grunted his standard packmule grunt. The new man in the travois weighed twice what the old Indian did. And it was hard, hard work hauling such added weight uphill. Red Weasel squatted and began to pin his ears. A hard-packed snowball flew through the night and hit the slowing animal in the back of the head. 'I know what you are thinking,' accused the shrill voice of Crowfoot. 'Forget such an evil thing. Besides, remember, if the travois goes over the edge, the mule goes with it. Eh, tiny brain?'

Red Weasel unpinned his flattened ears. 'Screeehawww!' he complained, and he put his honest Oglala muscle into the matter of dragging Con Jenkins up out of a certain death in the icy snows of Bad Face Pass.

CHAPTER TWENTY-FIVE

Upon his return to the post, McGillycuddy first made Tasina Sapewin comfortable in the infirmary and left her there in care of his acting orderly, trooper Sweeney. He also left Tuweni there, charging the Sioux boy to wait for him and meanwhile see to any wants of the Oglala woman, since Sweeney spoke no Indian tongue whatever. The doctor then went to the office of Major Lee and reported the disappearance of the two kinfolk of Crazy Horse, as well as that of his former orderly, W. O. Maggart. He also reported the story of the stolen Oglala herd as given him by Tuweni. The report was at once gotten off to Red Cloud agency and Fort Robinson and confirmed back by telegraph within the hour—the news would be checked out and acted upon. Captain South had already been alerted by post spies as to the stolen Oglala herd, but the McGillycuddy report substantiated that information nicely. General Bradley sent his compliments to Major Lee, his thanks to Dr McGillycuddy: The capture of the Indian fugitives and the army deserter would be added to Captain South's orders. With departure of the scout force assured no later than tomorrow morning, apprehension of the fugitives would be a certainty.

Gratefully, McGillycuddy was able to return to his medical service. The morning was by this time, of course, nearly gone. Noon came and passed and the afternoon wore on with the infirmary unusually busy.

Nothing could have suited Tuweni better. Sometime late in the day, he quietly disappeared.

* * *

Stealing the big bay horse of the soldier doctor proved an easy surprise. Also, the animal was not the devil described. All that he required from Tuweni was to be struck firmly between his stubborn ears with a good stout stick each time he laid back those ears. In this way friend Lucifer went along with the Indian boy very willingly indeed.

The only problem might have been finding just the right striking stick, and that trouble had solved itself.

In the good soldier doctor's office, as the afternoon grew late, Tuweni had found a knobbly cudgel, with a fine head of gold, standing by the front door. It was in fact Dr McGillycuddy's prized English walking stick, an heirloom by which he set considerable store. But Tuweni only observed that no one was using it and, more important to the moment, no one was watching it. He stole the beautiful cane, anticipating the correctional need with

Lucifer, and went out the infirmary door with it while the physician was wearily making last ministrations for the day to his several outpatients and carefully instructing replacement orderly Sweeney in the special care of Tasina Sapewin.

Accordingly, McGillycuddy first learned of his missing horse while he was searching the office for his missing walking stick, which he had plainly mislaid and which he now wanted for the pleasure of his nightly presupper stroll to quarters and to mess with Major Lee.

Still making no connection with the also missing Oglala boy, Tuweni, the doctor's innocence was shaken awake by the report of an angry stable sergeant coming into the infirmary for treatment of an enormous goose-egg behind his right ear. The lump had been the gift of a damned 'Injun kid' about the size of a rat terrier but carrying a crooked stick with a gold head that must have weighed as much as the boy himself. In any event, when the sergeant apprehended this urchin putting saddle to the doctor's personal horse and sought to question him, the Indian boy had pointed toward the infirmary and said in excellent English, 'Why, ask the soldier doctor yourself; there he comes now.'

The sergeant had turned to look, of course, and the Oglala youngster had laid the hardwood behind his ear when he did so. And that was all the sergeant knew.

Except, quite clearly, that walking stick, saddle horse, and small Indian orphan boy were not missing as separate, unrelated items.

'Did the boy say anything?' asked Dr McGillycuddy, daubing the wounded sergeant's contusion with tincture of carbolic. 'Anything at all. Think now, man.'

The sergeant, after yelping fiercely at the bite of the awesome antiseptic, at first said no, then recalled differently. 'Oh, yeah,' he glared. 'The little son of a bitch hollered "*hopo, hookahey!*" in Sioux, as he tooken off on your horse, sir. Then he hung another string of Injun jabber onto that, aimed at me personal.'

'Ah,' said McGillycuddy. 'You understand the language. Good.'

'Not so good,' winced the soldier, ducking away from the doctor's swab. 'He told me to go, well, you know, sir, do something to myself.'

'Aye,' nodded the doctor. 'It's the same in any tongue.' He did not seem to Sergeant Akers unduly disappointed in the small horse thief's behavior, prompting the soldier to inquire if he were not going to report the loss. 'Of course we must, sergeant,' McGillycuddy replied. 'I will see to it, though. Don't you bother. I must sign the stolen property forms in any event, mustn't I?' He paused, seeing that his patient was still frowning. 'Yes, well, off you go, Akers,' he said. 'Come back tomorrow. I'll want another look at that

188

hematoma.'

'At the what, sir?'

'The swelling on your head.'

'Oh.'

He got up from the office chair, forgetfully jammed his hat back on, bellowed like a branded calf at the pain. McGillycuddy had been treating the postwar frontier enlistees long enough to know their mental levels were no threat to average learning abilities. Ignoring Akers's laments, he frowned and said, 'I wish that we knew where the lad was bound. I'd truly like to get him back.'

'So would I!' gritted the wounded stable sergeant. 'But we never will, sir; he's aiming to go a far piece.'

'Oh?'

'Yes sir. Betwixt thumping the tar out'n Lucifer with that knobbly stick, whilst yelping *hopo* and *hookahey*, whicht means "let's get the hell out'n here," and then lastly outlining for me what I could go and do to myself, the little bastard—begging your pardon, doctor sir—he up and sandwiched in something else.'

'To you, you mean, Akers?'

'No sir, it was to Lucifer. He hollered at him in Sioux, "Come on you big bay coward! *Wagh!* Away to the Land of the Grandmother!" They're headed for Canady, sir, sure as your head-medicine burns like saddle-scald.'

'Are you certain of that, Akers?'

'Yes sir, doctor, sir. I run off with a Hunkpapa squaw onct. Spent a whole winter with them devils.'

'Canada,' sighed McGillycuddy, a look of rare contentment belying the seriousness of the theft and the flight from agency control. 'Ah, what a terrible long ways. Do you think he has any chance, whatever, to make it, sergeant?'

Sergeant Carl Akers was at the infirmary door. He glanced out at the blackening weather and shook his head. 'Can't see how,' he said. 'He's alone, he ain't but eight, ten, year old. No gun. No food. Coming on to storm bad. Trails will all be snowed in by tonight.' Again he shook his head. 'I'd best be getting along, sir. I still got my stable work waiting.'

'No chance, no chance, at all,' murmured McGillycuddy. 'Poor little tyke.'

Akers stopped, looked back in at the door.

'I didn't say that, sir,' he frowned. 'He's always got one chance, you know.'

'Ah!' McGillycuddy brightened.

'Sure,' shrugged career noncom Carl Akers. 'He's an Injun, ain't he?'

'You mean that's his chance, just *being* an Indian?'

'I told you I lived a winter with them, sir. They ain't like us. You know any ten-year-old white kid that would steal your gold-headed stick, brain the stable sergeant with it, lift your prize saddle horse and light out for Canady, all because you had took him in and treated him

190

good?'

'Ah, yes,' said the post physician, eyes dancing. 'You're right, absolutely right. Thank the Lord.'

'Thank him for what, sir? Begging your pardon.'

McGillycuddy looked at him gravely.

'For the fact, sergeant,' he said, 'that "they ain't like us."'

CHAPTER TWENTY-SIX

The bad weather, threatening from the north the past twenty-four hours, now closed in on Fort Robinson, Nebraska. The heavy ground-hugging clouds were cold as ice. They were plainly burdened with a big snow but had not yet begun to discharge it. In the early morning light of the parade yard just outside the headquarters building of General Lewis Bradley, shadows of mounted forms were drifting into loose column. An officer, short and brisk and looking like the young U. S. Grant, strode from this assemblage of ghostly horsemen into the office of the general's aide. The aide, a man who had never been near an Indian fight, greeted the officer huffily.

'Ah, South. About time, too. Now, sir, do you understand that General Bradley *will* have this deserter Maggart and these two Sioux fugitives taken and returned to Robinson

191

immediately? This is not a mission; it's an order.'

The disturbed briefing officer paused for effect. He was overage for his majority, a prisoner by marriage to Bradley's career—and protection—and presently aware that his illustrious in-law stood to lose the command at the fort as of that morning's telegraphed news from division headquarters: Crook was coming back. He had been ordered back, in fact, by the War Department. He had objected, much preferring his present assignment in the field, but the Division people had been firm.

The prospect of Red Beard, as the Indians called George Crook, returning to Fort Robinson just as the Crazy Horse mess, along with the discovery of the theft of the Oglala horses, had broken the surface of Bradley's customary iron control, had the potential of a career disaster. Add these two crazy Indians fleeing Spotted Tail to the desertion and flight of McGillycuddy's orderly to avoid lawful military punishment, and the general's next star might be a long time coming.

Captain Terrance South well understood the situation.

'Yes,' he said grimly. 'I've heard about Crook.'

'What have you heard?' The briefing officer demanded anxiously. 'Are you implying something here?'

'Put it this way, major. The general will look

192

one hell of a lot better to Crook if I can round up these fugitives *and* the damned missing Indian horse herd before old bristleface gets back in off the buffalo grass.'

The overage major commenced to sputter, decided the cool-nerved South was not the one to bluster with. 'Well, yes,' he said. 'Are you ready to leave, sir?'

'I've been ready since the news came up from Spotted Tail yesterday. Thank God Crook was recalled.'

'What do you mean by that, sir?' A commanding general's aide had certain prerogatives of power, even if he was passed by for promotion. Bradley's man was aware of this and now glowered at the younger officer who, for his part, was scarcely intimidated.

'What I said,' South rasped back. 'My men are ready to go, and so am I. Good day, sir.'

The two men saluted one another, and the brusque scout commander wheeled to depart.

'Good day,' the briefing officer called after him, the emphasis deliberately sharp. 'I'm sure I don't have to remind you, captain, who was in charge of security the night of the Crazy Horse affair. Or stress the fact for your own protection that this matter will appear in official full in General Bradley's accounting to Crook.'

South did not even break stride. But the barb had taken him painfully, nonetheless. It was not only the career of General L. P. Bradley,

Ninth Infantry, that rode out of Fort Robinson that cold, snow-flurried morning. So, too, at stake, was the service future of United States Cavalry Captain Terrance Smith South. If he and his one hundred much-publicized Cheyenne scouts could not get back the Indian horse herd and run down and return to post all three of the wanted fugitives from Spotted Tail, and do it before George Crook got back from the field, the years in rank were certain to stretch interminably for both the infantry general, Bradley, and the cavalry captain, South.

Captain South now barked irritably at his waiting Indian sergeants. They, in turn, shouted guttural Cheyenne orders to the long double line of mounted Indian riders sitting long-haired ponies in the blowing cold of the Fort Robinson parade ground. Captain South swung to saddle, heeled his mount hard about, and put spurs to the animal with authority. In moments only, the column was gone from the lonely post, westward into the low hills of Nebraska's north corner.

All eyes were on the trail ahead. All Cheyenne minds were on the agency rumor that said that the stolen Oglala horses of the hated warchief, Ta Sunke Witko, grazed hidden in the Wyoming roughs to the west. There, too, the rumor said, they would surely find the two fugitive Sioux from Spotted Tail, giving the Cheyenne Cutarm hunters one more vengeance coup to count on the people of Crazy Horse.

CHAPTER TWENTY-SEVEN

Tuweni, the Indian orphan boy, rode swiftly through the night toward Fort Robinson, watching all the while for friend or foe along the familiar trail. It was a hard ride, long and cold. If he were to come to the fort and Red Cloud agency before the Cheyenne scouts of Captain South departed on their mission, his heart and his luck must be good. But the boy believed that Wakan Tanka was on his side. Had the old Oglala god not given to Tuweni this great bay horse that went so powerfully and tirelessly beneath him? *Wagh! Woyuonihan!* Salute the big bay horse. With such an animal, any Bad Face boy worthy of the tribal name could catch up to those Cutarm scouts. And then, after that, he could follow them and use them for his real purpose— escaping to the Land of the Grandmother.

The hours fled. The great bay horse loped on. Darkness faded into false dawn. Tuweni was very tired, very sleepy, but the fort was just ahead.

He though again of Dr McGillycuddy and the lies he had told him. But McGillycuddy would forgive him. Tuweni knew, better than any white soldier doctor might ever know, the debt of spilled blood that Tuweni and his Oglala people owed the Cheyenne. The doctor knew as well the wasted vanity of thinking that Tuweni was going to collect any of that blood debt by himself from all those tough Cheyenne scouts over at Red Cloud agency. Tuweni was, however, just as sly in his mind as Dr McGillycuddy had surmised. Those scouts, when they departed from Fort Robinson later this day, would be going exactly in the direction Tuweni must take to reach his grandmother who was living with the Hunkpapa up in Canada. What surer way of making certain that one's own trail would not be followed by the Cheyenne of Captain South than to follow the trail of those very scouts themselves?

The plan worked, too, just as Tuweni had believed it must. Not only did he reach Fort Robinson in time, but he and the big bay horse had been hiding in the brush west of the fort for only an hour when here came the snowy column of Cheyenne riders out of the east. From this point, it was a simple thing to keep Lucifer on the trail of Captain South's men without being discovered. It became only simpler when, after a while, it snowed so hard they could leave the hills and ride squarely in the track line of the swiftly moving scouts, needing only to be careful to stay close enough behind the column so that the hoofprints of its horses did not fill

196

up with the heavy snow before they might be followed.

*   *   *

But the hours proved the enemy.

All that day the Oglala boy trailed the Cheyenne scouts of Captain Terrance South. In the course of the rash action, he was protected by the special fortune that attends the very young in their adventures, and he was not discovered. Hunger rode with him, however, and, increasingly through the long afternoon, weariness and cold. As the September dusk approached, the tracks of the hard-riding Cheyenne showed a slowing of the pace. But Tuweni did not see this. The small shaggy head was bent to rest upon the thin chest. Both dark hands laced themselves about the horn of the soldier doctor's big saddle. The bay horse felt the reins slacken. He bobbed his head, rolled an eye rearward. The tiny rider was still there. The bay turned his head again to the tracks of the Cheyenne ponies. When those tracks shortly veered from the valley trail to enter the surrounding hills and begin the steep upward climb to higher country, the bay veered with them. The Indian boy on his back did not object.

*   *   *

It was full dark when Captain South's

column reached its primary objective, the breaking camp of the High Meadow horse thieves. The commander, on the advice of his principal Indian sergeants, Ookat (Bareskin) and Voxkasz (Bent Over), ordered the halt made at this lower camp rather than going on to the meadow where their information said the stolen Oglala herd was being held.

In such snow and darkness the upper trail would be too precarious for wearied men and mounts. It would be better, the two chief scouts suggested, for perhaps one or two of the best men to go forward and reconnoiter. Under cover of the storm they could determine who, precisely, might be in the upper camp. Then they could return to Captain South with their report, giving the commander the advantage of surprise over the fugitives from Spotted Tail, or the horse thieves of High Meadow, or whoever should be found up there with the Indian horses.

For this sensitive mission Ookat and Voxkasz offered themselves. Captain South at once agreed, although he suffered some hesitations. He entertained suspicions aroused by the dead ashes of the cookfire at lower camp. Feeling the earth beneath the brushed-away fire spot, his dark-faced sergeants had told him the people had gone away from here at least one entire day since. There was only a detectable warmth in the dirt, that was all. Against the possible alarm of this estimate, however, was the fact that there was no corresponding sign of any sizable number of horses held in or driven out through this base camp of the thieves. Still, it was a tribute to his faith in himself and his Indian cavalry that South was so quick with his assent to the proposal of his chief scouts. 'Be careful,' was all he said to them. 'There must be absolutely no shooting, nothing of any trouble up there. *Nohetto!*'

Nohetto was the Cheyenne equivalent of the English, 'that's all,' or 'that's it.' Ookat and Voxkasz nodded, remounted, and were gone. The scout sergeants were back within the hour. Each of their shaggy ponies was carrying double. Behind Ookat was one frozen body, behind his friend Voxkasz, another. Both corpses were ice-sheathed and snow-crusted, requiring half an hour of fireside thawing to be identifiable as white men: trooper W. O. Maggart, Ninth Infantry, Spotted Tail; a civilian, name unknown, presumed one of the outland band sought in the matter of the stolen Oglala horses of the Crazy Horse band.

Frozen bodies told no tales. But Ookat and Voxkasz had taken the time to circle the death-camp and quarter out through the building drifts of High Meadow itself. The silence and the emptiness up there spoke in ominous tongues to the Cheyenne scouts.

There were no outlaws or any other people up in High Meadow. Neither was there one

199

Oglala horse remaining. No, they could not see all of the meadow. And, no, they had not ridden each rock and thicket of the pasture. But they were Cutarm scouts. They had other eyes than those in their heads. Captain South could believe it: High Meadow stood empty.

It was while the restless and ambitious South frowned over this intelligence, and while his Indian troops yet examined the grisly remains of the two *wasicuns* melting at the roaring fire of the bivouac, that a commotion was noted among the ponies of the company picket line.

The Indian ponies were pricking friendly ears and whickering in welcome to an unseen stranger of their own kind. All eyes swung to the picket line and the trail's mouth entering into the base camp from the east. Into the ensuing moment of tense stillness stumbled the snow-caked, big bay horse of Dr McGillycuddy, post physician at Spotted Tail.

Upon the animal's broad back, small hands laced about saddle's high horn, rode an Indian orphan of the storm. It was Tuweni, the runaway *wablenica*. Sound asleep.

CHAPTER TWENTY-EIGHT

On the trail, Crazy Charley sang in his high-cracked voice. It was a song without meaning, except to the mixed-breed wanderer himself. Charley was going home and Charley was happy for that, as well as for many other wonderful things he could not just now remember.

Hand-walking the rangy cavalry mount of the dead trooper Maggart, he played games in the still-falling snow with his very large feet, dancing and wheeling about like some grotesque trained bear.

The horse, which had surely never seen another man to match mad Charley Beckwourth, had long ago quit shying at Charley's gyrations. It had been such an easy, unforced retreat. No pursuit had developed and Charley had rested the horse four times and taken all of the following day to make the few miles to their present rest halt. Those lazy, strange hours with the new master had given the army mount an Indian view of traveling life quite different from the cavalry, with its spurs and tootling horns.

Given all that rest and the snow games, the horse was becoming playful in return, snorting and buck-jumping and giving every indication of being ready to once more travel all night, if need be. This renewed vigor was to play a part not yet designed in the mind of Crazy Charley—a part taking nebulous form in the strange man's thoughts as he paused now atop North Ridge. It was this thought, in fact, that had brought Charley to halt there.

He made warbled sounds in his throat, waved at the horse, patted him gently, frowned ever harder.

Something was wrong.

He had once again forgotten a thing that he should never have forgotten, a thing he must remember or find himself plagued with restless dreams along the way. The wind up on the ridge sliced through the mixed breed's greasy army shirt, chilling him to the marrow. Shivering, he made more mewing sounds and then, whirling suddenly about to stare back along the way he and the horse had just come, he gave a long, broken sob. He had remembered the thing. It was his old Crow blanket. His living place. His home wherever he was. To leave that behind was unthinkable.

But he had done it. It was left behind. That dear blanket was lying back there beyond the cookfire in the breaking camp of the tall, wolf-eyed white man who had stolen all of the Oglalas' horses.

Un-huh! it was a bad thing.

But Charley would make it all right again. There was no other way. Without the blanket he was nothing. He was naked. He could not hide anymore and everyone would see him and laugh at him and throw stones and chase him with sticks.

He patted the freshened horse again. With a mutter, he sprang to the animal's back. The horse wanted to go—he slid down from the ridge crest and back along the trail they had just traveled carrying Crazy Charley

Beckwourth as though he had never known another master. The long hours of retracing the trail hand-walked by himself and the mewing man were loped away in a third of their previous time. It was only just darkening into full night when they came again to the place where the trail turned off for lower camp. In the darkness Charley did not see the filling tracks of the Cheyenne ponies, but the cavalry horse from Spotted Tail smelled the shaggy mounts from Fort Robinson and Red Cloud and by his actions of alertness let his rider know that something was not as it ought to be with that trail going into the camp of the horse thieves.

Mumbling reassuringly to the horse, Charley took him away from the main trail and went by a secret way known only to the half-wit. It was a way that had a nice hiding thicket of willow and cottonwood scrub at its blind end. Here, Charley left the horse and went the short rest of the way down the slope to the flat of the breaking ground. He crept up through the timber to the brush fringe where he knew he had cast aside his priceless blanket. Unerringly, he came to a halt not ten feet from where he had left the garment. There it was, still there. Charley could see it as plainly as anything. He could reach it without being seen, too. But he did not do so. Rather, he again forgot the wonderful blanket in his astonishment at seeing Captain South and the famed Cheyenne scouts camped there about his old cookfire.

But it was not South and not the slit-eyed Cutarm dog soldiers that so took the eye of Crazy Charley Beckwourth.

It was the defiant small figure of Tuweni, the orphan boy of Spotted Tail, standing in the middle of all those enemies and telling them in perfectly good Oglala Sioux that he would never answer their questions and would die rather than admit one word to any of them.

All that he had for them, the boy cried with a spirit echoed in Charley's wild breast, was to spit on them, every one, as he would now spit on the two sergeants querying him with such Cutarm *waohala sni*, such damned Cheyenne discourtesy.

As good as his word, Tuweni expectorated full into the bent-down faces of the two chief scouts.

One of the scouts, a squat, powerful brave badly bent forward in posture by some past crippling accident, struck the boy a stunning blow, driving him to the ground. Before the other scout could likewise do harm to the small prisoner, the white officer barked an angry command at the Indian sergeants and himself strode over to protect the youth.

The captive was not out of spittle, however.

He instantly aimed and fired at Captain South's face. South leaped back with an oath, wiped off his U. S. Grant whiskers.

'Tie him up!' he stormed at the sergeants. 'Give him nothing to eat until he decides to be civil.'

Crazy Charley, watching from the brush beyond the fire, made an angry low sound in his throat. When he made the noises, he nodded in reply to them, as if he had understood what he said and agreed with it firmly.

Swiftly, he retrieved his abandoned blanket and was gone back into the deeper timber.

An hour later, with the Cheyenne scouts snoring in their blankets by the fire, a strange apparition reappeared from that same timber and stole out to the tall stump that anchored one end of the long picket line of Indian ponies. The stump also anchored the small orphan boy from Spotted Tail agency. The shrewd lad had not talked to the 'Two Bar Chief,' Captain South, and for his reward South had left him tied to the stump. In truth, the officer had not intended the boy to remain so bound all of the night. He had, in fact, left instructions with sergeants Bent Over and Bareskin—who again had volunteered for extra duty as guards of the camp and the young captive—that they should release the Oglala urchin within an hour, watching him only enough after that to see that he was given a blanket and a good place by the fire.

But the two chief scouts had other things in mind for the young captive.

205

Boy or no boy, this little botfly from Spotted Tail might make real trouble for Bareskin and Bent Over. It was a matter of guessing how much the nosy youngster had learned of the matter of the stolen Oglala horses. For example, did he know that Bareskin and Bent Over were trooper Maggart's principal fellow agents at Fort Robinson? That both of Captain South's widely known chief scouts had taken money from Maggart, ever since the original theft of the Oglala herds by the horse thieves dressed as soldiers? And, whether the boy knew that or not, could Bareskin and Bent Over take the chance that he *might* know? That he might, the very first thing next morning, stop spitting and start talking? That he might, indeed, thus put the rope about the anxious necks of Bent Over and Bareskin?

Un-huh! The Sioux being the Sioux, and they being Cheyennes, it was not a good gamble, at all.

The two had decided to do something with the boy during the night, so that he very surely would *not* be speaking with Captain South next morning.

The only question remaining was of the method of the harm. The two volunteer guards had been discussing this problem for the full hour of the camp's retirement. They were still considering safe ways and means of killing the damned *wablenica* from Spotted Tail when the strange apparition floated out of the nearby

206

brush fringe and stole up behind them and behind the anchor stump and the bound captive.

The apparition studied the two Cheyenne chief scouts briefly. His decision was reached when he noted, lying on the ground at the foot of the rope-tied boy where it had fallen in his short-lived defense of himself, the handsome gold-headed and crooked walking cane of the soldier doctor McGillycuddy. In his youth, the apparition had known no peers in the high Indian art of the wielding of the war club, and this looked like a beautiful, beautiful weapon of that same class.

Tuweni, who was not asleep, saw with a start the dark and unwashed hand appear from behind the stump and pick up the cane of the soldier doctor. Both Bareskin and Bent Over heard the boy's intake of surprised breath, and they turned to look at him. Neither of the famed scouts, however, took note of the fact that the gold-headed cane was missing. Since there was nothing else of a suspicious nature about the condition of the small captive, the two returned to their guarded discussion of how best to murder Tuweni Oyuspi.

The next thing Bareskin knew, he saw the flashing knob of the gold-headed cane strike out from behind the stump and hit his friend Bent Over across the skull with a sodden *thunk*. Before he himself might react to this assault, a second thunk sounded on his own side of the stump. But Bareskin didn't hear it. That was because it was his thunk this time, and his own skull being thunked. So it happened that the two great scouts were struck, as one, in the backs of their heads by Dr McGillycuddy's gold-headed walking stick. And that they then fell forward to lie unconscious across the ground in an odd posture that made it appear they were sleeping in each other's arms.

At this point the apparition stepped out from behind the stump and grinned at Tuweni Oyuspi, the orphan boy of Spotted Tail, and of course it was Crazy Charley Beckwourth. Tuweni greeted his savior with a gulp and a gasp. While he still gaped, the blanket-muffled figure cut him free, patted him on the head, presented him with the gold-headed cane, and made the sign-language suggestion that he follow his rescuer with all due care and noiseless speed. To this, Tuweni agreed thankfully.

But he had forgotten something. As he and Crazy Charley started for the brush, the big bay horse of Dr McGillycuddy saw the Oglala boy deserting him. The bay did not care for the Indian ponies on the picket line, and he had, as well, formed a genuine attachment for his seventy-five-pound rider. With a piercing neigh, he flung up his head, lunged on hind legs, broke free of the picket line, and charged straight through the rows of blanketed scouts on the ground toward where Tuweni and

Crazy Charley crouched frozen in despair at this announcement of their flight.

But Charley recovered and gave a staccato yelp of laughter. He caught the reins of the big bay horse as the animal charged up to them. Leaping to the bay's back, he drew Tuweni up behind him with a great swing of his long arms and drove Lucifer at a gallop into the brush.

They were plainly seen by several awakening scouts but were cleanly away before the first Cheyenne scout got out of his blanket to utter the wolf cry of Cutarm vengeance and run bowlegged for the picket line.

By the time the aroused scouts had gotten their ponies saddled, the last crashing sounds of Lucifer's retreat had died away.

Captain South's splendid manhunters had nothing to chase but the wind.

CHAPTER TWENTY-NINE

The jolting of the travois over the steep downhill trail returned Con Jenkins to the gray world of half-consciousness. He lay in this state for several minutes, then the grayness departed. He could see and hear and feel, and he was Con Jenkins again. Pushing himself upright in the travois, he was greeted by a friendly hail.

'Waste, owanyeke waste!' cried the old Indian. He waved reassuringly from the saddle

of Con's horse which was carefully following Red Weasel and the travois down the rocky track. '*Ha-a-u, hau kola!*'

Con, who understood some of the language, uttered a grunt of demurrer. His answering wave was one of patent disgust augmented by physical pain, even apprehension. The outlaw had no notion what part of the frontier world they might be in, except that it was an Indian part.

'Everything may be good for *your* eye, old one,' he said, 'but as far as I can see out'n this damn Injun dragpole snowplow, all I got to say is horse manure.' He felt his wounded head gingerly, winced, and cursed again.

The old Sioux laughed. '*Waste*,' he said. 'Horse manure.'

'Wonderful,' growled Con. 'The Injun talks white-man talk. Oh, how lucky I am.' Scowling, he grabbed for the dragpoles as the travois hit a bad place in the trail. 'By the way,' he asked Crowfoot, 'where at is it that all this great good fortune has befell me?'

The white-haired Indian shook his head. 'One does not wish to be thought *waohola sni*, without proper respect, but I do not understand what you have asked me to answer for you.'

'Oh, Jesus,' sighed Con. 'A goddamn Injun lawyer.'

'What?' said the old man. 'How do you say?'

'How I say,' answered Con, 'is two things:

210

Where the hell are we at, right now, and where the goddamn hell are we bound to?'

'Oh—' Crowfoot waved magnanimously. 'Why didn't you say so?'

Con, who to his amazement still had his Colt buckled to his waist beneath the buffalo robe that bound him to the travois, considered shooting the old bastard. He decided as quickly that friendly Sioux Indians were not that common in those lonesome Wyoming hills. Best for a white horse thief—leastways one specializing in Indian horses—to act cordial until he could find other work at better pay. '*Tahunsa*,' he said, using the Sioux word for cousin. 'I just did say so; it's just that I'm a poor ignorant white man what has lost his bearings in the snowstorm and don't know whicht way is his ass from his earhole. You savvy, chief?'

'Yes, yes!' cried the old man delightedly. 'Crowfoot savvies. I once knew a white who had holes in both his ears. But he wasn't lost—'

'Forget it!' pleaded Con, interrupting. 'Make out liken me and you never see'd one another.' He fell back into the travois. 'Look, I'm *telanunwela* again.'

He feigned unconsciousness but Crowfoot was not to be denied the pleasure of another male's company. 'Listen, *wasicun*,' he said, 'we will talk, you and I. I've heard nothing but the chatter of women since my granddaughter, who was the wife of Crazy Horse, came ill of

211

the lung sickness. It has been of no help trailing all the way out here into these hills with the other one, either. I mean the younger granddaughter, sister of Crazy Horse's woman. *Wagh!* It grows wearisome being a medicine priest. Even with the wife of a warchief. *Ha-a-u*, believe it, white friend. Horse manure.'

Con Jenkins could not help himself. He had to laugh. He had not heard himself laugh for such a spell of time that it came to him like the laugh of a stranger. 'Old man,' he said, 'you are a pistol. Jabber on. I'll haze you back into line wherever you quit the trail. *Woyuonihan*, Injun.'

Surprised, the old warrior peered at him. What was this? The respect word from a white man? Hmmm.

'*Ha-ho*, thank you,' he said, somehow feeling very proud. 'Let's go on. We can talk, but we must not get too far behind my granddaughter and the horses.'

Sliding down the drifted snow of the trail, lurching, cursing, hanging onto dragpole or saddle horn, the two began to talk, *shacun* to *wasicun*, red man to white, and the way was never quite the same again for Con Jenkins. By the time they reached the bottoming of the old Indian road, where it came down from Bad Face Pass to go over the headwater crossing of Sage Creek, the outlaw knew the story of Crowfoot and his girl-squaw granddaughter right to the present moment of their following the broad track of the Oglala horse herd led by the girl and the dowager white bell mare. In return, strangely affected by the old medicine man's tale, Con had laid it out straight for the old devil as to himself, Con Jenkins, being who he was and what he intended remaining—sole owner of the stolen herd.

'Them's my horses, by God,' he grimly told old Crowfoot. 'I don't give a damn what you Injuns say.'

The Indian only waved and said, 'Come on, *hopo*, *hopo*, *wasicun*. The snow is thinning down here, but it will still fill up our herd's tracks if we don't hurry.'

'*My* herd, Injun!' snapped Con. But his head suddenly hurt with a pain like a knife blade driven into it, and he fell back and seized the dragpoles and remembered no more.

'*Hookahey*, Weasel,' Crowfoot called softly. 'Pull him gently where the rocks are, and over the bad places. I don't want to lose him.' He slapped the old travois animal on the rump, straightened in the saddle of Con Jenkins's horse. '*He-hau*,' he laughed. 'I cannot wait to see the face of the granddaughter when she sees *this wasicun*.' The wide mouth lifted at one corner into a warming leer. He winked at the mule. 'For that matter,' he said, 'I cannot wait, either, until this *wasicun* sees the granddaughter. *Wagh—!*'

*   *   *

Twilight was having trouble with the herd. On the trail out of High Meadow and down this side from Bad Face Pass, there had been nothing to it. Once started along that narrow way, the horses either followed the trail or went over the side of the cliff. But now the herd was spread all over the wide valley of the old Indian road leading from Sage Creek to the main fork of Old Woman Creek, where the shelter timber and the winter-grass pasture for the horses was said to be. The slim girl rode frantically to try and bunch up the herd, but presently it came to her that her spurring back and forth, and the hazing of the leaders with her swung blanket, amounted to nothing at all of interest to the beautiful, slim ponies. They were following Speckledbird and the pony bell on the old mare's halter strap. Twilight laughed aloud and surrendered the herd to the leader of its Oglala days.

'*Hai!*' she shouted at the freckled white she-horse. 'Do you know that when we get home I am going to have a lodge pitched for you? *He-hau*, believe it, old lady. You will never know cold or snow again. *Hopo!*'

Speckledbird, who had been promised much for many winters by a lot of other Indians, only blew out in dubious reply through frost-rimed nostrils. Never mind, the sway-backed matriarch seemed to be saying. I will be just as happy as you, young squaw, to get back up there where we belong. *Hookahey*, yourself.

Soon the storm thinned and Twilight saw ahead the dark fringes of the creek timber. There was a considerable meadow of snow-hummocked old grass, too, exactly as Crowfoot had promised. Plainly, the horses would have no trouble pawing through to this fine and heavy pasture. It had not been grazed in years, nor overburned by fire. Their horses were going to be safe and warm in the timber, and their bellies fat-filled with rich grasses. *Wanica!* Wonderful! It passed belief how a man as old as the grandfather could still recall all of these twistings in the old Oglala road he had not ridden in twenty summers. *Wanica* again. Twilight must hurry and get a good fire going and a cozy campsite cleaned away of snow, to welcome the poor old warrior.

She found a set of hobbles hanging from the skirt-ring of Ben Childress's saddle. These she put on Speckledbird, adjusting the pony bell on the halter's chinstrap at the same time. 'There,' she said. 'I don't like to do that to you, faithful old horse, but these ponies are your children and will stay where you stay. Eat good now. Keep close.'

Speckledbird, who cared not the least about the hobbles, rabbit-hopped her way out into the tufted meadowland. Twilight saw that the other horses followed her and that, with her, all fell to pawing the snow and cropping the fat brown winter grass as if this were the pasture of their foaling.

'*Waste!*' called the Oglala girl. '*Owanyeke waste!*'

All was indeed good for the Siouan eye here in the shelter timber and the snow meadow of Old Woman Creek flats. Wakan Tanka was watching the young sister of the warchief. The herd was on wind-sheltered graze, the storm was abating. Behind them, the narrow crevice of Bad Face Pass would be blocked by drifts. No soldiers could come after them, and no white devil horse thieves. All she and Crowfoot must do was travel wide of the Bozeman Trail, the white man's road, watching always for the soldiers. In a matter of half a moon, driving hard, they would be up in their own country asking for word of Joseph and the Slit Noses. *Hi-yee! hi-yee—!* She uttered the Sioux battle shout ear-piercingly.

On the inbound trail, Con Jenkins, aroused from the depths of his faint, sprang half upright in the travois.

'Christ Jesus!' he said. 'What was that?'

Old Crowfoot, enjoying once more what he knew and the white man did not, answered calmly, 'Why that was the little girl, my granddaughter, who has helped me in all of this thing.'

'Sure enough,' sighed Con. 'I'd forgot. Must be a mite peculiar little girl. Part catamount, I'd say. Elst that, or she's been bit by a rabied coyote.'

'Just a child, *wasicun*; you will see.'

Only minutes later they had homed on the cheery fire winking at them through the timber of the meadow flat, and Con Jenkins was standing one foot in, one foot out, of the halted travois, staring at what Crowfoot had promised him he would see.

'Christ Jesus,' he said again, and softly. 'Some child.'

CHAPTER THIRTY

Iktomi, the Sioux call them. They are the tiny spidermen who make the flint arrowheads for the people and who also weave the web of sorrows that entraps the lives of men, tumbling all toward the center of the web with an ever-increasing speed. This web was closing now upon the scattered ones whose lives were caught within the warchief's dream of freedom, and the *iktomi* spun exceeding swift in old Wyoming.

Crazy Charley Beckwourth and the agency boy Tuweni were able to reach Beckwourth's tethered horse safely. From there, each now mounted on a strong animal, their track line led away toward North Ridge and an old Indian trail well known to South's scouts. This trail crossed the ridge to the drainage of Sage Creek north of High Meadow, striking that

217

stream at its juncture with Old Woman Creek. It then turned northeast following a succession of branches all tributary to Cheyenne River.

When, with first light next morning, Captain South sat with his two Indian sergeants at the foot of North Ridge frowning up at the difficult way his troops must go, he took pause to review his options.

Behind him, as his mind considered trail conditions and tracking luck against the career factor should he return to Fort Robinson empty-handed, the one hundred members of his Indian-hunting scout force waited impassively.

Here and there among the ranks a talkative brave commented on the delay. 'Isn't it interesting,' said one of them to his blanket-wrapped neighbor, 'how Bent Over and Bareskin take such loyal interest in finding those horses for our captain. See them jabbering away up there. You know very well what they are saying.'

'What?' grunted his companion.

'Why,' the other said, 'it's plain as the frozen drops at the end of your nose. Our captain shakes his head. He doesn't know. He wants to quit this foolish running after a small boy and that *mashane*, that crazy one, who took the boy from us. What good are such captives to our captain?'

'I don't know. What good?'

'None, I say. But our sergeants are talking

218

him into it. Why, you ask. I will tell you. They know where those horses went from High Meadow. They know where they are. So do you. So do I.'

'Where?'

'*Hun-uh!* Think about it.'

'I don't want to think about it. I want to turn back and get out of here. My assbones are freezing to the saddle in this morning wind.'

'Listen anyway. Can you take a herd of ponies—even Indian ponies—out of that meadow up there to the south? You cannot. Only a foot track runs there. Same to the north. As to the east, we know they did not come that way to escape. There were no tracks of a herd.'

'You are saying they went out to the west then?'

'Of course!'

'How?'

'That old Indian pass up there. The one the Sioux call the Oglala road. I've been over it on foot. It is closed with big stones, but the thieves must have gotten it open again in some way.'

'My assbones still ache.'

'They are going to ache more. See what happens there. Bareskin and Bent Over are riding on up the trail. Our captain rides back this way. Watch him; he will try to talk with this young lieutenant he is trying to make into a man tracker. Do you know that lieutenant is the husband of our captain's pretty sister? Sure. That's the reason for our captain working so hard to make something of him. But he will never rub enough salt in that weak hide to make it stiff like his own.'

'Who cares?' scowled his comrade-in-saddle.

'You will care. Watch Bareskin and that damned Bent Over up there sniffing higher on the trail. They're going to take us up there, sure as mule marbles are smaller than horse apples.'

'You watch them, nosy one; I'd rather watch Lieutenant Skinnybones. It's fun to see him turn pale when our captain tells him we're going over the ridge—or anywhere that he might fall off his horse.'

The other brave shook his head. 'I like him a little bit anyway,' he said. 'I think he's only young and afraid. He has good teeth and fine hair.'

'Shut up,' growled the negative one. 'Here comes our captain. Will you let me listen to him?'

'Sure,' said his friend. 'Go to hell.'

Up on the ridge's flank but a little way, the two chief scouts halted for the parley that Bent Over had known they must hold away from Captain South, and even away from their Cheyenne comrades of the ranks.

'Act as though we are working the trail,' Bent Over told Bareskin, 'but answer fast as I talk.' Bent Over glanced down to be sure South was occupied. He was laboring to persuade his unwarlike brother-in-law to take interest in the

220

chase. 'Now,' Bent Over swept on, 'you know where that crazy mixed breed Charley Beckwourth is taking the boy, don't you? You must.'

'Well, I don't,' denied Bareskin, not so brainy as his crippled twin. 'Where?'

'Wherever the white horse thief is, you fool. Don't you remember our spies said that Beckwourth worked in the horse thieves' camp cooking the meat and making the bread? And don't you know that, wherever the horse thieves are, there is where the horses will be found.'

'What else?'

'We must still reach that boy before Captain South does. You go back down there to guide the troop and I will go on to scout the advance. By noon halt, I will have caught up to them, finishing the boy. We cannot risk this thing further. The boy was a tipi-pet of Crowfoot. He will know whatever the old man knew.'

'Yes, yes,' broke in the other excitedly. 'And the old man knew everything, that we took the money from Maggart, and all the rest of it about us, eh?'

'That's right. Now go on back to our captain.'

'No,' said Bareskin obstinately. '*I* will go on after the boy and *you* can go tell our captain that this trail leads him to the Oglala horses.'

The two chief scouts fell into a violent argument. A resolution was reached only when

221

the canny Bent Over suggested a vote with the sticks, long and short, the traditional Indian way. He was certain he could hold onto the longer twig of the two he himself picked up and broke off. But Bareskin jostled his hand, and he had to clutch at the sticks to prevent them from falling and he could not then be sure which might be the longer. Even worse, Bareskin immediately reached and plucked one of the sticks from him, and it *was* the longer one.

'Goddamn!' exploded the cripple, but he had lost. 'Very well,' he said. 'I will go and tell the captain. Make very certain of both of them, now; you understand? Leave no trace that our brothers would see. *Nohetto.*'

Bareskin did not move. 'I don't like to harm the crazy one,' he frowned. 'It's against the laws of our people. It's not an Indian thing to do.'

'Who will ever know you did it?' Bent Over had been with the white man but a brief time, but he was learning fast. 'I won't tell anyone.'

'Maheo, our Allfather, will know,' said the other stubbornly.

Bent Over wanted to curse again but his cunning asserted itself. 'Just make certain of the boy, then,' he conceded. 'Leave Crazy Charley to me. I will slit his windpipe later. That way you won't need to worry about the Allfather. Agreed? *Nohetto?*'

'*Nohetto,*' sighed Bareskin, relieved. 'Here I go.'

222

He sent his pony on up the steepening trail over the North Ridge. Waiting a moment to ascertain that his comrade would not halt and call back another question of tribal protocol, Bent Over wheeled his own mount and clubbed the little brute between the ears with the butt of his rawhide quirt. The pony grunted its hurt but at once sprang into a downslope gallop. Moments later, the senior sergeant of enlisted Cheyenne scouts was spreading his Indian bait for Captain Terrance Smith South: If South wanted the Oglala horses, all he had to do was follow the North Ridge tracks.

South was at once excited, but, as quickly, he was cautious again.

'What exactly are you saying?' he demanded. 'What have you found up there to make you so certain?'

Bent Over was contrite. He was regretful as only a chief of scouts could be, but it wasn't anything they had found up on the ridge. It was only that his good friend Bareskin was not so agile in his mind as might be wished. He had only now, up on the trail there, remembered something the Sioux boy had confessed to him last night, while Bent Over had gone to the fire for coffee: The strange *mashane* who had freed the boy and carried him off was Crazy Charley Beckwourth, camp keeper and cook for the High Meadow horse thieves!

Captain South, an alert man always,

frowned at once. 'Wait just a moment, sir,' he said to Bent Over. 'How could the boy identify his rescuer *before* he was rescued?'

Almost caught, the crippled chief scout showed his wile by explaining without pause that this had not been the case. The boy had only told Bareskin that Charley Beckwourth was keeping the camp for the outlaws. Bareskin had not thought until this very moment, just past, to connect this bit of information with the blanketed rescuer.

'That's damned strange!' snapped South. 'Since no less than a dozen of our men identified the creature as Beckwourth last night when he jumped you two.'

Bent Over merely shrugged.

'Bareskin has a strange memory,' he said. 'He forgot all about what the boy told him in the pain of the wound on his head. We were both in the blackness, captain. It sometimes makes a man forget.'

This could not be argued. Moreover, South was now smelling what his head scout was really saying. Bent Over, watching him sharply, saw the wild light of the hunter leap to flame in the white officer's eyes.

'Yes, captain,' he said quietly. 'You think as I do. As an Indian. Where will this poor broken-minded creature run to but back to join the horse-thief people?'

'Ah!' rasped Captain South. 'And where the horse-thief people are, there will be our horses!'

224

Bent Over made him the respect sign, fingertips quickly touching forehead. 'I have sent Bareskin on ahead,' he said. 'That way we will not lose them.'

'Very good. Fassenby!' The barked call went to the wan lieutenant standing aside holding his own and the troop commander's horse. 'Column of twos, please. Tell your sergeants the men may smoke until we top the ridge. Any questions?'

Harold Fassenby knew there must be none. He saluted and said, 'No sir.' Turning to the four troop sergeants, each of whom headed twenty-five men of the force and all of whom were standing a little off from the lieutenant so as not to show their awareness of the junior officer's shame at being required by South to hold the horses—never an officer's work—Fassenby said to them in his low, gentle voice. 'All right, men, we're going on.'

He knew they had heard South's directions, knew as well they required no parroting of those directions by Harold Fassenby. It was the mark of the honesty in him that Fassenby made no pretense at being what he was not to these men, a commanding officer. Somehow, oddly enough, the Cheyenne respected the quiet youth for the lack of vanity so rare in a white man. The skinnybones one-bar soldier was no fighter, no hunter, no leader of pony soldiers except on drill. But he never lied.

The four sergeants went back to their units,

got them into loose column. Fassenby led the horses over to where South stood staring up at the rampart of North Ridge, the twisted figure of Bent Over by his side. 'Ready, sir,' he said. The commander took his horse, swung up on him. Fassenby, after missing the stirrup once and having the mount sidestep out from under his seat on the second attempt, finally got to saddle. 'My God,' said South dispassionately.

Without orders, the Cheyenne chief scout went aboard his Indian scrub like some broken-bodied monkey leaping upon a ring-tamed circus pony. He only glanced at Captain Terrance South, who only nodded and said, 'Let's go,' deep-set eyes burning. He and the senior sergeant sent their mounts into a gallop over the level ground to the trail's start up the sheer face of the rock wall. Lieutenant Fassenby, so that the following troops might not ride him down, belatedly urged his own animal ahead. To eyes hidden in the rocks nearby, he would have seemed to be leading the Cheyenne scouts. He was not; he was being pursued by them.

CHAPTER THIRTY-ONE

Crazy Charley Beckwourth and Tuweni crossed North Ridge by darkness. It was treacherous going and terribly cold. They spent most of the night getting down the far side.

Once into the valley of Old Woman Creek, where Sage Fork came to join it, the boy could go no farther without risk of the cold killing him. Charley found a snug cave he knew, big enough for them and the horses. They rested there until midmorning, when the boy felt fit to travel again. There was no pursuit and the demented camp cook did not hurry. He knew where he was going and made Tuweni understand this by handsigns.

The boy obeyed unquestioningly. This foolish one had probably saved his life. At very least, he had set Tuweni free to continue the search for his old grandmother who had gone to Canada with Sitting Bull. As well, there was no one else to trust in this fearful cold. Neither of them was armed, save for Dr McGillycuddy's crooked walking stick, returned to Tuweni by the peculiar creature hidden beneath the old blanket. The way was strange to the Spotted Tail boy. The blizzard, thinning a little earlier in the morning, was howling again. By noontime it had grown dark as full dusk, and Tuweni was going numb again in his hands and feet. What else could he do but follow his rescuer?

Shivering at the thought, Tuweni decided he might try one small prayer. It was about not freezing to death there in the saddle of the soldier doctor's stolen bay horse; it was about hoping the weak-brained one had made the handsigns Tuweni thought he had, the signs that said they were turning south upstream along the ice-rimmed creek because that way waited a fine wooded flat of which the grinning blanket-wearer knew and which he guaranteed would harbor them and their beasts through any ordinary blizzard such as this one. And the prayer was lastly about a thing beyond the blizzard, the old grandmother, old Turtle, far, far away up on Red River in the Land of the Grandmother; Tuweni prayed hardest to live to see her again.

As if reading these things in his small friend's mind, Crazy Charley Beckwourth patted the agency boy on the head and gobbled encouragement sounds to him.

Tuweni had scarcely time to be restored by this assurance when Charley suddenly straightened, halting his mount. The boy pawed futilely with cold-stiffened hands to rein in the bay. He could not. The big horse slammed into the rump of Crazy Charley's cavalry mount, which kicked at once. Lucifer would have taken the matter directly back to the other animal but for the fact that the powerful Beckwourth seized his bridle, literally pulled the bad-tempered bay back down from his up-reared anger, and held him to the halt with iron grasp.

By this time Tuweni had gotten his fingers unkinked and had the reins in check.

Charley let go of the cheekstrap and flung up

one long arm in the sign for absolute silence. His other hand made the follow-up sign, and a chill not of the cold went through Tuweni Oyuspi.

His companion had ordered with those signs: *Be still. Don't move. Someone follows us.*

CHAPTER THIRTY-TWO

Con Jenkins and the Sioux young squaw H'tayetu continued their staring match across the popping campfire. The white outlaw did not see the 'little granddaughter' of the old man's tale. This child was a woman grown. She had the body of a woman, the ways of a woman, and she was looking back at Con as a woman would. She knew it. Con knew it. The smoky-eyed granddaughter was telling him things to make any man shake.

From her side of the fire Twilight was feeling uneasy, strange, at a loss to know what she felt.

This was the white devil of them all. Crowfoot had just told her that in explaining the *wasicun*'s presence at their camp. This was the man who had used the soldier uniforms falsely to steal the best ponies from the Oglala of Crazy Horse. The man Twilight had vowed to kill before all other whites. Now he was there, close enough to touch. The knife was still belted beneath her camp garment, a doeskin dress into which she had changed from the rough winter trail-garb. It would be done in the snapping of an ember. Crowfoot could not stop her. The *wasicun* did not expect the blade. *Wagh*, all she had to do was do it.

She could not.

Something about the tall, hard-faced enemy of her people stayed her hand. Within the young squaw emotions were stirring which had no names in her brief years of life. It was certainly not love at first sighting. Twilight had known of love, at least to speak of it with the other Sioux young girls. She did not imagine that any white man, least of all this gaunt stranger from Red Weasel's travois, might kindle her heart-thoughts. But, again, what was it that moved within her when he stared at her as he was staring in this silence?

Sensing the confusion in the girl's mind, Crowfoot spoke to lighten the camp's air. '*Ih*,' he said to her. 'Where are your manners, woman? Take the mule. Unpack the travois. Tend to the head wound of this traveler. The *wasicun* is welcome here. I have promised him that.'

'Never mind all that,' said Con Jenkins, eyes never moving from the girl. 'Let her say the welcome herself. I want to hear it from her.'

Across the fire, Twilight could not find words. She could only go on returning his long looks.

'I stole your people's horses,' Con told her flatly. 'And I'm going to steal them back.

230

That's fair warning. But for tonight, let it be as the grandfather says; we are all friends when the White Wolf howls.'

The White Wolf was the blizzard. The girl seemed affected by the usage of the old Siouan term. Con saw the dark eyes lower at last. 'I will tend your hurt,' she said, and she went to the travois and got Crowfoot's war bag. From this, she took certain herbs and powders to make a poultice. Cleaning off the caked blood with snow rubbed vigorously, she applied the poultice to the freshly bleeding injury. The fire of it went into Con's head like a hot coal. But he ground his teeth and stayed with it. 'Sioux sister,' he said, 'I would rather be kicked by a mule than tended again from your grandfather's medicine pouch. But, in your hands, the cure begins already.'

He had thought to be cynical but even as he spoke the burning ceased and a great, drawing coolness invaded the wound. Within seconds, not only was the wound without pain, the pounding headache of the injury was completely subsided.

'I will trade you ten of my Oglala horses, yonder,' he told Crowfoot admiringly, 'for the recipe of this balsam.'

'No,' said the old man. 'You take twenty of *my* Oglala horses and I will keep the secret.'

'By God, we're big traders, ain't we?' Con asked. Then he laughed for the second time in sixty minutes. '*Okola kiciye*,' he said, offering

231

his hand to the old Indian.

'Yes, all right,' Crowfoot agreed. 'Friendship.'

They shook hands but after that it got very quiet around the fire. Twilight busied herself putting on snow water to melt for coffee and in other ways pretending to care for the old grandfather. It amused Crowfoot but did not deceive him. If his white-hating ward were not suffering friendship thoughts for the tall *wasicun* thief, an old, old man had learned nothing of young squaws in his lifetime.

'Girl,' he finally said to her, 'I am comfortable now. Go and tend to the mule. Get him out from between those travois poles. See to the *wasicun*'s horse also. We will wait for you here at the fire, the *wasicun* and I. Eh, *wasicun*?'

'Sure we will,' Con Jenkins nodded softly. He watched Twilight sway her way over to the drooping Red Weasel and his own dozing buckskin. 'Wait,' he called. 'I'll tend my own horse.' He turned to Crowfoot. 'Grandfather, you keep to the fire till you're sent for.'

'Aye,' said the old man. 'You don't need to instruct me on these things. Just watch out for what she carries under her dress.'

Con heard him but did not answer. Other matters were on his mind. He practically trotted over to take his mount from the Sioux girl. But Twilight, perversely, would not give him the buckskin horse. He hesitated, watching her lead both animals away and out of sight beyond the bend of the cutbank against which she had made the fire for grandfather and for the camp. After an anxious moment on his part, her low voice beckoned him. 'I am waiting over here, *wasicun*. Come and help me.'

Con shook like a wet dog and answered her call like one, cringing on his way for fear the damned grandfather would make some spoiling comment or come nosing along to see how things went.

Around the turn of the cutbank, Con discovered the girl had found an undercaving of the creek's low bluff which formed a shallow, open-faced cavern. Here, she had halted Red Weasel and unlashed the travois. Without delay and as though he now understood his part, Con took up one of the travois poles and helped the Sioux girl drag the buffalo-hide sling and its cargo over to the cavern face.

At this promising point, Twilight ordered him aside. 'You wait now, *wasicun*,' she said. 'The rest is squaw's work.' My God, Con thought, is that all she wanted? Some dumb ox just to give her a friendly lift with the heavy travois? But he had spent his time with Indians disdaining them, not learning from them. The girl all in the few moments he stood watching her, unloaded the travois and stored its goods back under the cavern's overhang, unsaddled

Con's buckskin and dragged the saddle into the same shelter, rigged a windbreak across the open face of the cavern with the emptied hide of the travois sling, and then turned soberly to the white man, holding back an edge of the hide for him to enter the snug haven she had created, murmuring in her low, husky voice, 'Our lodge is ready, *wasicun*.'

Well, by Christ, all right, Con nodded to the announcement and to himself. If the lodge was ready, so was he. A man, so far, couldn't say just what he might expect beyond that buffalo-hide windbreak, but for damned sure he could guess. Indian women were like that. It was no life decision with them. They took a shine to you, said 'come on in,' and you had best be prepared for something more personal than talking in Sioux about the White Wolf prowling or the pony bells tinkling. With a look and a leer that gave all the answer Twilight required, he started for the entryway the slender squaw had made for him.

But you didn't ride the owlhoot all those years, as Con had done, and live to reflect on it, unless you had acquired very nearly the instincts of the coyote and the kit fox. Just short of the entryway, Con Jenkins halted and stepped back from the young squaw. The owlhoot instincts had struck their spark to the tinder of his wary mind. He remembered suddenly old Crowfoot's parting admonition to beware of what his granddaughter carried under the cling of that doeskin campdress. He eyed the girl, now, as she looked puzzled and inquired in that throaty voice that had started all the trouble back at the fire, 'What is it, *wasicun*? Are you afraid?'

'Not of what you think,' he answered. 'Open your damned dress.'

'Why? My body is clean. I have no sores of the squawman's disease.'

'I'm not thinking about that. Open the dress.'

He could see the girl was upset, even angered, by his tone and the way it changed things. She had a temper to go with that beautiful face, and that wasn't all she had to go with it. When, next moment, giving him a hard Indian look, she flung open the soft-tanned garment, Con Jenkins forgot his owlhoot instincts, the grandfather, the grandfather's warning, everything.

For the moment that he held his breath and simply stared at that loveliness of glowing copper skin, no power could distract him. But then he saw what the grandfather meant. What his own instincts had warned him about. It was sheathed and belted beneath the doeskin campdress, and it was the only thing worn there. Con went cold. It was not the snug lodge that had been waiting for him, but the naked steel of the knife.

Too late, the girl unbelted and let slip the weapon. Too late closed the dress and dropped the luminous dark eyes. Too late murmured the throaty lie, 'Please, *wasicun*; it was not for you.'

Con Jenkins's senses were no longer in stampede. His outlaw brain was back where it belonged, up under his hat. He nodded bitterly to the soft denial, to the open plea of the waiting Sioux granddaughter of old Crowfoot. 'Is that what you told the others?' he asked.

The girl flushed, tried to speak again, could not.

Con gave her a last look and turned away.

He was a gunfighter, a hand-fighter. He hated blades and those who used them. They always came at a man from the dark. Or from behind. Or when they just smiled at you from the front. Knives were not the white man's weapon. And this particular skinning blade had recently taken the lives of two other off-guard white men. As surely, the young Oglala squaw had figured to make him number three with it. Con wanted to smash her up against the creek's bluff and beat her bloody. But he did not. He had his Indian ducks in a straight row now. He knew where he was with this one of his two new Oglala friends. Or where he had better be. And that was on guard against her every blink of the way that she and the old grandfather might try to lead Con Jenkins and the stolen Bad Face horse herd.

CHAPTER THIRTY-THREE

The Cheyenne scouts used more time than Captain South wanted in crossing North Ridge. Bent Over was nervous. He had planned to meet up with his friend Bareskin at the nooning. Now they were taking that halt only a little ways toward Old Woman Creek— and of course they had not come far enough. Bareskin was not to be trusted when he was by himself. He did foolish things when time grew long. Bent Over urged his captain to hasten the remount. 'See,' he pointed, 'the weather returns.'

In truth it did look as if the storm were lowering once more. The cold certainly was intensifying. 'How far to that wooded flat?' asked South, studying the sky. 'I don't like this chill.'

'Two hours more, captain.'

'Fassenby!'

'Yes, sir.'

'Mount the men up. No smoking, please.'

They moved out, turning up Old Woman Creek when they came to that stream, climbing south to the headwaters basin. The first hour passed. Then the second. No topping out came, and no timber and no flat. 'It has been many winters since I was here,' explained Bent Over. 'Another hour, captain. No more.'

They went on. Shortly before three o'clock they found Bareskin. He was waiting in the trail. But he would not talk to Bent Over, or even to Captain South. He would never talk to anyone again. His brains were beaten out of his skullbones.

A halt was made and searchers sent to quarter the area. They returned with the dead man's pony, which had run loose. They found where the madman had lain in ambush for their Cheyenne brother. The strange son of old Mulatto Jim had gotten up on a flat rock overhanging a narrowed part of the trail. When Bareskin rode underneath the rock, eyes bent downward following the tracks of the fugitives, *thwaacckkk*!

The scout telling this to Captain South made a clubbing swing and the sibilant sounding of the club—or cane—thudding home in splintered bone, then shrugged, '*Nohetto.*'

They sacked the body of the dead sergeant of scouts over the back of his saddled pony, and they forced on. 'One hour,' repeated the crippled sergeant, Bent Over, 'but they will be warned now, unless we crowd them closely, captain.'

'Can we do that?' asked South.

'The body had not yet gone stiff,' said the scout. 'It held warmth yet in the pit of the arms and between the legs up high.' He nodded intently, eyes stabbing at the clear track line of Crazy Charley Beckwourth and the Oglala orphan boy. 'Yes, we can catch them, if you will let me go ahead with a few men on the best horses. If we go on with the entire troop, then they will get away.'

South rode a few rods thinking it over.

'No killing,' he said. 'I want both of them in good health. Otherwise we learn nothing. What men do you want?'

Bent Over called certain names: Hat, Iron Cedar, Gray Corn, Paints Pretty, Horse Foot, and Bob Elk. The six men pulled out of ranks and came up. They were already checking their guns. 'Come on,' said Bent Over. 'No shooting now. The captain says no trouble.' The six men grinned and put away their rifles. 'No trouble,' echoed one of them. 'Let's go.'

'Wait!' called South at the last instant. 'I've someone to go along with you. Fassenby—!'

Bent Over winced and the lieutenant paled, but the commander would blood his man in the field. His sister was not going to be married to a nobody and a nincompoop. Fassenby could share in this pie without taking the plum away from Terrance Smith South.

Moments later, the young white officer and the seven Indian scouts had disappeared in the blowing ground-snow. Two of the remaining troop sergeants moved up to flank South. The bearded cavalryman ordered them back to their units with an eagerness they had seen before. No matter what their captain had said to Bent Over about not shooting, they knew what he was smelling for himself in that snow wind. It was blood.

CHAPTER THIRTY-FOUR

Trapped in their camp on Eagle Creek at the Bear Paws, the Nez Perce watched the soldiers come.

There was no time to run. There was no place to run to. The people had listened to Looking Glass rather than to Joseph. They had heard the chief who hated the white man, instead of the chief who loved the Indian. Now Eagle Creek would be the last water. They would never reach Milk River. Never see the Sioux of Sitting Bull. Never live in the Land of the Grandmother. It was *hindkasa*, the finish.

But the old fighting chiefs White Bird and Toohoolhoolzote had gotten below the rim of the hollow in which the camp lay. The advancing soldiers did not see them there until too late, when they arose in front of the shouting bluecoats firing only at officers. The blast of the Indian Winchesters withered the middle of Nelson Miles's overconfident charge. Many of Bear Coat's commanders were dead or wounded badly in that fusillade. Without officers, the soldiers broke back and scattered.

On the west side of the camp, however, the Seventh Cavalry swept on. On the east side, the

240

Second Cavalry did the same, except that it continued its sweep past the camp to carry away the Nez Perce horse herd. Caught in the rushing herd were Joseph and the loaded packtrain. At once the fighting became general and the dead were falling everywhere.

In that brutal first shooting, more Nez Perce died than in all of their way from the Wallowa to Big Hole. The roar of rifle and the stink of powdersmoke was blinding. No one could see to aim. The Indians were firing at anything that moved near them.

At noon the main body of soldiers pulled back to potshoot at the camp from the high ground about it. Joseph had meanwhile fought his way out of the running horse herd and was back in the camp. He reported that the great fighter Yellow Wolf had come up just in time to delay the soldiers, permitting most of the packtrain to escape northward. There were fifty women and old people with it. Joseph was happy that the women and few children with them had gotten away, but he was furious with twenty grown warriors who had fled behind them.

Yellow Wolf, coming in a little after Joseph, reported the final disaster: As to the stampeded Indian pony herd, he said, only about one hundred remained in the camp, another one hundred fifty had run with the packtrain. It was certain from this that the soldiers of Bear Coat Miles now held over one thousand of the

Nez Perce horses. Without those horses the Nez Perce were done. They could run no more. The lodges of the Manure Fires would never be moved again. Tsanim Alikos Pah would be the last camp of Joseph and the Nez Perce people.

* * *

In midafternoon Bear Coat sent three companies of cavalry to drive the Indians free of the stream, thinking to thus force their surrender for want of water. It was an extremely bold, extremely foolish gamble; the Nez Perce drove them out in wild disorder. Three red men died, but six dead and seven sorely wounded soldiers were left inside the camp. The Indians treated these men fairly, giving them water and caring for them as they could. Two of them were strong enough to stand. Old White Bird, still aroused from the short fight, let the two men go over to Miles with a message: 'Don't send any more soldiers in here like that or next time we will kill them all. If you want to fight you had better get ready and fight; otherwise get out of the way and let us go on.'

Miles sent in no more soldiers after that. Neither did he get out of the way, however. As night came on, the Indians saw him direct his bluecoats in digging with picks and shovels all along the hilltops and high ground about the hollow. They were making rifle pits. They had decided to dig in and wait for the people to starve or freeze. When this became clear to the Nez Perce, a war council was held.

Strangely, this meeting was called at Joseph's lodge. This puzzled many. Joseph's young brother Ollikut had been the Wallowa warchief from the beginning, and the leader of the young men of all the bands since White Bird Canyon. Why the war talks, previously held at Ollikut's lodge, should now be changed to his older brother's was questioned uneasily. The answer came soon enough.

Word went out for all remaining able-bodied men to attend. The term by this time meant any between sixteen and sixty who were not yet so badly hurt they could not walk, or at least sit to fire a rifle. When the last had come in, or been assisted in, Yellow Bull turned to Joseph and said, 'Fifty-five, Heinmot,' and Joseph nodded and replied, 'All right, Chuslum. Thank you. I will speak now.'

He studied the waiting men, getting all his facts in his mind as was the Indian way when a dark place had come.

'My brothers,' he began, 'this morning early I was in the horse herd with my little daughter, twelve years of age. I had dreamed of pony soldiers coming. I sent scouts as you know, and you know what news they brought.'

He did not say how those among his listeners had ignored that news, or how he had pleaded with them.

'When I saw the soldiers coming, I gave my daughter a rope and told her to catch a horse and join the others with the packtrain. Even as she obeyed me, the horse herd began to run all about us and I was there alone with my horse.

'I thought of my wife and other children who were surrounded by soldiers, and I resolved to go to them or die. With a prayer in my mouth to the Great Spirit who rules above, I dashed unharmed through the line of soldiers. It seemed to me that there were guns on every side, before and behind me. My clothes were cut to pieces and my horse was wounded, but I was not harmed. As I reached the door of my lodge, my wife handed me my rifle, saying, "Here is your gun. Fight."'

Joseph looked toward the west hill where the soldier tents stood gray and thin-walled against the cold slant of the rain that had begun again.

'I fought,' he went on. 'We all fought. You saw this old friend fall; I saw that old friend fall. How many soldiers fell does not matter. They will get more soldiers. Our people who are gone will not come back.

'A great tragedy has come upon us today. In our wildness and fear we killed even our own men. Naked Head shot Koyehkown and Kowwaspo and Lone Bird, all three in the same shelter, thinking they were scouts with Bear Coat. By the same manner Lean Elk was killed. But they are only four of the many who are gone. We mourn all alike who fell by our own or by the soldiers' guns. Yet there are two who went down today—' Joseph could not go on. He waited until his voice steadied.

'If you will look about the circle here,' he said, 'you will see that Peopeo Hihhih, chief of the White Birds, is not among our number. That is because he is at the lodge of his dear friend Toohoolhoolzote, saying *taz alago* to the companion of his lifetime who fell in the last shooting this afternoon.' He stopped again, then went on. 'Now I must tell you my own great sorrow. Then I, too, must go to a lodge that is not mine and sit outside it in the dark grieving for the life of one I loved.'

His comrades had never seen such sadness on his face. For long moments he did not or could not continue. Then he lifted his head and said it very quietly. 'I must tell you now that Ollikut is dead.'

It was a thunderstroke. Joseph's own brother. The premier fighter of them all. Gone. None of those present spoke. All got up and filed out. The meeting of war was ended. But as each chief arose, he placed his voting stick in the center of the ground. It was a memory to Ollikut; the vote was *not* to surrender.

That night the women dug trenches facing the soldiers on every side. They worked the whole night using only camas hooks, knives, trowel bayonets, and, when they had nothing else, their bare fingers. The men roped and dragged up dead horses to fill the gullies of the camp's center and to make higher the breastworks being raised by the squaws. Joseph directed all of this. He was in all places at one time, and he never slept. The thought that they might be digging their own graves came to many of the Nez Perce. But their faith in Joseph's power to 'see ahead' was constant. They tore on at the sleety earth tireless as burrowing animals. And the marks they put into that flinty place are there to this day, standing mute and eloquent under the Montana sky.

But it was not all done for Ollikut's death, or for faith in Joseph.

Fifty of the people had escaped to Canada with the packtrain. Up there was Sitting Bull with as many as four hundred lodges of Hunkpapa Sioux—so the rumor said—and if the Nez Perce people reached those Sioux up there in time, those Sioux would be racing down to help their Nez Perce brothers to defeat Bear Coat Miles there on Eagle Creek, as the Sioux had killed their own nemesis Long Hair Custer, on the Little Horn. Joseph also clung to his belief in the coming of the Oglala Sioux from the south, from Cow Island, led by Crazy Horse and surely bringing Sioux ponies to replace the precious Nez Perce ones lost that morning.

Thus the cold gray morning found the Nez Perce ready to die for time, for four or at the

246

worst five days more, when the Sioux would come. They had nothing to eat but dead horseflesh. Very little ammunition remained. No warm clothing against the fearful wind. More than half the men and many women and small children were seriously wounded. Already they had found the bodies of forty-four of the people killed that first gruesome day. Some of the wounded would die before another sun. They had only old White Bird and Joseph left to lead them. There was no medicine, no cloth for bandages, not even blankets to cover the hurt ones. The little children huddled four and five to each of the few worn buffalo robes. The only warmth came from the handful of manure-chip fires kept feebly alive in the most sheltered of the standing tipis. The thin line of young and old men waiting for the dawn at the rifleworks had only the heat of their bodies pressed together to warm them. Here and there a lucky one lay at the belly of a dying pony which still gave heat for an hour.

But the vote of the council had been against surrender. The bleeding fingers of their mothers and sisters and daughters had gouged the trenches into the frozen earth. With torn and blackened hands their wives had held forth to them their guns and said, as had Joseph's wife, 'Fight.'

Sepekuse. If that was the way that it was, let it be. They were ready.

247

CHAPTER THIRTY-FIVE

All the next morning following his rebuff of the young squaw outside her makeshift lodge under the cutbank, Con and his new partners in the Oglala horse herd lay safely in camp. The storm was passing over. Although the cold still bit like a cornered she-bear, it looked like excellent driving weather upcoming for tomorrow's sunrise. *Owanyeke waste*, as old Crowfoot said, all was beautiful and good; time to be moving on.

Sometime after four that afternoon, the forecast changed.

Into camp rode the snow-caked figures of two horsemen. Both were old friends, one of Con's, the other of Crowfoot's. 'Christ Jesus,' said the tall white outlaw. 'What the hell you doing here, Cookie?' And the old medicine priest stared hard at the second, very small horseman, crying, '*Ih!* can it truly be you, *wablenica*?' So it was that the news of the great Captain South and the close-following advance of his feared Cheyenne enlisted army scouts was brought into the snowbound stolen-horse camp at Old Woman Flat, Wyoming, that thirteenth day of September, 1877.

Tuweni announced the warning, adding that the scouts might be angry because the *heyoka* (Crazy Charley) had killed the chief sergeant

Bareskin only an hour back. Anyway, they had better hurry.

'Good God,' said Con, 'why'd you have to kill the damn sergeant, Cookie?'

Tuweni explained for the jabbering Charley that it was because the simpleton had overheard Bareskin and Bent Over, the other chief scout, planning to kill him, Tuweni, in the camp of the horse thieves. 'Back there just now,' the boy told Con, 'Bareskin simply came up too fast behind us, and the *heyoka* broke his head open. He did it for me.'

'Oh, Christ,' gritted Con. 'Wonderful.'

The old-faced orphan boy shook his head, not smiling.

'No,' he denied, 'not so wonderful. Now the other one, Sergeant Bent Over, he is coming up too fast behind you in this camp. He has six men with him and a lieutenant, running ahead of Captain South and the troop. We saw them when we looked back from a high place, in a moment that the snowfall blew clear. Come on, big *wasicun*,' the boy urged. 'The *heyoka* says you have less time than two dogs require to sniff noses. That's not much time.'

'Not a hell of a lot,' Con agreed. 'What do you suggest we do?'

'We've got to flee,' Tuweni insisted. 'All of us.'

'No, no!' cried Crowfoot, alarmed. 'We can't leave the horses. We can't run away from the warchief's dream.'

249

'Maybe you can't,' Con said. 'Watch me.'

'Hah!' the old man snorted. 'You won't do it.' He pointed at Twilight. 'How about her? You think she will leave the horses to go off with you?'

'I don't give a damn, grandfather, but I'll ask her just for the hell of it.' Con wheeled on the girl. 'Will you?' he said. 'The pay'll be a lot better than hot-trailing a bunch of damned Injun ponies.'

'No,' the girl answered, scowling at him. 'The grandfather does not lie. We must go on with the horses to Cow Island. We must get them there.'

'Why?' Con demanded. 'For God's sake, why?'

'Crazy Horse promised Joseph and the Slit Noses to meet them at Cow Island. It was the warchief's dream to bring these horses to our Indian brothers at that place. I will die for that dream, and for him.'

Con was trapped. He had two options, both red of skin and life-risky. He could throw in with these pipe-dreaming Sioux hostiles who thought they were going to trail that big pony herd half a thousand miles to Cow Island, Montana. Or he could give himself up to the Cheyenne scouts and go back with them to Fort Robinson, Nebraska. There, he would be hanged as a horse thief, if not as a suspected murderer. And if the army didn't want to swing him, they could turn him over to any one of

250

half a dozen territorial sheriffs who held hanging-paper on Con Jenkins, and they would be more than pleased to do the job for the boys in blue.

Christ, a man in front of a firing squad had a better choice than that. He could at least ask for a smoke and it would be real tobacco, not the old Indian's treebark special blend of *kinnikinnic* and shredded buffalo chips.

But off in the nearing distance a thin wolflike yelping arose as the lanky outlaw wavered, and Tuweni pointed fearfully and whispered, 'The Cutarms come!'

Con glanced at the stricken faces of Twilight and the old grandfather and knew he had no choice at all. These people, red Indians or not, had saved his life. He owed at least Crowfoot on that precious score; and Con Jenkins always paid his owings.

'All right,' he said, 'we're going to Montana.' The gray eyes flared. 'But first we're going to set us a Cutarm wolf trap.'

Crowfoot nodded appreciatively. 'Thank you, *wasicun*. What will you use for bait?'

Con Jenkins gave him the cold trace of a smile. 'Some halfways Crow meat,' he said, 'and a little Sioux.'

'What? What's that you say?'

'Why, Crazy Charley and your Injun kid,' the outlaw answered. 'That's what the Cheyenne been shagging ain't it? *Hopo!* Get the girl and yourself out of sight around the bank

251

corner. Wait for me there.'

Crowfoot delayed no more. Twilight looked at Con who nodded sharply at her. She did not return the nod but went with the old man.

'Now then,' Con said to Tuweni and Crazy Charley, 'you two gather up close and listen hard. Here's the way we're going to make them Cheyenne cousins of yours wish they had never enlisted to hunt down good honest Injun sons of bitches like you two poor bastards.'

'All right,' Tuweni consented. 'I will listen hard and then explain it for you to the *heyoka*. I understand him and he knows what I say. Go ahead.'

'Thanks,' Con said, eyeing him. 'You're a true comfort.'

But he laid out his plan for them, forced to trust them, and in moments after that the camp and the earthen bank behind it were at peace. The tall outlaw was gone and only the figures of Crazy Charley Beckwourth and Tuweni Oyuspi were crouched to the cheery blaze of the fire, watching the coffee water boil. Ten minutes passed, no more. Then the thicket beyond the camp was filled with shadows moving up behind the motionless pair at the fire. The shadows were Lieutenant Harold Fassenby, with Bent Over and his six Cheyenne wolf-yelpers.

Down, all of you. Bent Over made the sign and the six Cheyenne dropped to their bellies. Lieutenant Fassenby was the slow shadow to

252

obey, not understanding the handsigns. The same thing happened when Bent Over passed the signs to his henchmen to rise up and rush the figures at the fire. *Remember*, he motioned to them, *no shooting. Just capture them, unharmed.*

The men nodded, grinned, got themselves ready.

Now, signed Bent Over, leaping to lead the silent charge. Behind him came the others, all save Lieutenant Fassenby, who fell down when he jumped up, then could not see for certain, because of the blowing ground-snow, which way his Indians had gone. Having counted on this, indeed, planned it so that the officer would *not* be in on the thing at the fire, Bent Over now threw rifle to shoulder and yelled in Cheyenne to his comrades—deliberately loud for the delayed lieutenant to hear and remember in his testimony—'Look at the boy, he is getting away! Don't let him get away!'

With the command, the crippled brave himself fired his Winchester into the small form of Tuweni Oyuspi. The heavy bullets ripping in from such point-blank range literally tore the thin body apart. Sticks of propping wood, bunches of dry stuffing grass, and cloth bits of Tuweni's agency jacket which had covered the dummy of the boy flew in every direction. In the same moment, excited by their leader's false cries, the others shot wildly into the blanket-shrouded reconstruction of Crazy

Charley Beckwourth. The second dummy toppled forward, dropping the gold-headed cane of Dr V. T. McGillycuddy, which Con had thought to add as a faithful touch to Crazy Charley's scarecrow body.

The six Cheyenne and Bent Over were still standing in a half-circle about their victims only just understanding how they had been false-baited, when the bullets from the top of the cutbank exploded into their real bodies from not fifteen feet away.

The executioners were Con Jenkins, Crowfoot, and Twilight, with two Winchesters and trooper Maggart's trapdoor Springfield carbine. Three Cheyenne fell dead or dying into the fire, Bent Over one of them. The remaining four scouts staggered away wounded, and Con shot all four, with great care to anchor them without further fatality. They went down short of the timber just as Lieutenant Harold Fassenby came blundering up out of the trees to find his command and to fight with what was left of it, dying with his men if need be.

Need, fortunately, was not.

'Don't shoot that one!' pleaded Tuweni, seizing Con's arm where they lay together in the snow atop the bank. 'He is kind, a good man.'

Con scowled but nodded agreement. 'Lieutenant!' he called to the bewildered Fassenby. 'Up here.' The officer peered upward through the fire's smoke and found the gaunt face of the outlaw. 'Lieutenant, sir,' said Con, 'please don't move. Just drop your piece there in the dirt. You're a prisoner of war. I reckon.'

Fassenby reckoned the same.

'Gladly,' he called up to Con Jenkins, letting go the big Colt revolver that he did not even have on the firing cock and sitting down with a weary sigh on the nearest rock. Con slid down the bank, poked the dead Cheyenne in the eyes with his gun barrel, picked up the lieutenant's Colt, and handed it back to him. 'Oh,' said Fassenby, accepting the weapon, 'I must have dropped it.' He did not mean it to be humorous. He was just exhausted, glazed of eye, utterly done out. 'I knew it had to come to this one day,' he said. 'Poor Terrance; he'll never understand.'

'Terrance?' said Con, returning from his brief inspection of the groaning wounded.

'Captain South,' said the young officer.

'Yeah,' said Con. 'That reminds me. We better get a move on. *Hopo!* everybody out.' Twilight, the old man, Crazy Charley, and the boy Tuweni came slipping over the bank's top in a tumble of dislodged snow. 'I want all those wounded hauled into the girl's hollow back of the travois hide,' he told them. 'Leave the hide where it is. I got nothing against these poor hurt bastards. Besides, we ain't going to have no time to be holding up for that spavined old mule to drag along the travois. Load all of them supplies onto two, three pack animals out'n our herd. Hop it! *Hookahey!*'

The wounded men were Hat, Iron Cedar, Paints Pretty, and Bob Elk. All four talked with Con Jenkins, saying they were sorry for what had happened, and that it was the bloodlust of Sergeant Bent Over that was to blame. One of them, the record says Iron Cedar, asked for a word in private with the white outlaw. This granted, he told Con that it was well known to the Cheyenne scouts that their leader Captain South was also a blood hunter. He was coming fast behind now and Iron Cedar, who had a Sioux wife back at Fort Robinson, believed that the fugitives should leave at once and not be there when the main troop came up. Say it was something in his Cheyenne heart that called to what they were doing, driving all those Indian horses back to where the wind blew free, but Iron Cedar wished he might go with them. 'Go at once, stealer of horses,' he begged Con. 'Our captain will kill you, surely, if he catches you here.'

Con saw them all safely in the bank-hole behind the shelter of the buffalo hide, thanked Iron Cedar, went back to the fire and the problem of Lieutenant Fassenby.

'Iron Cedar tells me we got time to round up the herd and get it out of here if we hustle,' he said to Fassenby. 'That agree with your timepiece?'

'I don't know,' said Fassenby. 'I surely hope so.'

'The hell,' said Con. Then, frowning, 'What am I going to do with *you*?'

'I wish,' said the young officer almost wistfully, 'that you could take me with you.'

He did not mean it literally, of course, but a grateful light was growing in Con Jenkins's gray eyes, nonetheless. He reached over and fetched Harold Fassenby a clap on the shoulder which spilled the lieutenant's steaming coffee from both cup and mouth. 'By God, lieutenant,' he said, 'you done just promoted yourself to a new tour.'

'What?' blinked the youngster.

'How would you like a transfer to the Department of Montana?' said Con.

'Me? Montana?'

'You, Montana,' nodded Con Jenkins. 'On your feet.'

Fassenby got slowly off the fireside rock. 'What if I refuse?' he said, looking about as though for an avenue of desperate gamble.

'You can't refuse,' said Con soberly. 'You're a hostage. It ain't legal to refuse.'

Harold Fassenby looked at him a full five seconds, during which a dress parade of his past life with the great Captain South's army-reared sister trooped past in draggletailed array. At the end of the sorrowful review, he reached out and took Con Jenkins's hand.

'You're right,' he said. 'We've got to keep it

legal.' Then, happily, 'Let's go—!'

CHAPTER THIRTY-SIX

The evacuation of the Oglala herd from Old Woman Flat was a 'genuine Con Jenkins.'

Everyone had an assignment and was running it out within sixty seconds of Lieutenant Fassenby's final surrender. The tall outlaw didn't bark his orders, he wolf-grinned them. He was getting the real feel of this 'heist' professionally now. And what he was feeling was that it just might be the greatest job of his notable career. Of course it was costing him twenty-four thousand dollars, but he could afford it. Where could you gain experience like this for any amount of cash money? Besides, a man had to look at all the money he was saving, too; like whatever those sheriffs were offering for his hide back yonder. Hell, that could run as high as five hundred, right there!

Con had to laugh. And did. As a matter of fact, he wondered if he weren't possibly getting a little flabby between the ears. He had laughed three times now in only the past two days. 'Happy sounds,' old Crowfoot called them. Whatever they were, Con felt each one of them to be worth about a thousand dollars of that big payday he and Blue Slattery and Frank Gavilan had missed at Fort Robinson on the remount deal. Christ, he was getting rich. At that rate he'd be owing himself money by the time they reached Cow Island with the herd. He had already laughed more in forty-eight hours than he had the last five years along the owlhoot. Maybe it was that he was getting crazy like the Indians. A man had to be slipping his head hobbles when he got to thinking that stealing horses from himself was funny.

But this was different. God knew it was. And Con Jenkins laughed again and waved his *hopos* and *hookaheys* to his fellow thieves, happy as though he still had good sense. When they all laughed back—even the girl—and gave him their damned Indian *he-haus*! and only went the more spiritedly about their tasks, he knew they had him roped and tied. Lieutenant Fassenby wasn't the real hostage of the Cow Island horse drive. Con Jenkins was.

But the job itself was still a beauty.

Twilight went out into the grazing herd and, putting fingers in mouth like a boy, whistled up the old white bell mare and got the herd to mill around Speckledbird and herself so as to have its hundreds of animals 'compacted,' as Con put it, when they were ready to push out of there.

Meanwhile, he gave his lasso to Tuweni, instructing the Oglala boy to go and get the ponies of the dead and wounded Cheyenne scouts. He was to string them all on a lead-rope made with the lasso and be prepared to 'put 'em in tow,' when Con gave the word. As well, the Oglala boy was to take the collected Winchesters of the scouts—seven precious brand-new models—and stick them back into the saddle scabbards of Bent Over's men, along with the ammunition belts taken from the scouts. Tuweni would be in charge of their 'armory' and responsible for the artillery 'all the way up to Cow Island crossing.'

The old man, Crowfoot, was given woman's work and did not care for it. But Con convinced him that it was only because the granddaughter was needed to call the horses in that Crowfoot had to supervise the loading of the travois supplies onto the pack animals. 'Besides,' Con told him importantly, 'Tuweni tells me you used to be chief pack-master for the warchief, "just like Joseph with the Slit Noses,"' he added offhandedly. The last part about Joseph did it, and the old man fell to his work with fierce will and deep Oglala pride.

And why not? Crowfoot had never before understood that the great Nez Perce chieftain was a lowly Master of the Packs for his people. Con Jenkins didn't know it, either; he never did understand how near to the historic truth he had struck by pure inspiration.

Crazy Charley was put to guarding the Cheyenne prisoners in the cutbank covert. The idea was that the captives would not require any lectures to get it into their minds that what had happened to their friend Bareskin could even more easily befall them in their handicapped condition. The prisoners made no problem. They were only grateful when Con came hurriedly to their shelter and did his best to clean and bandage their hurts for them. When Iron Cedar tried to express this debt to the white outlaw, Con grinned and said, 'Hell, chief, it ain't charity. I need you bastards alive and kicking. Dead Injuns don't present no problems to live Injuns.'

They knew what he meant. In the Indian warfare mystique, the wounded were rescued and cared for at all costs. No man was knowingly left to suffer in the field of a fight. Countless unwounded and well-mounted red men had died trying to save a fellow who would not last the hour after he was 'scooped up' and given a double-ride to safety. It was an Indian weakness—of courage and morality—which had cost them a deadly toll through the white man's knowledge of it.

Iron Cedar, however, even while recognizing the advantage the tall white man had gained by wounding him and his fellows, remained an Indian.

'Nevertheless,' he said gravely to Con, 'we will remember you. An enemy who cares for the injured of his enemy cannot be forgotten.'

'Pony droppings,' shrugged Con Jenkins.

'*Nohetto*,' waved Iron Cedar, with Cheyenne dignity.

And that was the note of the parting, the day

Con Jenkins drove out the Oglala herd from under the eager nose of Captain Terrance Smith South.

It was a very cold day, but clearing.

September 13, 1877.

An Indian day—the day that began the historic 575-mile running of the Bear Paw horses.

CHAPTER THIRTY-SEVEN

As nearly as it may be located on modern maps, the drive started somewhere immediately north of Lusk, Wyoming, most likely from just south of historic old Hat Creek stage station. From there, the way points, in the surviving Indian account, were Old Woman Flat, Lance Creek, Twentymile Creek, Lightning Creek, Dry Creek, Dry Fork, Antelope, Porcupine, and Little Thunder Creeks to the headwaters of the Belle Fourche River, north of Pine Tree, Wyoming. Then, going still north and west, past Savageton into the Powder River drainage, twice crossing the forks of the Powder east of Crazy Woman battlefield and north of Old Fort Reno, proceeding through the roughs northeast of the TA ranchhouse, where the Johnson County War was to end fifteen winters later, to Crazy Woman Creek's old crossing outside Buffalo, Wyoming. Thence, past old Fort Phil

Kearney and Massacre Hill to swing south of Sheridan, skirt Fort Mackenzie and turn due north into Montana past Tongue River and the place where the Arapaho of Black Bear and Old David had humbled General Connor twelve years before.

In its entire line of flight the drive paralleled the Bozeman Trail by as much as forty miles in the beginning, tapering constantly nearer to the main track throughout Wyoming, to virtually join it at the Montana border. In all this way there were many near things, some of them shooting clashes with both federal troops and civilian posses, the latter alerted to the rich herd to be taken as a right of salvage by any enterprising white group along the way. Con and his companions were able in each case to win free and to drive on. But the cost was not little. Four white townsmen were killed in the chase, and two soldiers. The charges escalated from stock stealing to wanted for murder. Horses were lost, too, at each place where a trap was set by settler or military. The beautiful animals had dwindled to 275 head at the Montana crossing. Yet they were growing stronger, if more gaunt, with each mile nearer they came to the old pastures of home. Like Crowfoot and Twilight, the ponies could smell the winds of freedom. Going over into Montana on the black midnight of September 23, 1877, they had come 250 crow-flight miles in ten precious days, a true average of over thirty miles per day—and still they were barely halfway on their perilous journey. But *now* they could smell the wind!

An hour after leaving Wyoming, where they had freed Lieutenant Fassenby at the territorial line, they picked up the Little Big Horn River and Con Jenkins called the halt; they were many a safe mile beyond Sheridan and the last of the settlements, with nothing but buffalo grass between them and Cow Island.

*　　*　　*

The rest halt made that first night in Montana, high on the Little Big Horn, was the first opportunity since drive's beginning to lay over for twenty-four hours. Stock was there taken not alone of beast, but of man. Yes, and of woman.

The company had found a rocky campsite where piled boulders and some shelfrock of local strata provided a perfect wind and fire screen. It was hence risk-free to have a cheering blaze, good hot food and drink, with beckoning dreams of secure slumber and an all-day rest to follow. Within the hour, the camp was dark but for the dim flickering of the banked fire. Old Crowfoot's snores vied with those of Red Weasel who was dozing but a pebble-toss away. In their separate places Tuweni and Crazy Charley Beckwourth also slept the sleep of the totally exhausted. Only Con and the young squaw Twilight stayed at the fire.

It was Con who broke the silence.

'Well, Sioux sister,' he said in her own tongue, 'we have come a long way now together. What are your thoughts tonight?'

Twilight looked into the fire. 'What thoughts do you mean?' she asked.

'The thoughts for us,' Con said.

The girl shook her head and still would not look at him. 'I don't know,' she said.

'Have you held the idea in your mind, H'tayetu?'

It was the first time he had spoken her name in Oglalan. When he said it, she brought her eyes from the fire to stare at him a moment, as though in confusion. Then, she looked away again. 'Yes,' she said.

'Did it frighten you?'

'At first.'

'Why?'

'I did not know what it was.'

'Do you know yet?' Con asked gently.

'Do you?' said the girl.

Con sighed, shook his head. 'No,' he answered honestly. 'But I will say this to you, my sister; it is *something*.'

'I know,' she answered wearily. 'It is something for me too, and I do not know what it is either.' Twilight paused, trouble in her face and yet a shadow of some deeper excitement rising there, too. Her slant eyes found Con's, and held them. 'I do know this one thing, however,' she said in that low voice, 'it is not the feeling of a sister.'

Con shivered. He had never before in his lifetime been where he was right then. Still, he was wary.

'Listen,' he said. 'I have learned many things about you and the grandfather on this ride. Yes, and about the boy Tuweni. Even about that *heyoka* Charley, and he is no more than half an Indian. I have never known any Indians before.' He shook his head and, in his intentness, forgot and finished in English. 'You're the damnedest people ever a man run into!'

'What?' said the girl, frowning.

'Excuse it,' Con muttered. 'I said the Indians are not as I thought they were.'

'And this Indian,' she said to him, 'me?'

'You?' Con said, and he could not answer her.

He reached across the spiraling smoke, both hands offered to her. She took them and he raised her up and she came around the fire and stood with him. He did not touch her but said softly in Sioux, 'Will you be my woman, H'tayetu?' and she answered, with a simple nod, 'I have always been your woman.'

Down the stream, past the boulder pile, they found an old fallen cedar circled by a thicket of aspen upon a beachlet of old, high-water sand.

Beneath this covert was a wind-still and warm-aired place carpeted with mosses and dry grass, seeming as though placed there by Wakan Tanka for these people and this night.

Twilight was the one who saw it and led Con Jenkins to its shelter. 'Our lodge,' whispered the throaty voice. 'Will you enter this time?'

'Yes,' Con said. 'I know you now.'

'You knew me then, *wasicun*,' she murmured. 'I am not the same one.'

'Nor am I,' admitted the tall outlaw.

They crept beneath the ancient cedar tree, its warm dark a welcome thing to both. Women had not woven themselves into the harsh fabric of Con's life. They did not ply their wares along the owlhoot and, where they did, were of a shared kind not hungered after by tall Con Jenkins. As for Twilight, she had known no man nor, until this man, wanted one.

So in the cedar's fragrant gloom they lay, the white outlaw and the Indian girl, saying the things neither had said to other woman or other man. The loving was sweet and of a great strength and their sleep, when it came, dreamless. The trail had been far to this place and still was far to its ending. But for them it fell away. They knew it not, nor cared for any danger in it.

CHAPTER THIRTY-EIGHT

Laying over one full day on upper Powder River, Con Jenkins drove on along the Little Big Horn with the following dawn, September 25. In his mind a growing uncertainty spread. The brief happiness of the rest camp changed nothing for his little band of Indian people. They might laugh and shout to one another all the nearing-home things they wished. To speak with nomad's joy of the smell of the pines and the yellow-brown buffalo grass and the curly cows themselves, and of all the homesick wonder of coming again into the beloved Land of the Shining Mountains, was just fine with Con Jenkins. These people were simple in heart and head. They did not know anything of what Con Jenkins did. The very fact that Crowfoot and Twilight had even thought they could steal this big herd and bring it up to Montana showed just how simple they were. The idea they both would thus share Crazy Horse's refusal to understand that his time of freedom in that country was forever gone, only proved their ignorance of the white man's world. The daft scheme to join Chief Joseph at Cow Island just to bring him a gift of horses and the word that they came from the dead warchief who had once promised the Slit Nose brother to *be* there, was the final cow flop in the entire trail of red Indian buffalo chips. At the noon halt, these doubts having redoubled themselves in the worried, hard-driving hours since daybreak, Con summoned Crowfoot. While the others gathered at the coffeefire trying to eat what Crazy Charley had prepared from his stocks of spoiling horsemeat and weevily pinto beans, Con and the old man sat among some boulders atop a nearby rise, watching and talking.

Con reviewed the way they had come. Beginning with the inspiration of taking the willing lieutenant along as hostage—four times along the desperate trail the exhibited presence of Fassenby among their ranks had gotten them safely away from cavalry attacks—and ending with the handshakes and good wishes with which they had left the young officer in the inky blackness of the Wyoming-Montana line two nights gone, he laid it all out for the gravely nodding Crowfoot.

They both well knew, he reminded the wrinkled medicine priest, that there simply was not enough time remaining to them, all other problems aside.

The few roving Indians they had met and spoken with the past days of getting up into the home ranges of Sioux and Cheyenne, Crow and Arapaho, had told various stories about the Nez Perce retreat, true. But these 'wild coyotes' were themselves bountied outlaws, as certainly with prices on their hostile heads as were Con Jenkins and the Sioux grandfather. They would say whatever they thought would get them a free meal or a twist of trade tobacco. How could a man winnow out what was fact from what had to be pure *shacun* bull hockey in their reports on Joseph's whereabouts now? Which same information he and the old man *had* to have to lay their Montana track line. God Almighty, for all Con and Crowfoot knew for sure, the Nez Perce might never have gotten to Cow Island, might be way past it, might have crossed a hundred miles above or below it, might, Christ knew, already be dead, turned back, captured, or safe across the line into Canada. How in God's name could they know? They had heard every one of these stories in the past four days. And every 'red bastard' swore on the sacred navel of Wakan Tanka, Maheo, Tiwara, Jesus Christ, or whoever, that his story was the straight-tongued one.

The old man nodded again. 'An Indian will always lie,' he said. 'The truth has no hope in it whatever. But an Indian will always tell the truth, also. He just leaves it up to you to understand the difference.'

'And you understand it, I suppose?' Con snapped.

At this point, Crowfoot made his own review. Think, he said, of how they had come to where they were. Look back at *that* trail and shake the head.

Who would ever have thought that the

cursed Captain South would take twenty picked men and come after them from Old Woman Flat? And who would believe that a skinny old Oglala man and his young-squaw granddaughter and a ten-year-old agency boy and a half-witted mixed-breed Crow Indian could then ambush that bad officer, kill three of his scouts, and wound seven more of them, to the point where the great Captain South was finally beaten and had to creep back to Fort Robinson with his sorry little story of how he had rashly done it all to rescue the brave and dashing Lieutenant Harold Clarence Fassenby who, in the hands of the bloodthirsty Sioux hostiles, faced a fate far worse than simple dying?

And who would then ever have conceived that the white man's newspapers would so fall upon the story and so multiply the plight and heroism of their nice, kind, and quiet officer guest as to make of Terrance South ten times the legend he already was and make of Fassenby a hero to match Kit Carson, Long Hair Custer, Big Throat Bridger, Yellowstone Kelly, and Bear Coat Miles? Making him so big, in fact, that they had had to cut him loose in the night and leave him on the trail in the dark, because if they kept him they would have more cavalry chasing them than were pressing poor Chief Joseph.

Eh? the old man finished. Who would have believed all that? And who would now believe, he challenged his silent white listener, that where Wyoming had failed to defeat them, Montana was going to do it?

'Why!' he cried, finally, rheumy eyes flashing, 'this is my home, here! I know it as I know each seam and wart and fissure of my old dried-out body. I can lead you to Cow Island through this Shining Mountain land by ways no soldier will see and no Indian reveal. Where in all of this can you lose heart, *wasicun*?'

Con's narrow, bearded face only hardened.

'You ain't said what you set out to say,' he told Crowfoot.

'What is that?' frowned the old man.

'Whicht of them Injun yarns to guide on; I mean the ones we've been told abouten where Joseph is.'

'Why, the last one,' said Crowfoot. 'The one the Crow told us.'

'You mean that crooked-eyed bastard that claimed he'd been with Custer right here on the Little Horn last year?'

'He wasn't crooked of eye. You only say that because your young squaw found him so handsome. The *heyoka* Beckwourth vouched for him, remember? He even knew his name before the Crow gave it. You recall it?'

'Bushway,' said Con. 'Who could forget an Injun with a name like that? Curly? That's a redskin name?'

'Hah!' cried the old man. 'You're still jealous!'

'Forget that.' Con glowered at the wizened Oglala, then grudgingly yielded with only one more growl and one more 'bushway.'

'All right,' he said. 'The crooked-eyed bastard was a scout with Custer last year. He did just come that night into our camp from old Fort C. F. Smith over yonder on the main Big Horn. And all that's left over there, mostly, is a few soldiers and a new "talking wire" machine. And the telegraph did say something about Chief Joseph and Cow Island. How the hell do we know *what* it said?'

Crowfoot spread wrinkled hands.

'Curly told us,' he smiled.

Con could have shot him gladly. But that smile and that wonderful old sun-creased, battle-scarred red face defied anger, destroyed reasonable argument. Instead of shooting him, or even shouting at him, the weary outlaw concentrated on recalling to his mind the picture of the message that the Crow scout Curly had said came relayed over the wires for Colonel Clendennin at Fort Benton—the first hard word of the Nez Perce whereabouts since Canyon Creek above Laurel Crossing of the Yellowstone.

Rifle Pit
at Cow Island
Sept. 23, 1877
10:00 A.M.

Colonel: Chief Joseph is here and says he will

273

surrender for two hundred bags of sugar. I told him to surrender without the sugar. He took the sugar and will not surrender. What will I do? Michael Foley

But even that shocker, its date showing the Nez Perce far, far ahead of them at Cow Island the same night they had crossed out of Wyoming, was not the final crushing extent of Curly's intelligence. The much-maligned Crow survivor of the Custer fight had another 'talking wire' message to report. He did not have the exact words of this one, but only its chilling content, dated many days before down on Canyon Creek. It was to Colonel Nelson Miles waiting at Fort Keogh to go glory hunting. The sender was General O. O. Howard, smarting after the bloody defeat of his junior, Colonel Samuel Sturgis, at the hands of the fleeing Nez Perce caught in Canyon Creek.

'*Bear Coat*,' said the message, in Curly's Indian translation, '*I have little confidence that Sturgis will catch the Nez Perce now. You have fresh men. You are a better Indian chaser than Sturgis. Where you are on the Yellowstone, you are closer to the crossing of the Missouri River than is Joseph. I think you can beat those Indians to that crossing. I order you to go and do it. I am One Hand.*'

Seeing these things in his mind now, understanding what they meant should they

274

believe their Crow informant, Con Jenkins stood up, still undecided.

'I don't know,' he muttered unhappily to the old Sioux medicine man standing with him on that lonely hill of grass above the Little Big Horn. 'I just plainly don't know.'

Down below, the noon halt was over. Crazy Charley was kicking out and burying his fire's embers. The orphan boy Tuweni was mounting Dr McGillycuddy's big bay horse and going to his place on the drag at herd's rear. H'tayetu, Twilight, the slim girl-squaw who dreamed the warchief's dream, was gracefully swinging up on her pony and going with old Speckledbird to once more ride the point, guiding the herd home.

Coming to her place, the girl looked up at her grandfather and the tall white outlaw on the grassy hill and saw them watching her. She waved happily and they both saw the white teeth flash in the sunshine. Crowfoot nodded and said softly to Con, 'Follow your heart, *wasicun.*'

And Con Jenkins laughed and knew that he was done for and that he was going on.

'*Wagh—!*' he yelled aloud, echoing the stillness of the sunlit buffalo pasture. Turning from the hill, he ran in his awkward bowlegged cowboy lope down the grassy slope, the old man war whooping behind him.

CHAPTER THIRTY-NINE

Driving on down the Little Big Horn east of the Rosebud Mountains, the little band went northeast across what is now the Crow Reservation. They passed first the Reno-Benteen and then the Custer battlefields, still following the river. Where the Little Horn turned west to join the Big Horn, however, Crowfoot became hunchy and turned due north to drive out over what is blank paper on the map today, as then, striking the Yellowstone east of Big Horn ford, midway between present-day Billings and Miles City, Montana. The stratagem saved them from half a regiment of United States Infantry waiting on telegraphed orders to ambush the 'murderous hostile Sioux Indians' who had just released the fearless Lieutenant Fassenby and were reportedly 'racing to get behind and hamstring the redoubtable Colonel Nelson A. Miles on his vital march to end the bloody forays of Chief Joseph and the pillaging Nez Perce.' How long the three hundred soldiers sat at Big Horn ford is not remembered by an embarrassed army. But they were still there (according to old Yellowstone County settlers) when, two days later, on September 29, they received a second telegraphed communique: Miles was not even in the country; he was up in the Bear Paws trying to kill Joseph before General Howard or Colonel Sturgis might get up there and beat him to the bloodshed.

From their crossing of the Yellowstone, the Oglala horse herd and its drovers simply vanished. For eight days they were neither sighted nor reported sighted. Then, on October 2, a scout force under Lieutenant E. E. Hardin (from the relief garrison at Cow Island under Major Guido Ilges) had a brief scare in the cold dusk of day's end.

Said one account of the time: 'Without warning whatever, the light being dim and a strong gale blowing, the soldiers rode into the flanks of some two to three hundred native ponies being moved westerly toward Cow Creek, and at a rapid pace. The Indian herd broke and began to run. Almost at once, a cross fire of Winchester, or other repeating rifles, burst over the startled troopers. "We broke off," said their officer, "not knowing the strength of the foe, nor his kind."'

Another local source said merely, 'The troops run like rabbits. They was scairt crazy.'

It was a fair exchange, nonetheless.

Neither did Con Jenkins or the girl-squaw H'tayetu, whose Winchesters they were that welcomed the mounted soldiers, know the number or the nature of the enemy.

Their ignorance, however, was short lived. As well, it would never appear in print, local or official.

The Oglala herd quit running when it came to Cow Creek in the near darkness of that second day of October. By the time Con and the others had gotten the horses collected and spread out in a meadow swale some five miles north of the Cow Island crossing of the Missouri, the full night was down.

Only then did they realize that Crowfoot was missing.

Almost as soon as his absence was noted, they heard his cracked voice singing a brave song off in the distance toward the big river. Since the sound was coming their way, they waited. Presently, the grandfather wandered in off the prairie, bringing a guest for dinner.

'I caught him down the stream a little ways when I became lost in the pony running,' the old man explained, giving his terrified prisoner a shove with the muzzle of his Winchester. 'He says there are another thirty-five *wasicuns* just like him helping the soldiers at Cow Island. They volunteered to save the country from Joseph and the Slit Noses. He must have the heart of a grizzly bear in that little rat's body of his.'

They tied up the captive white settler, offering to swap him his life for some straight talk. Con warned him that they knew several things for themselves and that, accordingly, if and where his tale might stray from the track of the truth, as they knew it, why, they would just have the young squaw cut him in the kidney of his choice, the way the soldiers had done to Crazy Horse down at Fort Robinson.

'You can tell us which one you want, right now,' said the bearded outlaw. 'I'll guarantee you we won't cheat you. You say the one, and that's the way they'll find you. Start lecturing.'

The citizen-soldier was of small stature and even smaller spirit; he was under death-oath, and he knew it.

His news, by courier that same afternoon from the Bear Paws, was two days old. But as of the nightfall of September 30, forty-eight hours ago, it was all over but the promotion of Colonel Miles to General Miles. Old Bear Coat had caught the Nez Perce, shot the hell out of them, taken Joseph as hostage-prisoner under a flag of truce—all's fair in war!—and had no doubt, by the present time, got his surrender and was marching back down Cow Creek to put the details of his great victory for civilization on the telegraph wires for Washington, D.C.

Con could not bear to look at Twilight or the old grandfather in that moment of brutal silence.

He did move to relieve Crowfoot from his guarding of the prisoner, fearing the old man might shoot or knife the settler out of pure Indian frustration. He also watched H'tayetu closely. But the young squaw was as shattered as her beloved warchief's dream. And how could her will be less than broken?

279

They had come nearly six hundred miles driving the herd like furies. Killing ponies every day. Losing uncounted scores to lameness, breakdown of wind, the wanton attacks of greedy ranchers. They had made the greatest drive of Indian horses in the red man's history, only to be fifty miles and two pony rides late.

Nor was that even the full extent of it, as they now learned from the captive's continuing information.

They had 225 sound horses remaining that dark night above Cow Island. Up at the Bear Paws, Joseph and his walking wounded from the eleven-week blood trail of the Nez Perce search to find freedom, stood all dismounted, their beautiful Appaloosa horses swept away by the charging Second Cavalry. All of the Slit Nose people not wounded and fit to sit a mount, when the soldier courier rode out two nights gone, numbered no more than two hundred souls. Another two to three hundred lay badly hurt and would not leave that place except in death or by army wagon. But it was the tragic number, two hundred, that stayed in the numbed mind of the Indian girl: If the Oglala herd had reached the Nez Perce two suns earlier, every able-bodied one of Joseph's people would have had a Sioux horse to ride out to freedom and twenty-five horses left over to serve in full-running pack usage!

No Indian could face a bitterness like that,

280

thinking to go on when everything was already lost up in the Bear Paws.

Well, wait. One Indian might. One very small Oglala Indian not considered in the sorrow, not consulted toward its solving. Said Tuweni Oyuspi, standing forth to hail his silent comrades onward, '*Hopo!* Didn't you hear the little nervous *wasicun* say it only now? The Slit Noses need these horses very bad. *Hookahey—!*'

A gust of cold wind blew through the darkness.

Con looked at Crowfoot. The grandfather gave over the glance to the granddaughter. She returned it to tall Con Jenkins. Three hearts quickened and three heads nodded as one to Tuweni's statement of simple Indian brotherhood.

'Let's go,' said Con Jenkins.

And they went.

CHAPTER FORTY

The first of October, the second day of Colonel Miles's surround of the Nez Perce at the Bear Paws, was taken by the Indians to expand their hand-dug fortifications. The soldier fire was light and long range only. The work in the Nez Perce rifle pits went forward under cover of a light snow that began in the afternoon. When darkness fell, the Indians had created a perfect

281

network of buried bunkers, slit trenches, interconnecting tunnels, and raised breastworks. If Bear Coat Miles was to make a siege of this thing, Joseph's people were ready. They could not know, as Miles did with that nightfall, that both Sturgis and Howard were coming up fast from the Missouri. Had the Nez Perce understood this, they would have tried to break away for Canada that same night. But knowing only what they knew—that they had stopped the great Bear Coat and driven him back and that Joseph's six messengers to the Sioux of Sitting Bull had been on the trail to Canada since the previous night, September 30—Joseph's wounded survivors believed still that they could win.

This faith took a great blow on the third day, October 2, when Looking Glass was killed, as he stood atop the piled earth in front of his rifle pit, by sniper fire from Milan Tripp, one of Miles's chief scouts.

The death of the Asotin chief, in its manner of coming, struck the chill of prophecy into the cornered people.

Aleemyah Tatkaneen, chief of all the Clearwater people, called Looking Glass in the white man's history books, stood up above the pit to show the power of his personal *simiakia*, his faith, his own medicine. Nothing could harm him and, thus, nothing could harm the people who would listen to Looking Glass. He placed himself up there on that rifle pit breastwork with his arms folded over his breast, his black peaked soldier hat—his strongest *wyakin*, or war charm—jammed straight upon his head as he always wore it. His gun lay in the trench behind him. His face was turned to the west toward the soldiers who at once raised their rifles and fired heavily upon him. But he stood there like a rock, nothing moving on his body except where the wind whipped the ragged buckskin fringe of his leggins. No soldier bullet could touch him, and none did. Then Milan Tripp's long buffalo gun boomed, and its heavy bullet whined over the frozen brown grass and laid the Asotin dead upon the naked dirt of his defiance.

Now all of the people fell into their first mood of real gloom, and not falsely so.

White Bird, seventy-four winters, was the only fighting chief left alive. Of warriors of first reputation, any age, there now remained but Yellow Wolf, Wottolen, No Feet, Naked Head, Otskai, Black Eagle, Sun Necklace, Yellow Bull, Band-of-Geese, Ten Owls, Dead Bones, and Tabador. There were perhaps seven or eight others of lesser skills.

As well, the weather again turned evil; a falling wind and rising temperature thawed the Nez Perce rifleworks, rendering them a hell of slushy ice and mud. A worse chill yet was coming. In the afternoon Bear Coat sent a white flag of truce: He wanted to see Joseph.

A buffalo robe was placed on the freezing

ground midway between the soldier lines and the rifle pits of the Nez Perce. Joseph, with that uncanny prescience that was his, made a final arrangement before going out to sit with Miles upon the robe. Calling to him the courier Timuni, Fire Rifle, who had taken Joseph's message to Crazy Horse that summer, he spoke urgently.

'You went another time on a perilous journey for the people and for me. Now I want to send you on a second journey. We do not see Sitting Bull with our Sioux brothers coming from the north. They should be here and they are not. My heart says something bad has happened. Now there is only the Oglala Sioux who may be coming from the south from Cow Island where we missed them. Go and see if you can find them. Bring them up here. Tell them Looking Glass is dead, and all the chiefs save White Bird are dead. Tell them to come with what they have and help us.'

He paused here, being sure he and the messenger were not heard. 'Do not tell any of our people what I've said to you. Just make your way out of here when I have gone to talk to Bear Coat. None will be watching then. *Taz alago*, farewell, Timuni. *Tukelukse!*'

'*Taz alago*,' nodded the courier. 'I will find the Oglala.' Then softly, 'Take hope yourself, Heinmot.'

Joseph only said, 'Remember, do not speak to anyone. Go quickly when I have gone.'

With that, Heinmot Tooyalakekt, Thunder on the Mountain, went out to see why Bear Coat waved the white flag. He found out very swiftly.

By a quirk of fate, what happened was seen by Timuni, Joseph's secret courier. The message-rider could not immediately find his pony, which had been repicketed by his wife. He was thus still in the camp when he heard a great shout go up from the Indians and saw many of his fellows running in the rifle trenches toward the parley ground. Dismounting, he went atop the nearest elevation of dug earth, holding his pony by its bridle rope behind him.

What he saw rode with him for his lifetime.

Over there, the soldiers of Bear Coat Miles had seized the arms of Joseph and were dragging him as a prisoner back into their rifle lines.

By the buffalo robe on the ground, still planted on its stick and waving limply, was the white flag of truce.

* * *

Joseph's messenger, Timuni, found the Oglala pony herd about eleven o'clock the following morning. The herd was driving east of Cow Creek in broad daylight and only God himself had kept the five brave people that were with the herd from blundering into some soldier patrol on the way to that place.

Calling himself by his name in English, Fire Rifle told the drovers that he came from Joseph. When they did not seem to believe him, and when the tall, mean-looking white man with them cocked his Winchester, the Nez Perce courier reminded the others that he had come to the Oglala before. Did they not remember their own Sioux courier Long Fox? Well, he, Fire Rifle, was the Nez Perce messenger who rode back with Long Fox to Joseph, bearing Crazy Horse's word that he was coming to help the Slit Nose brother.

'*Ih!*' cried old Crowfoot when the courier said this. 'Of course. I remember you now. Don't shoot him, *wasicun*,' he advised the gray-eyed white man. 'He comes from Joseph, all right.'

Once accepted, the messenger exhorted them to get the herd away from Cow Creek. There was soldier traffic up and down the stream. They must at once veer away to the north. He would go with them to show them the way to get their Oglala horses to the Bear Paws in a big circle, avoiding all soldiers. It would require more time, but they had no choice. Meanwhile, the Nez Perce courier wanted to know, which of them would ride back and tell Crazy Horse and the Oglala people where their horses had been taken to?'

'*Wonunicun*,' said Crowfoot sorrowfully. 'Excuse it, Slit Nose brother, but Crazy Horse is dead and there are no more Sioux back there.

We three,' he pointed to Twilight, Tuweni, and himself, 'are all of the Oglala that have come.'

Fire Rifle seemed unable to believe this.

'It's true,' the gaunt white man told him in passable Sioux. 'The horses are all that we could bring you.'

The courier from Joseph then explained his despair. In getting away from the surround up there, he had gone out to the north. Circling up there to turn back south, he had found a dying Nez Perce hiding under a snowbank. It was an old woman who told him that the Assiniboin, blood brothers of the Sioux at Red River, had murdered all six of Joseph's messengers to Sitting Bull. Worse than that, the Sioux were not coming to help them from up there anyway. Some of their young men, even, had attacked the packtrain of escaped ones. These brother-killers, the old woman said, murdered ten of the packtrain people and took another ten captive. The remaining thirty-odd Nez Perce escaped into the snow. These survivors of the treachery of Indians turning upon Indians—to curry the favor of the overwhelming army of white troops that was killing Joseph at the Bear Paws—were presently hiding in a cave that the old woman had been trying to reach when her wounds forced her to quit. She had lived only long enough, then, to tell Fire Rifle how to find those hidden cave-people. The messenger of Joseph had thus come all this way to find the

Oglala Sioux coming from south, knowing that they were the only people left who might save these cave people as well as those others trapped with Joseph along Eagle Creek, which the white man called Snake Creek, up at that terrible Place of the Manure Fires.

'Listen,' Con Jenkins said to Fire Rifle. 'Is it true that you have lost all your horses up there? All swept away by Captain Carter on the right side of the camp?'

'Yes, that is true. We have only some old bonepiles in the camp. Nothing like the number needed to break away with any chance at all.'

'Well, then, brother, don't you think we had best get along with moving these Sioux horses of ours up there for your people to make a ride-out on?' Con's eyes were blazing. 'Or did your heart die with that old woman under the snowbank?'

Fire Rifle looked hard at the white man. Whatever he saw in the lean, dark-bearded face of the stranger, it was not despair to match his own. He felt the pride come back into him. He was a man, this white drover who had helped the three Oglala to come all of this way with the Sioux horses for Joseph and his people. It did not matter the color of his skin. Or the alien way that he spoke the Sioux tongue. What mattered was that he had brought these Indian friends and more than two hundred good Sioux horses a score of journeys from faraway

Fort Robinson. He had done it to help Fire Rifle's people, *and he was a white man!*

Fire Rifle put out his hand. '*Hohe*,' was all the Nez Perce said in Sioux to the pale-eyed outlaw, 'my brother.'

CHAPTER FORTY-ONE

In the same hour that Miles treacherously seized Joseph under flag of truce, Hunyewat, the Nez Perce Great Spirit, sent to his children a nearly equal gift. Yellow Bull, on guard at the north perimeter, caught a soldier spy. This young officer apparently also sought to take advantage of the white flag and to sneak into the Indian camp while Joseph and the ambitious colonel parleyed, but he had delayed too long in the effort and was not safely returned to the soldier lines by the time that Bear Coat had Joseph seized and dragged away.

At first, White Bull, a comrade of Yellow Bull and a known killer of white men, wanted to slay the captive—slowly and out in full view of the lying Bear Coat and his troops.

But the officer (Lieutenant Jerome) behaved bravely under the threat, and Joseph's nephew Yellow Wolf, aided by Wottolen, saved him. More than that, realizing the value of their hostage as trading bait against the return of their chief, the two Nez Perce mounted guard over Jerome. As well, they had the women put him in a dug-hole underground, so that he would be out of the line of soldier fire. Here, the Indian wives and sisters of the dead and dying Nez Perce kept Jerome warm and supplied him with water and all of the food they had to offer. It was not the way of Joseph, or his Wallowa people, to mistreat a brave man.

Meanwhile Yellow Bull, understanding that his own life would be protected by that of the hostage officer, went over to see Bear Coat Miles about releasing Joseph.

Miles began the conference on a hopeful note, by telling Yellow Bull he would permit him to speak with Joseph alone. But when Yellow Bull then haughtily informed Miles he had captured Lieutenant Jerome and would kill him if harm now came to Joseph, the commander turned white faced with anger. Rescinding his promise to Yellow Bull, Miles had Joseph brought to the conference tent where everything spoken could be recorded and witnessed. Said Joseph long after:

General Miles would not let me leave the tent to see my friend alone. Yellow Bull said to me, 'They have got you in their power, and I am afraid they will never let you go again. I have an officer in our camp, and I will hold him there until they let you go free.'

I said, 'I do not know what they mean to do with me, but if they kill me you must not

290

kill the officer. It will do no good to avenge my death by killing him.'

Miles, in his rage at what he called 'Yellow Bull's trickery,' ordered immediate shelling of the Nez Perce camp with the twelve-pound fieldpiece, which had only then been brought up from the rear. He had Joseph hobbled like an animal, his hands cuffed behind his back, rolled up in a filthy horse blanket, and left on the ground outside the tent among the mule droppings.

For their part, the Nez Perce treated Jerome humanely. The young officer did not forget this debt. Next morning, October 3, he sent Miles a handwritten note. It was cryptic:

I am treated like I was at home. I hope you are treating Chief Joseph as I am treated...

Abrupt or not, Miles got the message's implied rebuke. He ordered Joseph raised up out of the mule manure and his hands released. Within the hour, the exchange of hostages was executed at the lonely 'Place of the Buffalo Peace Robe' out between the lines. Here, Jerome offered his hand to Joseph in full view of hundreds and hundreds of soldiers. The Nez Perce chief shook hands and there were tears in the eyes of both men. A rousing cheer went up from the ranks of watching troops. From the rifle pits of the Indians, no sound came.

As a final act of decency, Lieutenant Jerome took down the truce flag and broke its staff over his knee, dropping its dishonored rag into the mud beside the buffalo robe.

Five minutes after Joseph came back, the artillery shelling resumed, the soldier guns renewed their popping.

Until night, the firing continued. It was nearly all long-range rifle sniping, no advance by either side. The twelve-pounders were ineffective because their lowest setting still carried over the Indian camp. But the Nez Perce spirit flagged lower, nonetheless. A black snow cloud was forming and moving in on them from the north. They knew their choices; they understood their two ways out. They could leave the wounded with the women and children in the pits, the warriors slipping away on the handful of unwounded horses they might find left. Or they could stay and all surrender to Bear Coat Miles, as the soldier chief demanded.

Joseph shook his weary head, his deep voice giving his followers one more brave speech.

'My people,' he said, 'we can do neither of these things. Have you ever heard of a wounded Indian recovering in the hands of white men? Can you forget the scalping done by Red Nose's Bannock and Shoshoni scouts to our aged or sick when we had to leave them along the trail? No, we cannot leave the wounded again. Neither can we all surrender to Bear Coat. To One Hand personally, were he up here, we might give our guns in safety. He is not a squaw killer like Bear Coat Miles and Red Nose Gibbon. His scouts do not defile our dead. But I would rather see my women and children die in the fighting than to give them over to Bear Coat Miles and see his soldiers shoot them down like slaughter animals.'

Almost until twilight the Nez Perce clung to the stirring words of Heinmot Tooyalakekt. But those were the hours when the artillery soldiers finally dug the deep hole for the tailpiece of the twelve-pound cannon. Before that, they could not get the cannon's nose pointed down enough to fire directly into the Indian camp. Now, with the big gun's snout pointed up at the sky, they were mortaring the Nez Perce positions. The powerful shells were coming into the rifle pits like rocks being tossed into a hollow stump. As full darkness came, the bomb bursts of their steel fragments had brought the people to the last edge of their courage. The brave words of their chief made a thin blanket for that night's fitful sleeping.

*　　*　　*

In the earliest light of the fifth morning, October 4, a cannon shell blew up in one of the Nez Perce pits which held an old woman and four small children. The burst made bloodied, sightless things of three of the children.

Twelve-year-old Atsipeteen and the aged grandmother Intehtah were killed. Their own people did not know who they were when they saw them. They were just meat and blood.

With that one shell, the Nez Perce gave up. They had never been able to accept the deaths of their women and children as a part of the white man's way of war. What a thousand soldiers could not do, that one cannon burst accomplished. When Joseph came to stand above that terrible hole in the earth and looked about him at the people standing there in open tears, he wept with them.

The day passed in a strange quiet. Both sides made only token fire. No one else was killed in the Indian camp. But the men met and took council and the women grieved softly, and, when night drew near, the feeling was that all was lost. Joseph would still not surrender to Miles, insisting death in the pits was better. The others knew they could fight no more. Yet they agreed with Joseph that Miles would kill them if they trusted him. All sensed the end was near.

Then something happened. With that day's darkness, One Hand Howard arrived in the camp of Bear Coat Miles. In their pits the Nez Perce welcomed the news of his arrival. They knew he had with him Indians of their own Lapwai and Wallowa peoples. Indians to whom they might entrust a surrendering, knowing their words would not be twisted in translation, or deliberately changed. Also,

General Howard had brought with him their old white friend, Ad Chapman, to whom they would talk when even Howard might not be trusted. All of these people who came up in that night with One Hand Howard were from the old Fair Land they had left and for which they now all mourned. Nor was that all: One Hand wore a star on his coat, Bear Coat only had an eagle. One Hand had the power over Bear Coat, and One Hand was the friend of the Nez Perce. The word was passed to the soldier lines that Joseph would gladly talk now.

At noon the following day, the white flag came out again. With it this time were Ad 'Narrow Eye' Chapman, to interpret, and two old 'treaty' Nez Perces. These two were well known to the people. They were Captain John, called in the native tongue Jokais, Worthless; and Captain George, called Meopkowit, Know Nothing. But both men had daughters with the fighting Indians, so they were accepted.

Jokais spoke: 'Heinmot, you must realize your position. Bear Coat has six hundred soldiers. One Hand brings four hundred more. The soldier chiefs know the number of your dead and the fact that your horses are gone. You must surrender.'

Joseph said quietly, 'To Bear Coat?'

'Yes.'

'I will never do it.'

'Heinmot! Think of our women and

children.'

'I will not surrender to Miles.'

'One Hand says you *must* talk to Bear Coat.'

'No. Only to One Hand. Tell him that.'

The two treaty Indians, Jokais and Meopkowit, understood where it had come to for their people. They went back to the soldier lines. Watching them go, Joseph said in a low voice, 'Call all who are yet alive. We must get ready. One Hand has deserted us.'

CHAPTER FORTY-TWO

The spidermen now spun the last of the web that was to be the story of the Bear Paw horses. Only they, the *iktomi* of Sioux folklore, knew the ending. Their tiny hands flew faster, faster, for what they saw was darkness coming down. And the horses of the warchief's dream were still not met with the Slit Nose brother.

The reason was a bad luck thing.

Fire Rifle led the Oglala herd, skillfully and well, past two cavalry patrols and, with great trail craft, completely around the troops on the east, to come driving back down on the Place of the Manure Fires from the north. He gauged the approach perfectly. The cover of darkness was needed for the actual entrance into the Nez Perce camp and, as they came into the final mile, night was settling. But they were all terribly tired and the horses had gone unrested for seventy miles. No human or beast among the gallant company had slept in two days. Fire Rifle had ridden ninety miles in thirty-eight hours. It was too much for luck alone to carry them farther. At the confluence of two unnamed dry gullies, within sight of the beleaguered camp's pickets—and with no soldiers visible to stop the driving in of the horses—the *iktomi*'s flying hands missed a thread, and their spider weaving trapped the wrong people.

Con was riding point with Fire Rifle and Twilight. Riding the rear were Tuweni, Crowfoot, and Crazy Charley Beckwourth. None rode swing or flank on the herd because the high banks of the gully did that for them. Those high banks did more than that. They hid the Oglala herd from soldier view, and they were high enough to get the herd into the Nez Perce lines without being seen by Bear Coat's men. All that the weary drivers had to do now was to keep going. Five minutes more and the Bear Paw horses would be delivered. The warchief's dream would be reality. It was unbelievable.

'Jesus, Jesus,' breathed Con Jenkins, seeing the open avenue ahead into Joseph's bunkered fortress. 'It ain't possible, but yonder they are—the Neppercy—!'

Fire Rifle nodded. Yes, he answered the tall white man. There were the Nez Perce, his Pierced Nose people. And here were Con and his Sioux friends with horses for all. No soldier had seen them. No soldier would know they were there. All night the horses could rest and then, just before the dawn, *Wagh!* out they would go, carrying the people away.

Con laughed softly. He had never pulled a job to touch Twilight's and Crowfoot's crazy scheme and now he had completed it for them. It was more than a genuine Con Jenkins. It was something a man couldn't put a name to. Not a white man, anyway.

And he had been right about the price it paid, too.

Way, way back yonder at Old Woman Flat, Wyoming, he had joked when he told himself he would get rich on the deal. But he would, by God, he would. Maybe he had laughed at himself for a damned fool back there, turning away from all the real gold dollars that hard-broken herd was worth in soldier or settler terms. But Con Jenkins wasn't laughing anymore. Riding through the lowering dusk of northern Montana into the silent camp of bleeding, freezing, hopeless, huddled, and dying Indians, bringing them the horses that would let them go on, get away and beat the army and it headline-hunting hero, Nelson Miles, Con knew a reward that no army gold, no white man's money of any color could ever pay him.

When he turned to Twilight as they started into Joseph's camp and saw the look on her dark, exultant face, that was Con Jenkin's price. It had a Sioux name: *wolkota*, peace.

He touched heel to tiring mount, called softly to the shining-eyed young squaw riding with him. 'Come on, by God. We've made it home.'

But they had not.

It was when the words left his lips that they came to the place where the fatal side gully entered the main wash that they followed. And it was as they came to this place that the ambushed Cheyenne scouts of Bear Coat Miles burst from it with their terrifying wolf yells and fell upon the Bear Paw horses.

CHAPTER FORTY-THREE

Within minutes of Joseph's pronouncement that General Howard had deserted the Nez Perce, Jokais and Meopkowit came back into the Indian camp. One Hand had changed his mind. He wanted to talk to Joseph.

A day sooner, or with some good horses to ride, or had the cannon shell not shredded the old grandmother and the children in one pit, the Nez Perce leader might yet have taken heart and fought on. But with One Hand's word that they might see him and not Bear Coat, the council of war Joseph had called now became a last meeting of the fighting chiefs to hear the terms of their surrender which Jokais and Meopkowit now brought them.

One Hand gave his word that they would all be sent back to Lapwai, or the Wallowa, and they could keep all of their horses captured by Bear Coat. This return would be in the spring, as snow already closed the Bitterroots and the Lolo Trail to home. If they understood this, and agreed to it, General Howard was ready to see Joseph.

Was Joseph ready to see General Howard?

The chiefs leaned forward as tensely as the two emissaries from One Hand. They knew no more than did the treaty Indians what answer Heinmot Tooyalakekt would make.

Their number now was pitiful. White Bird for his White Bird people. Wottolen for the Asotin of the dead Looking Glass. Naked Head for the Palouse of Hahtalekin. Band-of-Geese for his people, and Black Eagle for his, then Yellow Wolf, Yellow Bull, and the others who, not chiefs of rank, were of the blood of chiefs.

That was all, yet there was not even one of this reduced listing who had not limped or tottered to that meeting, or had come with blood-soaked rag about head, or arm or leg or chest. Only Joseph was hale of the entire council.

Joseph spoke in answer to Jokais and Meopkowit and the offer from General Howard. He told them that his own heart was gone, his people dead and gone, and that the

300

fight was over. He was eloquent, if brief, and the two old men from Lapwai went again back to One Hand. Lieutenant C. E. S. Wood, who witnessed the entire proceedings, says that both oldsters wept unabashedly as they told Howard of Joseph's words.

The rest of it went in a terrible stillness.

Howard and Miles, with three staff officers and Ad Chapman to interpret, left the tent to stand outside it in the thin swirl of coming snow. Joseph saw them and called for his pony. Neither the fleet Joshua nor the noble Ebenezer was led up for him then. The beautiful Appaloosas were gone with all else that the people had run and fought for and died to keep. But Joseph sat proud on the thin, starving pile of bones they brought for him. Five of his warriors who were able to walk went with him on foot, following his horse up the long slope of the hollow.

The words of Lieutenant Wood are again the white man's best testimony to what came then.

Joseph's hair hung in two braids on either side of his face. He wore a blanket and moccasin leggins. His rifle was across the pommel in front of him. When he dismounted he walked to General Howard and offered him the rifle. Howard waved him to go to Miles. He then walked to Miles without a word and handed him the rifle.

Then Chief Joseph stepped back and began his formal speech...

That speech was to ring down the buffalo trails of the red man's memory.

Tell General Howard I know his heart. What he told me before I have in my heart. I am tired of fighting. Our chiefs are killed. Looking Glass is dead. The old men are all killed. It is the young men who say yes or no. He who led the young men is dead. It is cold and we have no blankets. The little children are freezing to death. My people, some of them, have run away to the hills and have no blankets, no food; no one knows where they are, perhaps freezing to death. I want time to look for my children and see how many of them I can find. Maybe I shall find them among the dead. Hear me, my chiefs, I am tired; my heart is sick and sad. From where the sun now stands, I will fight no more forever...

The company, all about, stood silent for the time of a snowflake's alighting and then melting. General Howard made his reply. The words, coming through Ad Chapman, fell with a peculiarly Indian sound.

You have your life. I am living. I have lost my brothers. Many of you have lost brothers, maybe more than on our side. I do not know. Do not worry more.

It was Miles's turn. From some deep well of dignity Bear Coat said it, also, like an Indian.

No more battles and blood. From this sun, we will have a good time on both sides, your band and mine.

Here there was a last stretching of the silence before the tent of One Hand Howard. It was Yellow Wolf, finally, who, looking from Howard to Miles to Joseph, found the words that had to be spoken and that, all knew, Joseph could not bring himself to utter.
Said Yellow Wolf:

Now we understand these words, and will go with General Miles. He is head man. We will go with him...

The Nez Perce returned to their rifle pits and the bodies of their dead. They did their best to tell the others waiting for them that the soldier chiefs had changed. All would be well now. They could believe what had been promised.
Hinakasa, the war was finished. The people went away to begin the gathering of the camp things that remained to them. In minutes only, all were gone. All except one. He was a very ancient one. White Bird. Seventy-four winters.

In his life, he had never known a white man to honor a treaty, to keep his word.

He stood up slowly, for his bones ached with his age and the wounds he had taken. But his face held a look of the darkest pride. The fierce eyes were not defeated yet.

'No,' said the old man to the rising night wind.

And that is all he said.

CHAPTER FORTY-FOUR

Miles's prowling Cheyenne attacked the incoming Oglala horse herd with a fury of yells and rifle shots fired wildly in the cold darkness. They were not a separate unit such as Captain South's famed Cheyenne, but they were attached to Bear Coat's personal command, as had been Custer's scouts. They were wanton killers of their own kind. Officerless, they hung like packs of buffalo wolves about the fringes of the diminished Nez Perce herd, waiting for the unfortunate strays and cripples of the camp to wander out or the healthy ones to attempt escape of the surround. Now they fell on Con Jenkins and his exhausted comrades, intent on scattering the horses and scalping the herdsmen, whoever they might prove to be. One thing was clear to Highback Wolf and his pack of painted 'army Indians': These were not Nez Perce bringing in the fresh herd; some

304

other Indians were trying to help the Slit Noses.

But in the blowing of the snow, coming on now harder all the while, the Scouts could not find the herdsmen. After the first rush and volley, Highback Wolf shouted them off, saying, 'Get the horses! get the horses!' and so they came away without scalps but with 'all of the horses, except for ten or twelve which got shot or broke their necks running in the dark.' But as old Crowfoot long ago told Con Jenkins, 'An Indian will always lie, and always tell the truth; it's up to you to understand the difference.'

The difference in the present case was the 113 Sioux horses that Con Jenkins got past the Cheyenne ambush; the 113 good, sound Oglala ponies presently corraled in a widening of the gully, *inside* the Nez Perce perimeter.

Fate had set her hand to repair the bad weaving of the *iktomi*.

That night, the north curve of the camp was in the guard of Black Eagle. With him were four or five of his band, all that remained of it. It was they who intercepted and calmed the incoming horses, their leader seizing the bridle of Twilight's mount and dragging the lunging animal to a halt. Black Eagle caught the young squaw as she fell, fainting from a wounding of the head by a Cheyenne bullet. She lay still in the Nez Perce's arms as Con slid off his horse and came running up, followed by Crazy

Charley Beckwourth. But the scrape of the bullet bled deceptively. Twilight recovered in seconds, to gasp out their story to the Nez Perce subchief. While she did this, Con and Crazy Charley searched in vain for Tuweni, Crowfoot, and Joseph's courier, Fire Rifle. 'They ain't coming in,' said Con to Beckwourth after several minutes. 'Let's get back to the girl and them Neppercies.'

There was, in footnote, another member of the original company who failed to be counted with the survivors of the Cheyenne attack that cold night: Itunkasan Luta, Red Weasel. But then who would think to count a twenty-one winters' aged and decrepit travois mule among the missing of any encounter?

Con arrived back where Twilight and Black Eagle were talking animatedly in time to hear the Nez Perce say abruptly, 'No, not Joseph, little Sioux sister. Your horses come too late for him. He has surrendered.'

'But I must see him.'

'You cannot. There is only the old man, White Bird, and some few others of us left who will not go in tomorrow. Joseph touched the hands with Bear Coat this afternoon. He is done. He will never change his word.' The Nez Perce paused. In that moment, several tough-looking tribesmen drifted up through the dark. 'Moreover, sister,' Black Eagle concluded, 'we cannot let you go to Joseph. He would surrender your horses tomorrow. We must use

306

them tonight. And we will do it.'

Con Jenkins, glancing at the silent fellow warriors of the Nez Perce spokesman, said guardedly to Twilight, in English, 'Go slow, these babies mean business.'

Either Twilight didn't understand what he said, or she didn't care. She stood there still arguing, still battling to hold together Crazy Horses's dream of reaching Joseph. Con feared she might get them all killed in the process. One look at the skulking forms of the Indians about them, one listen to the low sounds coming from their dark lips, was all a white man needed. These Indians were not going to let them near Chief Joseph. And Joseph was never going to see the Bear Paw horses of his Oglala cousins. 'For God's sake!' he whispered desperately to the stubborn girl, 'don't stall them. They ain't playing no Crazy Horse dream games, you hear me? Wake up!'

Black Eagle put deep-voiced affirmation to Con's fears and said, 'Come on, little Sioux sister. We have no time now. Forget Joseph. He walks the white man's road. We will not. Come with us.'

Con could have shot her. She still stood there arguing the dream of Crazy Horse to reach Joseph.

In that final hesitation, a lean figure slunk up through the night on foot.

'Is that you, Hemene?' rasped Black Eagle.

'Yes,' answered Yellow Wolf. 'I am going

307

with you.'

'What did Joseph say?'

'He said to go. He wants me to find his woman and the little daughter Running Feet out there in the snow.'

'Did you tell Joseph the White Bird people will not surrender with him tomorrow?'

'No.'

'Do you think he knows it?'

'He knows everything.'

The newcomer turned on Con and Twilight. 'Who are these people?' he said quickly.

Black Eagle told him the story of the 113 Oglala horses being held in the gully beyond. Then he said to Con and the Sioux girl, 'This is Yellow Wolf, the own-nephew to Heinmot Tooyalakekt. Ask *him* what you should do.'

'There is no need to ask,' interrupted Yellow Wolf. 'The answer is run hard, run fast. The Cheyenne murderers will soon find out these are Sioux horses they have caught coming in here. They will tell this to Bear Coat, and the soldiers will swarm to the north before you could even find Joseph. They will trap us in here, unless we go *now.*'

This Indian fact struck them all. In the excitement and the small time that had passed, none had thought of it. Now Black Eagle said, 'But the herd is two days sore for sleep. Give them two hours.'

'Not two breaths!' said Yellow Wolf. 'We don't have the time that it takes a bear to leave his sign in the trail. Go! I will stay with these people.' He gestured with his rifle to Con and Twilight and Black Eagle turned away.

'I will get White Bird and the rest up here. Did you bring any people with you?'

'None. Hurry.'

With a grunt, Black Eagle and his fellows disappeared. Con could hear their running feet for a few seconds, then the snowfall cut off everything. Yellow Wolf poked him with his rifle and said ominously, 'Don't try anything, you two people.'

'Two?' said Con. 'What happened to my half-wit? Hey, Cookie—'

He called into the darkness, so they might include Charley Beckwourth in the safe-keeping arrangement of Yellow Wolf's guard, but he called in vain.

Crazy Charley was gone.

CHAPTER FORTY-FIVE

At eight o'clock, on the night of October 5, 1877, the Bear Paw horses, unrested and unfed, were put on the last-mile drive to freedom. The Sioux ponies went out of the darkened, sorrowful camp of Joseph's people, north into the teeth of a blasting storm. With them went fourteen men and seventeen women of the White Bird band, with twelve children of all bands, then Black Eagle and Yellow Wolf, the

309

own-nephew of Chief Joseph. Forty-five Nez Perce in all, with one Oglala young squaw named Twilight and one gaunt white squawman who called himself Con Jenkins.

The history books of the *wasicun* were to say that twenty-eight Nez Perce escaped from the Bear Paws with White Bird. But Con Jenkins could count. His tally, that black and storming night, matched the number the Indians later gave in their own stories of the White Bird breakout, 'forty-and-five of our Slit Nose people, with two strangers.'

The fleeing Nez Perce followed the same gully out of the camp that the Sioux horses had used coming into it. They cleared the abandoned battlefield by the grace of their red gods. As the last of the people and the Oglala herd passed the ambush site and were safely gone into the blizzard beyond, the muffled wolf yelling of the Cutarm scouts arose in pursuit behind them.

'You bastards!' bellowed Con Jenkins. 'You dirty bastards!'

His answer was the thin blaring of a cavalry bugle knifing through the Cheyenne cries, plus a hard-swung blow to the side of his mouth from the hand of Yellow Wolf, and the tall outlaw decided he was not the chief here anymore. This was Indian business. It didn't require a genuine Con Jenkins touch. Least of all did it require a *wasicun* brother to be sending out cursing voice calls to guide the hated Cutarm Scouts down onto his fleeing Nez Perce friends.

'*Waste!*' he said to Yellow Wolf, wiping the blood from his split lip. 'I see your raise, and chunk in.'

'*Sapasauza,*' growled Yellow Wolf, 'shut up!'

They went on, beating their mounts, whipping the tired drag of the loose herd. There were no more options remaining. It was straightaway drive now. A horse race. They got away, or they killed the last pony trying.

After another two miles, with no more wolf yelps and no more bugle calls to jump their hearts, Yellow Wolf swung his pony in beside Con Jenkins where the two rode the drag with six picked warriors. 'Back there I saw something,' he said. 'It makes me know you do not lie. Fire Rifle did bring you in here.'

'I never doubted it,' Con said grimly. His lip was beginning to hurt, and he resented it. 'What brung you to believe it?'

The other told him he had almost ridden his pony over the body of Fire Rifle 'lying back there' in the side draw near the ambush site.

'My God!' Con said. 'Now he can't show us where the snow-cave people are!'

Quickly he told Yellow Wolf the story Fire Rifle had related about the murderous attack on the fugitives who had escaped from the Bear Paw camp. Yellow Wolf's dark face writhed.

'They are truly lost then,' he said. 'We will
311

have to pass them by, and they will freeze.'

'Yeah,' said Con, 'I know. We lost some, too,' he added, mentioning Tuweni, Crowfoot, and Charley Beckwourth. 'Nothing like your people, though.'

They rode on. After a moment, Yellow Wolf's frown lightened.

'Beckwourth?' he said. 'Do you mean that wrong-brained one that the Crows punished? That son of old Mulatto Jim?'

'That's him; Crazy Charley.'

'Good. There is still some chance, then.'

'How so?'

'The Crows say he is their most cunning hunter. We see the Crows every year. They wouldn't lie to us.' Yellow Wolf nodded, finding hope. 'You will see. That crazy one knew something, all right. He may have gone to get help for us.'

'Nope,' said Con. 'He just loved the Injun kid and went looking for him, is my guess.'

Yellow Wolf did not reply. But another mile farther on into the blizzard Con Jenkins had his second lump, and was forever happy to feel it. The herd slowed suddenly and Yellow Wolf, telling his braves to stay back, said to Con, 'You see? I told you. Come on.'

They reached the head of the herd in time to witness a tableau coming in out of the snowflakes which made of Joseph's nephew a prophet, and of Con Jenkins a believer.

There came Crazy Charley Beckwourth on

his horse, an Indian woman behind him riding double. Following Charley was Tuweni on Dr McGillycuddy's big bay gelding, also with an Indian woman behind him riding double—a very young Indian woman. Behind both horses came yet a third animal: old Red Weasel dragging a Nez Perce travois picked up abandoned along the trail. And in the travois, of course! was the last Indian of the missing friends of Con Jenkins; Kangi-siha, himself, old Crowfoot.

The Indian woman with Beckwourth was Heyoom Yoyikt, Joseph's missing wife. The girl with Tuweni was Kapkap Ponmi, Noise of Running Feet, Joseph's beloved twelve-year-old daughter. They had been found wandering through the storm by the half-witted Charley. And the others, Crowfoot and Tuweni, had been shoved into a dark place beneath a windfall pine by Crazy Charley when the Cheyenne rifles first began to bark. All they had needed to do was wait for the *heyoka*, Charley, to come back for them.

Red Weasel? Well, naturally, where old Crowfoot went, there went old Red Weasel. Like a dog. Even better. What dog could drag a travois big enough to carry a worn-out Oglala grandfather through the snow?

In later years, led astray by the white man's flattery, Yellow Wolf was to devise a story that made him more the instrument of the finding of Joseph's wife and child than Crazy Charley

313

Beckwourth. But on that dark night on the snowstorm trail away from Tsanim Alikos Pah, where freedom almost died, the famous warrior of the Wallowa had naught but an Indian's praise for the addled son of old Mulatto Jim.

As well he might. For Crazy Charley bore more than Joseph's wife and child in out of that blue norther blizzard: He knew where the snow-cave people were!

He had found the dying Fire Rifle after putting Tuweni and Crowfoot under the downed pine. Fire Rifle had told him by sign and some words of Absaroka, the Crow tongue, how to find the hiding cave. The half-witted one had had to wait until he found Tuweni again before he might convey to Con and Twilight, or to anyone else, the secret of the brave Nez Perce's dying trust. Now, with Tuweni's excited translation of Charley's news, the cavalcade cut away east from the trail and, within half an hour, were embracing the thirty-three half-frozen survivors of the Assiniboin treachery.

With everyone on a good horse, the march was resumed. The night hours wore away tensely. With daylight, a halt was made, a fire risked, a lame horse killed, and fresh meat prepared for all. The camp was in a willow and alder thicket, giving browse for the horses, too. The starving creatures stripped bough and branch and even main trunk, feeding like snowdrifted deer or elk. Settlement horses, or those of the army, would have gone hungry and failed. They never would have reached Canada, or even gotten beyond Milk River. But the Indian ponies were of that land, and they ate of that land. When the signal came from Yellow Wolf to go back once more on the forcing march, they were ready.

Coming to the fork of Battle Creek with Lodge Pole Creek, Yellow Wolf split his caravan. He took half the people up Battle Creek. The other half went by way of Lodge Pole, under Black Eagle and White Bird. The rejoining was made that afternoon and a common course set to the north. They rested again at dusk but could build no fires. Near midnight, Crazy Charley roused up the camp and said he had had a dream to go on. In the cold darkness, the people blundered to find mounts and to be in the line. Within the hour of Beckwourth's vision, they were gone on. And the manure of the Bear Paw horses yet held some heat in it when the savage Cheyenne scouts of Bear Coat Miles swept in on that empty camp to fill its black, cold loneliness with Cutarm curses.

The Cheyenne followed on, but fate had truly taken away the closing of the final web from the clumsy-handed *iktomi*. When the day came again, the scouts of Highback Wolf halted to look north over nothing but a hundred miles of freshly fallen snow. There was not a Nez Perce moccasin track upon its unbroken whiteness. Nor was there the solitary hoofprint of an Oglala Bear Paw horse. The Cheyenne were thirty miles inside the Land of the Grandmother and they could sit there and wolf howl until every redcoat in Canada was brought galloping down upon them. The Nez Perce were gone and the Cheyenne had better be likewise.

'*Nohetto*,' said Highback Wolf. 'Turn around.'

And that was the way that the story ended in the white man's history books.

CHAPTER FORTY-SIX

The real ending, the Indian ending, was yet to come. In justice, a red man tells it. The painter of the words is Lame Bull, adopted son of the Hunkpapa leader Sitting Bull. A sober man of thirty-four winters at the time, he was not given to the Indian fault of 'seeing happy'—wishful thinking. His account of the arrival of the Nez Perce in Canada is accepted among red men as the Indian truth of the matter.

Here, then, is Lame Bull remembering:

. . . It was a fine morning such as Wakan Tanka would send when he might be pleased with us. After many days of blowing snow and cold, the sun had returned. On the big hill south of the camp, it shone through the snowdust to make the eye squint with its brightness. It was there that the Poge Hloka [Pierced Noses, the Nez Perce] appeared. They came of a sudden out of the sunburst in the blowing snow up on the hill.

First, rode a small Sioux boy on an exceedingly large bay horse of white man's breeding. An old woman of our band, seeing the boy, gave a joyous cry. The crone had bad hipbones and was called by us Keya, or Turtle, from the way that she waddled. Now she ran out toward the boy, who jumped down from the bay horse and embraced her. The two sat right down in the snow and cried together. They were grandmother and grandson, separated by the parting of the tribes when Sitting Bull fled to Canada and Crazy Horse went with his Oglala people into Fort Robinson to surrender.

Since my father, Sitting Bull, was not in camp, it fell to me to greet these strangers. Going forward past the boy and the grandmother, I saw many more people struggling out of the dazzle of the sun on South Hill. Leading them was a white man riding with a young Oglala woman—very beautiful, the girl. The man was gaunt, heavily bearded with whiskers, and of a mean look. Following them in a travois drawn by an ancient red mule was an elderly Oglala man much used by exhaustion. After him, came the main body of the wounded people, whose band I did not yet recognize.

‹ When we Sioux of the Hunkpapa saw these poor ones, we wept as children for them. All had hurts upon them and were covered with mud, slime, and filth. Some rode alone. Others were carried in the arms of friends or kinsmen. Some did not have one hand. Others had the part of one foot missing or an arm shattered and dangling. Still others were blinded from pieces of the face blown away. All were hollow-eyed, with swollen bellies. They had eaten nothing but the raw flesh of horses dead along the trail. They had drunk only melted snow water. It made the heart cry to see them, yet they rode proudly, like Indians.

One of them turned his horse out from the ranks and came to me ahead of his fellows. I knew him. He was Yellow Wolf, a blood nephew of Joseph. He had been many times in our buffalo camps down home in the old days. I myself had ridden lance and lance with Yellow Wolf upon the curly cows. I gave him the greeting shout in a glad voice. But he did not reply to it, telling me rather of the terrible thing that had happened to his people.

My shame darkened over me at his words.

Sitting Bull had not been able to go and help the Pierced Nose people when Joseph's messengers had reached our camp. This was because the redcoats had told him that, if the Hunkpapa went down to help the Pierced Noses get away from Bear Coat Miles, they would then have to stay down there in America. The Land of the Grandmother could not take sides against the soldiers of Miles. So Sitting Bull had to decide. He chose to stay with the people in Canada, though his heart bled for Joseph.

Yellow Wolf would not understand this. He looked back at me with eyes of stone.

But the others, coming out of the snow whirl on South Hill led by fierce old White Bird and dark-faced Black Eagle, sobbed with their joy to see us. I counted seventy-and-eight of them, and everyone of these forgave us, as Yellow Wolf could not. Many told us it was the first time their hearts had been warm—and their backs!—since Yellowstone River. I bid them all welcome and led them to our lodges.

Oh, yes, and wait; there was one other of them to come out of that snowburst with the Poge Hloka that day. He came last in the line, singing a cracked song and sounding as if he had a piece of hot meat in his mouth and was rolling it around to keep from burning himself. He had his head buried in a rotten old Absaroka blanket and was riding without eyes to see the trail, yet his horse did not miss a step of the way.

We found out later that this one had no tongue and a broken mind. Yet he was the same one, the Bear Paw people told us, who had awakened Yellow Wolf and White Bird in the middle of the night to save the people from

319

the Cheyenne scouts of Miles. We Indians always gave a special reception to those with injured brain. So we named this one Pa t'e Wowicake, True Head, because he could see through his blanket better than most men with eyes fully uncovered. We never treated him unkindly.

When all the poor Poge Hloka were safely counted into our camp, we made them warm and filled their bellies with good meat. The only ones of Joseph's own family who were there were his older wife and a small daughter of twelve winters. So that all would be treated equally and feel at home, we 'mixed up' our guests, putting one of them in each Hunkpapa lodge, letting them live as we lived, as one of us. This was the thinking of my father, Sitting Bull, a wise man who always put the people first, even as Joseph did among the Pierced Nose brothers.

Later, my father, who remained fearful that Miles still might come after him up there in Canada, moved our camp [the Hunkpapa] ten long pony rides to the north [about five hundred miles] of the camp of the Slota. The Slota were called the Grease People and were the main band of the Red River Mixed Bloods who had traded many winters with the American Sioux. It was their camp that the Poge Hloka came to that first day, and they did not move with us to the north. Some of the Pierced Noses stayed with them, others went with us Hunkpapa, fearing Miles as did Sitting Bull.

One who stayed with the Slota at the first camp was the handsome Sioux young squaw, H'tayetu. She was younger sister to Black Blanket, the wife of the great Crazy Horse. Actually, these two women were not of Oglala blood, but Slota. It was the older one marrying the warchief that caused the confusion. After that time, the white people came to think they were Oglala. They never bothered to ask the Indians about it.

The tall white squawman stayed with the younger sister, and they seemed to love well. They had a man-child the following summer. I heard they lived happily and the boy was sturdy.

The waddling grandmother Turtle and the white-haired old medicine priest Crowfoot built a lodge together there in the Slota camp, living next to the white squawman and the handsome girl, H'tayetu.

The orphan boy Tuweni, a rascal not whipped nearly enough, stayed with the old people.

Up on a small ridge behind the two lodges was an outcropping of rock. Beneath it was a snug small cave. On that rock, sitting there in snow or sunshine, lived the strange-minded man, Pa t'e Wowicake. He sang his tongueless songs and watched night and day for Bear Coat to come from the south. My people still know that cave below the rock. Two times a year, food is left there for True Head in reward for his vigil. Some old Sioux insist that, if the wind is right and all talking subdued, he still can be heard singing there. I don't know, I never heard him.

The Pierced Noses stayed with the Mixed Bloods of Red River, and with us Hunkpapa to the north, for two winters. Then they went home again to America, down into their own old lands of Winding Waters, the place they called Wallowa.

I heard that the white man and the young squaw, the old couple, and the brat of a boy stayed on with the Slota when the Pierced Noses went home. But, of course, I cannot be certain. About this time, we Hunkpapa moved to yet another new camp in Canada and, after that, I never saw any of those Bear Paw people again...

So ends the story of Lame Bull. It was, as he always concluded graciously to a white listener, *bala'he lo*, the time to be going on. God rest and feed everyone.

A safe journey, and peace, to all.

AN INDIAN FOOTNOTE:

The tale of the Bear Paw horses bears a postscript. It is written with the fine irony of an Indian hand. Reading it, as the Sioux say, each will have to decide in his own mind as to its truth.

In the hard winter of 1890, just before the tragedy of the Ghost Dance and Wounded Knee, a wild Sioux drifted into the agency at Pine Ridge, South Dakota. He had come a far journey, the traveler said, all the way from Sitting Bull's old camp on Witsa River, in Canada. He was looking for Dr V. T. McGillycuddy, the former soldier doctor at Spotted Tail agency. Some Sioux friends of the old days had told him that Little Beard was now here, at Pine Ridge. Was this a true thing, brothers?

The agency Indian police who had intercepted him explained the problem. Dr McGillycuddy, who had been agent at Pine Ridge since 1879, had recently been replaced by agent Royer. McGillycuddy yet worked on the reservation as a doctor but was away just then tending the sick in the outer lodges. *Hau tahunsa*, the Indian police asked, what did the blanket brother want of Little Beard McGillycuddy?

The wild Sioux, a comparatively young man but showing the age of many cold and hungry winters, got down stiffly from his old horse. The day was late, the snow blowing a cloud upon the ground. The ancient horse was an unusually large bay, rheumy of once-dark eye, gray of muzzle, caved of spine, worth only to be wolf bait. The ice of the cold was in the bay's coarse coat. His wheezing breath made frost trails in the twilight. But the strange Indian held him proudly by a frayed rope halter and stood very straight beside the old horse there in front of the agency police.

Would the soldier doctor McGillycuddy return soon? he asked the red policemen.

He would, yes.

Waste, good, the tattered one nodded. He put both arms about the old horse's neck, hugging him as only a man can who loves an animal as a brother. In the split and ragged ears, he whispered Sioux words of courage-in-farewell to an old companion. At the last he murmured fiercely, *woyuonihau*, the highest Oglala word of respect.

When he turned back to the Indian police, the ragged visitor coughed and made to sniffle as from a bad cold. The police saw that he was weeping but did not let him know what they saw. The stranger was grateful for this Indian thing.

Haho, thank you, brothers, he told them.

Awkwardly, he gave over to one of the men the knotted rein of the halter rope, which was all the harness worn by the rheumy-eyed bonepile standing rump-tucked and shaking in the December wind.

'Here, take him,' the wild Sioux said, just before he slipped away into the whirl of ground-snow whence he had come. 'When the soldier doctor returns, tell him I brought back his fine big bay horse.'

324